# THE FIGHTING MEN

Other novels by Willard Manus:
  The Fixers
  Mott the Hoople

THE FIGHTING MEN

A novel
by
WILLARD MANUS

Panjandrum, Inc.
Los Angeles   1981

Requests for permission to make copies of any part of this work should be mailed to: Panjandrum Books, 11321 Iowa Ave, Suite 1, Los Angeles, CA. 90025

Library of Congress Cataloging in Publication Data
Manus, Willard, 1930–
    The fighting men.

    1. Vietnamese Conflict, 1961–1975—Fiction.
I. Title.
PS3563.A575F5   813'.54   81–14092
ISBN 0-915572-55-9   AACR2
ISBN 0-915572-54-0 (pbk.)

This book funded in part by a grant from the National Endowment for the
    Arts, Literature Program.
Printed in the United States of America

First edition

"Why are the armies marching still
 That were coming home to me?"
—STORIES OF THE STREET, song by Leonard Cohen

This book is dedicated to my aunt, Mrs. Marion Sachs, and to my friend, Stanley Diamond.

Eli

The road was no better than a mule trail. Slashed into the stone face of a canyon whose bottom lay a thousand feet below, it corkscrewed down to the desert floor in a series of wild twists and turns. The lumps and potholes in the road were murdering the car, but I didn't give a damn, as El Cortez was within sight. Hot dawg, there she was, sitting off in the distance, white walls shining and sparkling in the sunlight. Shangri-fucking-la!

I stopped the car and jumped out, blowing kisses at that white lady sitting on the far side of the desert floor. It was time to celebrate, even though the car sat sagging on its busted springs, radiator pissing away. A week of fighting these roads had destroyed the vehicle, but no matter; happiness was mine. Once down out of these mountains it was a straight flat run through the valley to El Cortez. I was laughing out loud now, king of the hill.

It took me an hour to wind my way down to the desert floor. That's when I saw the girl. There was an adobe hut by the side of the road; the kind of place that sold gasoline and tequila out of the barrel, both so strong and raw you could hardly tell them apart. She came rushing out of the *rancho* and at first I thought she belonged to it and wanted to sell me a bunch of flowers. But she was no kid and she didn't belong to the *rancho*, not in those designer jeans and with that red hair.

She looked about twenty-five. She was small and plump and had a round, pretty face and lively eyes under a rag mop of hair. She shoved her face close and asked, "Habla usted English?"

"Hey," I said, "I not only habla it, I understand it."

"Of all the luck," she cried out. "A bluidy Yank."

1

"What the hell are you doing hitchiking here?"

"That's exactly what I was just asking myself."

As we bounced along, her backpack on the rear seat, she told me that her name was Doreen and she was from Glasgow and had for three years been working her way around the world, doing odd jobs for a month or two, then moving on. She'd been waiting on tables in Los Angeles when someone told her about the possibility of an office job in El Cortez. She'd written, was sent an air ticket, and here she was.

"What happened to the air ticket?" I asked as we bumped along.

"Och, I cashed it in," she said in her Scottish brogue. "I wanted to leave L.A. in style so I had a wee booze-up for me pals. Did we ever get skunnered! We each had a jug apiece and a steak as thick as a vicar's bum. And then we went jiggin'."

"You had a jug and then you went jigging. That's a funny language you talk, girl. You're gonna have to use subtitles to be understood."

"Jiggin's dancin' and jug is jug, just like Little Brown—How I Love Thee. So ye see, we *do* talk the same language."

"Didn't anybody warn you about hitchiking in a country like this? There are bandits and other armed men in these hills."

"What's the matter, you think I'm a wee feartie?"

"A wee what?"

"*Feartie.* A scairdy-cat."

"You shouldn't take chances like that with your life."

"That's what life is," she replied. "Takin' chances. You should know, you're doin' the same. You and this clapped-out car of yours."

"Cars don't have clap," I said, "only people."

"I hope you're not speakin' for yourself," she deadpanned. Then she pointed to the car radio. "Can I play it? I havnae heard any music in days."

"Be my guest."

She fiddled with the dial but could only find a commercial babbling in Spanish: "*Tome, tome,* ALKA-SELTZER!"

"That's exactly what I need," she said. "I wouldnae half enjoy an Alka-Seltzer. I've eaten so many beans lately, my farts would float a balloon."

"You and me both. The food sure is hot and heavy down here."

"Even the chicken's on fire. God, what I wouldnae give for a wee cuppa tea and a nice slice of roastit bubbly-jock."

The woman made me laugh.

"Roastit *what?*"

"Whatsa matter, cin ye no handle the tongue? Don't ye know that roastit bubbly-jock is just another way of sayin' roast turkey?"

"Wonderful. I can just see them when I go into a diner back home and ask for a roastit bubbly-jock on rye."

We both laughed at that, feeling easy and good with each other.

Up ahead someone was standing by the side of the road. He flagged us down and came over, a small guy with the hard, chunky features of an Indian and a shock of ragged black hair sticking out of his fatigue cap. I didn't like his looks and would have taken off had it not been for the thing in his hand. It was a .45, pointed straight at us.

"*Vaya,*" he said.

"Guid lord," Doreen gasped.

He had two others with him. Clad in worn camouflage uniforms, they had been crouching behind a clump of rocks, but now they approached, carrying weapons, both pale and black-bearded and showing shoulder-length hair. They had hungry, mean eyes. Suddenly I didn't like the feeling in my scrotum. The last time I had felt it was when my old man was in hospital with gangrene and the doctor said they would have to amputate his leg.

"I said get out."

"Why?" in English.

"I said get out."

The car radio began to play music, a song with these lyrics over and over: *te Amo, te Amo.* Now one of them yanked the door open and hauled Doreen out roughly. My instinct was to go for him but the .45 was still in evidence. *Te Amo, te Amo,* the radio crooned.

They searched us, going through our pockets.

"What are you doing here, Yankee?"

I said nothing.

"You, *muchacha?*"

"Whatsa matter? Afraid to talk?"

"CIA?"

Nothing

One of them slapped me.

"Who are you? One of Mulligan's soldiers?"

Again, "CIA? CIA?"

"Fuck the CIA," I said in Spanish. "And fuck you, too. Bandits. Sons of whores."

There was a scuffling, a blow, and I was going down, being kicked and hurt. Doreen was yelling and trying to help, but one of the men hit her, too.

"We're not bandits," the little one said, standing over me. "If we were, we'd murder you the way the government murders us. They're the bandits, the killers. But we're going to overthrow them," he swore. "The time is not far off. We'll show them that they're not the only ones who can kill."

Dizzily, I watched as they searched the car, bringing out my suitcase, the brandy and the big salami I had brought for Mulligan. They seemed disappointed at not finding anything out of the ordinary. I sat up, face pounding, and waited for their next move.

"Whatever we're taking from you is for the revolution," the little one said. He got behind the wheel and slammed the front door.

"Adios, CIA."

He backed the battered Chevy up and turned around, scoring some last points by employing an old hot rod trick. Reversing the rear wheels furiously in the dry white sand, he slammed the transmission into drive and took off fast, beating up billows of dust and pebbles.

I put thumb to teeth and flicked a Sicilian farewell: *"Va fongul."*

Then it was quiet again and we were alone. My body hurt from the beating and my legs were trembling under me. Doreen had gone pale and there was a blotch on her face where she'd been smacked. But she was a stand-up chick, all right. She didn't cry and she didn't whine. All she said was, "What the fook was that all about?"

"Don't ask me. They said they weren't bandits, they were revolutionaries."

"They still ripped us off, though."

"You're goddamn right they did. They took a hundred bucks from me, and change. They even stole the salami I was bringing Mulligan."

"And my Maggie Bell tapes," she said, checking her backpack. "The bluidy bastards," she cursed. "The rat-faced coves!"

Before us stretched the desert floor, a long sweep of land without a thing showing but the odd tree or boulder.

The sight of all that desolation was just too damn much. I dropped where I was, right back on my haunches, and reached in my shirt for a joint.

As we passed the smoke between us, she asked, "Where'd you learn to speak Spanish like that?"

"Driving a truck."

"You mean you worked with Spanish?"

"Nah. I had my own rig. Used to run Interstate, from California to New York and back, over two hundred thousand miles a year. That's a lotta time to fill. I did it by playing language tapes. Two hours a day, seven days a week, and you can handle español with the best of them."

"Guid show. But dincha ever listen to any rock n roll?"

"That cab of mine was wired with four speakers and sounded like the inside of Mick Jagger's head. But you can't listen to rock all the time. It scrambles your brains. You gotta listen to something intelligent too, books 'n stuff."

"Buiks?"

"Yeah, *buiks*. They've got everything on tape, Doreen—Shakespeare, Hemingway, James Joyce. You can really improve your mind, if you've got the time."

"Crikey, imagine that—a truck driver listenin' to Shakespeare."

"Yeah, and look where it got me—smack on my butt in the middle of nowhere."

"It's a bugger, ain't it," she said, taking a big hit of maryjane. "It's a real thump in the arse."

We sat smoking and looking out over the desert. Then I stood up and brushed the dirt off my pants. "Let's get this circus moving."

"Maybe we should just kip down here," she said. "It's getting late."

"We need shelter. We've got to try and make El Cortez."

But it was slow going and soon the sun began to angle down behind the hills on the horizon, throwing shadows over us. It began to get a little spooky out here in the desert. It was the trees, I realized, there was something weird about them, with their dark trunks and long spiky branches twisting themselves around each other like so many witches. Suddenly I began to shiver. *Adios, CIA!*

Up ahead a man was crouching by the side of the road, over a fire.

Doreen saw him too. We stopped short. "Who's that?" she asked. "Another guerrilla?"

Nothing to do but keep going, risk it.

The man had a rifle under his arm and a big black dog by his side. A horse was tethered in the shelter of a nearby tree. The man came toward us, showing a red, scabby face that looked as if someone chipped away at it every morning with an icepick.

I knew that face: it belonged to a first sergeant named Turk Kohler. We had done some killing in Viet Nam together. Turk was a career soldier working on his third war, but he'd shot his wad eventually, just like the rest of us. He'd built up such a hatred for the VC that he used to take the butt end of a bayonet to a dead slope and hack away at his teeth. The bits of gold filling went into a leather purse which he wore on a string around his neck, like an amulet.

It was no surprise to see him here. Five months ago Mulligan had started hiring a lot of army buddies of his, all retired NCO's, with the idea of installing them as a security guard against the guerrillas. He had even offered me a job in his private army, but I'd written back that my soldiering days were over. Ain't gonna study war no more.

"Well, I'll be goddamned," Turk said as we came up. "So there you are, Eli. We been waitin' on you, man. Gave you up for lost, you dumb maggot."

While he hustled over to his field radio and called El Cortez, Doreen and I crouched by the fire, warming ourselves.

"We're all right," I told her. "With Turk here, there ain't a thing can happen to us. He's the toughest son of a bitch on God's earth."

"*Guid,*" she said, "maybe he can get my Maggie Bell tapes back for me."

Turk looked a hell of a lot better than he did the last time I saw him, when we were both on short time, waiting to make it out of Nam. We had done two tours by then and his eyes had gone dead and white, like Little Orphan Annie. They looked out but they didn't see.

But now he was okay. Still ugly as sin, but back in control, some life in his eyes. He wouldn't look at Doreen, though. Probably she was too much woman for him, with that fiery red hair and those big boobs bouncing around in her t-shirt. Turk was a puritan at heart. He had never once shacked with a woman during the war, not even on R & R. "I hate whores," he told me once. "I hate all unclean women."

We heard the sound of a plane coming close, circling overhead, searching the plateau for a place to land. The pilot finally chose the north side and brought the plane down skilfully, blowing up the dust.

It was Mulligan. Picking up and shouldering Turk's rifle, I marched out to meet him, stood waiting at attention as he climbed down from the Cessna 310. When he came close, I did a snappy present-arms. "Staff Sergeant E. J. Brickman reporting for duty, sir."

Taken aback, Mulligan stopped short, gaped, grinned and said, "Turk said you'd just been robbed by Che's boys. But here you are, still full of piss and vinegar."

I told him about losing the salami to the guerrillas.

Mulligan made a face and said, "The last good salami I had was in Nam. Remember Dave Lifschitz's famous CARE package from home?"

Dave's mother, the quintessential Jewish mother, had sent this package from Miami Beach with a can of pickles, two beef salamis, and a jar of chicken soup inside it. Everyone in the company ended up having a crazy kosher feast in a bunker on a hill north of Quang Ngai city.

"Good old Dave. Hope there's a delicatessen up in heaven for him. But tell me, why didn't you warn me about the guerrillas?"

"You were supposed to call me from the capital. I would have flown up and picked you up."

"I decided to drive down. It was only four hundred miles on the map. I thought I could do it in two days. It was a chance to see the country and all that."

"Well, now you've seen it, buddy. And now you know that even with a jeep it takes a week to fight through these mountains. You know what they call this road? The Frijole Freeway," Mulligan grinned. "I'm sorry about the car. Will the insurance cover it?"

"Are you kidding? Have you ever known an insurance company to pay off in full?"

Matt had aged. His face was leathery and wrinkled around the eyes and mouth, signs of mortality and worry. His hair had gone grey, the color of steel wool, but at least he showed a full head, even if he did wear it short, and his big body was still lean and strong and upright, and he carried it smartly, exuding the old feeling of power and precision.

"Which way did the guerrillas head?"

"North."

Mulligan turned to Turk. "Stay close to the radio. If I spot them from the air I'll let you know. Maybe you can pick up their trail."

"Hell," Turk said, "they'll be long gone by now."

As we started toward the plane, I introduced Doreen.

"She says she's got a job with you. If you think I'm dumb, get a load of her story. She just hitchiked down here."

Mulligan smiled and took her arm. "You didn't really?"

"Och," she said. "I realize it was daft of me, but y'know, I've hitch-hiked through Turkey and Pakistan and if I could get through all them Muslims and live to tell the tale, I figured this country would be a cuppa tea."

"We're fellow-countrymen," Mulligan said to her. "My great-grandmother came from Scotland."

"It all depends on what fitba' team you support."

"Fitba?"

"Football, or as you Yanks so quaintly call it, soccer. So which is it—Rangers or Celtics?"

"With a name like Mulligan need you ask?"

"Wouldnae know it," Doreen sighed. "Come all this way, only to end up in the enemy camp!"

We had reached the plane. Mulligan helped Doreen up first, then turned to me, happily.

"I'm glad to see you, E.J. I've thought a lot about you over the years."

"Same here."

"I wouldn't have recognized you in a crowd," he admitted. "Not with that Zapata moustache."

"Well, it's the right part of the world for it."

"How right you are. Every half-ass in the province is trying to make like a revolutionary these days.

"What's going on? What have these guerillas got against you?"

As he began explaining things the motivation of the MNR—Movimento Nacionalista Revolucionario—became clear. Mulligan's copper mine was the only successful enterprise for hundreds of miles around. That made him the natural target of the MNR, particularly as the leader of the guerrillas, a guy named Jesus Maria Salvatierra, used to run the miners' union here.

"Che Guevara was killed in Bolivia a long time ago, but Jesus Maria decided to take his name, with a pledge to carry on his struggle. Right now he's trying to bring me to heel, make me pay protection money," Mulligan said.

"Will he make a revolution?"

"He couldn't make bread," was Mulligan's scornful reply. "He can't have more than two dozen men with him."

"But Castro started out with the same numbers."

"Che's no Castro. He's just a high-class thug."

Mulligan's wife Alicia was sitting and waiting inside the plane, smoking a cigarette. She was in her late thirties, with strong good looks and eyes that were dark and bold and proud—the eyes of a lioness. She said hello quietly, then turned away as we took off. We climbed a thousand feet in the Cessna and swept out over the mountains, turning south, picking up the shoreline. The Pacific showed bright-green below, shading off into darkness further out to sea. The wind here and there was whipping up white curds of foam.

I asked Alicia how many of my old buddies had shown up for the reunion.

"Well, you're the fourth to have made it down. Matt's a little disappointed at the turnout, but we're a long way from civilization.

But I think everybody's having a good time. They're out fishing right now.''

Alicia was a Latin beauty: dark-skinned, with a sumptuous body and fine straight features and a beehive of black hair. But the first two fingers on her right hand were blotched with nicotine and she kept fiddling with her lighter, turning it round and round in her hand.

The plane ran into some turbulence which shook us from side to side. I put my head back and closed my eyes.

"You all right?" Alicia asked.

I nodded. "Ever since 'Nam, I get airsick."

"That war," she said.

"Yeah. But you've got your own war down here, don't you?"

She shrugged her shoulders.

"What's going to happen to the guerrillas now that the military junta has taken over the country?"

"I wish I knew. We've had military coups before. The generals don't seem any better at running things than the civilians."

"What a mess."

"Never mind. We shall overcome."

Below us a stretch of barren white flats ran from the sea to the deepest reaches of the interior. Then there was more turbulence. Closing my eyes, I sat back, fighting down the nausea. In my mind's eye I saw the white-clad peons sitting along a mud wall in the river town I had stayed in last night, their faces ravaged and consumptive. Hovels, whore-houses, a jail filled with political prisoners. Swine and fowl roaming the streets. Mosquitos—

"—nothing I can do about them, señor."

"—spray the room?—"

"Sorry," the hotel clerk said. *"Son las cosas de la vida."*

That's life, jack.

What a place: large dead waterbugs on the floor of the hotel room, a putrid stench from the toilet; the hungry wide-eyed children running after me, begging for centavos.

"Things are much better now that the army has taken over," said a man in the bar. "We have all been saved from the arms of communism."

And then: "Have you ever seen a whale?"

What?

But it was Mulligan now, shouting over his shoulder. I opened my eyes.

"Have you?"

"What?"

"Ever seen a whale?" .

Befuddled, I just wobbled my head.

"Keep your eyes peeled."

Mulligan pushed the wheel forward; we headed down, skimming over some high sand dunes ringing a lagoon which sat mysteriously inland, right in the center of the flats.

"Look."

It was a whale, all right, swimming on the surface of the lagoon, huge and black and unmistakable. He was whipping along at a surprising speed, carving out bow waves that bubbled all around him. He seemed to be chasing his own shadow, a submarine shape skimming across the bottom. Sensing us, he breeched, heaving his massive body high and crashing back down and diving deep. Mulligan pulled the plane up and made a long slow turn which put us into position to see the whale break water minutes later and leap again, snorting a cone of vapor high into the air. At its peak the vapor caught the sunlight and blazed like white fire before curling over and dissolving.

We discovered a whole family of whales in another part of the lagoon, swimming around in a circle, ten or twelve of them. Mulligan brought the plane down low and we saw a mother whale lying within the circle floating on her side, giving suck to her calf. Mother and baby both poked their gray-green heads up and looked at us from the shallows. We could see the white barnacles on their backs, the expression in their eyes. It made me break out with goosepimples.

"They're California grays," Mulligan explained as we flew toward El Cortez. "They come down each winter by the hundreds from the Arctic Circle for courting and calving. The lagoon is some kind of natural phenomenon. It's hidden from the sea by kelp beds and a heavy surf, but the whales have learned to work their way a mile inland to the safe waters."

"Didn't I read somewhere that the gray whale has been exterminated?"

"Almost, but not quite. There weren't any for a long time, but then they suddenly came back. Now they're protected by international agreements and the whalers can't slaughter them the way they used to."

Whales! I sat back, healthy again, rejuvenated. "Goddammit," I said to Mulligan, "no wonder you like it down here. This is some country, things are happening everywhere you look!"

Soon we came to El Cortez, recognizable by the coastal waters around it, which were stained a reddish brown from the adjacent hills of copper. The iron-rust color saturated everything, not just the hills but the valley in which the village sat, even the stones, the trees, all of which glowed in the last light of the day like the dying embers in a fireplace.

The village itself looked simple but good: white-washed houses, adobe huts, and shacks with thatched roofs. The main road ran right through the heart of the town, a wide dirt street branching off into a network of footpaths and narrow lanes. A stream of reddish water moved sluggishly alongside the road. Two bare-assed kids waved to us from their backyard, blowing kisses.

We were circling over the air strip. On a nearby hill stood Mulligan's copper mine: crowned by a big sooty redbrick chimney and a conglomeration of work sheds, it appeared to be thriving; trolleys were running down a narrow-track railway to the sea, men were moving around, grey smoke was oozing out and streaming across the valley, covering it like a coffin lid.

Mulligan dropped through the thick hanging stuff and landed the plane like a pro. We taxied toward an adobe shack sitting between two dusty date palms. Half a dozen men came out of the shack, armed with carbines, showing the tough wary look of men on the alert.

So Mulligan did have war down here.

Doreen

Fab, everything was fabulous about the place. Imagine me, wee Dorrie, up in an airplane and all that, a *private* plane, like a bluidy industrialist or movie star, with these two gorgeous fellas. I took a real fancy to the Major, he was so handsome and manly, the kind of older fella every bird dreams of marrying, but of course he was already married and Alicia was something too, with her olive skin and long black hair piled up on her napper, like a bun. She was right out of a Spanish painting, kinda regal, but nice. If I did anything it would have to be with Eli. He was single, or at least I think he was, and I wasn't half attracted to him. He reminded me a lot of the lads back home. He was built small and stocky, but tough and chipper, a free spirit. No hiding what he felt. He yelled when he was mad, laughed when happy. Even better was his crazy moustache, like the handlebars of a motorbike.

I couldnae be sure what he felt for me but, from the way he kept copping squints, chances were he liked me, found me funny, anyway. Of course, nearly every Yank you met thought a Scots accent was a giggle and tried to take the mickey outa you. All foreigners were funny to them, though Eli was different with his languages and all, he had a noodle on him, all right. That was the thing about American men, they had brains *and* bodies, which is what made them so sexy, Eli anyway. That and his Viva Zapata moustache.

We were taken to town together in an old army jeep. El Cortez looked aw'right to me. There were some big old wooden houses with tin roofs and deep porches built by the French company that once worked the mine, and the center had lots of restaurants and cantinas

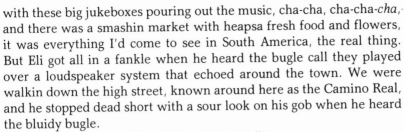

with these big jukeboxes pouring out the music, cha-cha, cha-cha-*cha*, and there was a smashin market with heapsa fresh food and flowers, it was everything I'd come to see in South America, the real thing. But Eli got all in a fankle when he heard the bugle call they played over a loudspeaker system that echoed around the town. We were walkin down the high street, known around here as the Camino Real, and he stopped dead short with a sour look on his gob when he heard the bluidy bugle.

"Do you hear what I hear?" he said to Mulligan.

The Major just sniffed a little. "Yeah, that's right, it's five o'clock recall."

"You use American army bugle calls to mark off the day?"

"It's odd, I know. But what can we do, we've got to defend ourselves against the MNR. I've been obliged to run the entire village on military lines."

Eli was an ex-soldier too but he seemed pissed at that, right shirty. And as we walked on his anger began to grow. The sidewalks were jammed with squatters—hundreds of skinny unshaven unhappy lookin' coves, mostly Indians from the mountain villages down in search of work, said Alicia. There were bags of federal soldiers loungin about too, fat ugly cheuchters in these dirty shabby uniforms. Lots of wains were also runnin about in the dust and there were beggars galore and even a half-crippled idiot that came stotting toward us, dragging his game leg and droolin' a plea for money.

"How long have things been like this?" Eli asked, with a look on his face like a runt that's just shat his knickers.

"Ever since the army took over the country."

"If there's no work why don't they go elsewhere?"

"There is no elsewhere. The real wealth is up north, in the big copper and tin mines. Around here everything is all sand and stones, except for up there on the hill."

We all took a wee shufty up at the mine. The work day was over and the navvies were leaving the pit, stumbling down the slope in a long queue that snaked its way toward the check-out point, where they paused to turn in their crowbars and picks before movin on again, slowly and wearily, like beasts of burden. It reminded me of my own da', who used to load coal on the docks of the Clyde. Like him, the miners were all covered with soot and muck and stooped over from the weight of their work. But this wee town was a damn sight better than Clydeside. Instead of all those dricht and drear streets in the rain, here everything was warm and alive, jumpin with music. And the sun was still shining gloriously on the mountain peaks, painting them orange and pink, and over our heads drifted homing flights of pigeons. They filled the evening air with their cawing and clattering, and when they turned over and dived their breasts caught the same fiery colors of the hilltops.

Mulligan showed us where we were going to stay. The house didn't look like much from outside, just a high wall and a dirty old door that hadn't sniffed paint in a century, but inside there was a smashin' courtyard with flowers and grapevines and a lemon tree resplendent with fruit. Eli and I each had rooms off the courtyard, with a private loo and all and bags of space and a nice view of the mountain.

Even more marvelous was the bowly bachal who owned the house and was being paid to look after us. Her name was Señora Blanca and she was a tiny stooped-over woman with about two teeth in her skull. She didnae speak a word of English and of course I spoke even less Spanish, but thank God Eli waŝ there to help out. Even to my ears his accent sounded atrocious but the old biddy was so delighted with him that she cackled like a daft chicken at his every word. Then, giving his cheek a tweak, she scuttled off sideways, like a crab, to make us some coffee. She paused in the doorway of the kitchen to flash Eli a smile that could only be called coquettish.

"Looks like you've got yourself a girl friend, fella."

Eli grinned and leaned back in his chair, turning his face up to the sun. Several minutes went by before he opened his brown eyes and sought mine out. "I dig this,'' he said. "I dig sitting here in the sun and being with you." Something nice and warm passed between us, until the moment was shattered by the sound of another bugle call coming from town.

"I wish they'd quit blowing that fucking thing," Eli grumbled. "The sound of it really upsets me."

"How come? You're an old soldier, ain'cha? The Major told me you were one of the best fighting men he had in Viet Nam."

"There was a time when I would have been proud of that. But now the thought makes me sick."

"Why?"

"It's like telling a man he's a machine, a machine for killing."

Eli broke out a black, stinky-looking cigar and put a match to it, puffing away furiously to get it going. "This damned thing must be stuffed with donkey shit," he muttered. Then he looked sharply across and said, "Get this straight. I'd do anything for Mulligan, but I'm sure as hell not proud of what I did in Viet Nam. The way I look

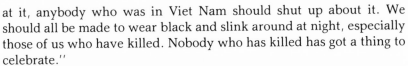

at it, anybody who was in Viet Nam should shut up about it. We should all be made to wear black and slink around at night, especially those of us who have killed. Nobody who has killed has got a thing to celebrate."

He started chewing on his cigar again but changed his mind in favor of taking a wee nip of tequila from the flask he'd been carrying on his hip.

"You want some of this?"

"Guid lord, no, it tastes like the stuff you fill cigarette lighters with."

"What made you take a job down here?" he asked suddenly.

"It was the lure of gay carefree South America," I deadpanned. "I wanted to dance the bossa nova under sunny skies with the friendly happy natives."

"Some happy natives," he growled, fingering the bruise on his cheek.

"It's no joke, this guerrilla warfare," I said. "But I was more frightened for my life when I live in East Los Angeles."

"Los Angeles. You've been around," he said.

And around and around, I added privately. Like the spirals of a whirlpool.

"What are you wandering around the world for?" he asked in that blunt, out-front way of his. "What in hell are you running from, girl?"

"Who says I'm running?"

"You do. It's in your eyes, if you'd like to know. Maybe you don't realize it but all it takes is one look to know you're in trouble."

"I'm just travelin'," I said.

"Same thing," he replied. "When a man's at the end of his rope, he either commits suicide or travels."

"What a thing to say. You mean all the millions of tourists in the world are really wantin' to stove themselves in?"

"You're not a tourist," he said. "You're a nutty bitch, wandering around like this, putting your life in the hands of strangers."

"Och, you'd better shut your mouf," I told him, "or you'll get a gobful of dandruff!"

Eli laughed out loud at that and asked, "Are they all like you back home?"

"You'll haftae come to Scotland and find out for yourself."

"I'd like to," he said. "Before I die, I'd like to see the Loch Ness monster."

"Easy. Next time you're shavin', just open your eyes in the mirror."

"You sure are one salty lady," he grinned. Then he put his head back and threw down another shot of tequila. It made him cough and wet his eyes. "Christ, this stuff is strong, it's real kickapoo juice. You sure you don't want a taste?"

I shrugged. "Och, what the hey, give us a wee sook."

I tried to get a swallow down, but the stuff was so raw and rough I nearly puked it all out.

"How can ye drink that plonk?"

"I can't," he replied, knocking back another snifter. He was trying to get pissed, I realized. Something was eating him out.

Then the Señora returned with our coffee and a plateful of corn bread and fried bananas, which turned out to be delicious. While we ate, she hung over me, makin' a lot of daft faces and gestures.

"What's she goin' on about?" I asked Eli.

"She's trying to tell you the water's heated up for your bath."

"A bath! I've forgotten what one's like," I cried, jumping up excitedly. "That's me awae," I said. "I'll try and leave a little water for you."

"Don't bother," he said. "I'm off to town. See you later, you roastit bubbly-jock!"

"Gobble, gobble to you, too," I sang back.

Alicia

Caray!, what a muchacha that Doreen was, one in a million. Anybody else just off the road would have slept late, but she made it a point to report to work at 7 A.M. And how that girl worked. Maybe she looked like a leftover hippie, but when she sat down to type a letter—*Hijo!* how she made that machine chatter, just like a machine-gun. She finished all my correspondence in one hour flat and then went on to attack the filing with equal speed and efficiency. She was out of the ordinary, the way she worked, talking a mile a minute all the while, laughing and cracking jokes. She hit that office like a bomb shell and all the girls loved her right off. I loved her too, with her round laughing face and flashing eyes and Scottish brogue.

She was full of questions, wanting to know about this person and that, but especially about Eli Brickman. Obviously, that *chica* had more than just a casual interest in him, though when I ventured that the two of them seemed to have hit it off, she replied, "Och, I doubt whether I'm really his kind of lassie. A fella like that, been everywhere and all, probably likes the fancy stuff, if y'know what I mean, cocktail waitresses or go-go dancers, the kind with big bulgers and a bloated bottom."

As if on cue, Eli came into view from the office window. He was an unmistakable figure in his leather jacket and jeans and big flowing moustache. He showed curiosity about everything, first stopping to poke his head in a blacksmith's shop, then studying an old woman grinding herbs in a three legged *molcajete*, then moving along and buying *pan dulce* from a street urchin and standing there eating and chatting with the child.

17

"Where'd he learn Spanish?" I asked Doreen.

"While driving his truck, listening to language tapes. That's just like a Yank, isn't it—puttin every minute to work."

She sat down behind the typewriter again and bashed out the last paragraph of a letter that Matt wanted redone. "Here y'are, hen," she said, handing it over, "it's ready to be signed."

The army commandent, Colonel Tito Cota, was inside with Matt; jacket unbuttoned and showing his dirty underwear and blubbery belly, he sat over a glass of *pulque*, making effusive gestures as he spoke. He had two sullen-looking *pistoleros* with him, and when he saw me he jumped up hastily and began buttoning up. With his paunch and tiny legs and sideburns he looked more comic than ferocious. But a week ago he had kicked and pistol-whipped one of his soldiers for insubordination.

After the colonel left Matt said, "Do you know what he wanted today? He wanted me to write to Washington, to my 'friends' in the Pentagon and ask them to supply his army with jet aircraft, tanks and napalm. How's that for a laugh? He wants America to supply the means for a bunch of fatheads like him—colonels and generals who have never even seen a war—to start bombing and napalming villages and suspected guerilla hideouts.

"Christ, what an imbecile," Matt fumed, "a real *cholo cabrón*. Instead of whipping his soldiers into shape and sending them up into the hills to fight, he sits here with his belly hanging out, drinking my booze and dreaming of napalm and jet fighters."

"All right, but isn't that another reason to avoid trouble with the MNR? Go and talk to Che, give him what he wants. He may come out on top next year."

"We could give him every penny we own and still it wouldn't help us when the revolution came," Matt said. "They'd not only take our mine away, but they'd dump you and me out in a field and riddle us with bullets and spit on us and chop us to bits with machetes paid for with our own money."

"I don't believe it."

"Of course you don't, you've never been in a war, you've never seen what men can do to each other."

I turned away.

Fnally, "Pour me a drink, Matt."

"What about your stomach?"

"I've decide that my ailments are psychosomatic."

He came over and slipped an arm around my waist. "I was worried about you last night."

Almost every night now I woke at three or four in the morning, trembling, full of dread. It took me hours to fall back asleep; I'd just lie in the dark beside Matt, shivering, fretting, feeling the pain moving from my womb to my chest and back again; and when sleep finally came dreaming agonizing dreams—Che appearing before me, body twisted into a melted-plastic shape, Matt aiming a pistolete out the window. "Don't hurt anybody with that," I had pleaded, "there are children in the streets." The dream sequences followed each other rapidly and mechanically, like records in a jukebox.

"Just a touch of the midnight sweats."

"As bad as when the baby died?"

I shrugged.

"That's rough, kid. Can I do anything?"

"Of course you can, dammit. Stop fighting with Che."

"How? By asking him to play nice?"

"Find a way. There's got to be a way."

"Look," he said quietly, carefully, "you're asking for the impossible. We've got war down here. I don't want it, I've had enough of war, a sickening lifetime of it, but we've got it whether we like it or not. And in war there's only one thing to do: kill your enemy. If you don't he'll kill you—it's as simple and despicable as that."

From outside came the blast of a horn; stepping to the window and looking out Matt said, "The boys are back. I'd better go and meet them."

"Remember what we agreed last night."

He scowled his displeasure.

"Look, Eli took an awful chance coming through the hills alone like that."

"When the invitations went out, I had no idea we'd be having this hassle with Che."

"We've been through all this. You've no right to jeopardize their lives. This fight with the MNR has nothing to do with them."

Matt mulled it over, then shrugged his shoulders. "All right, I'll make an announcement: anybody that can't stand the noise of the bells should quit the church."

"I'm sorry, Matt. I know how much you've been looking forward to the reunion."

"What the hell," he said, "fate laughs at probabilities. Meanwhile, give us a smooch." He took my face in his hands and held it tenderly like that for several moments, not saying anything, just looking into me. He kissed me, just once, and everything that was in him seemed to flow into me, his strength and resolve, his vanity and truculence, and I felt at once replenished and diminished, as if both the hosts of heaven and hell had laid simultaneous hands upon me.

"Hey, *mi corazón*, I'm still crazy about you," he whispered. "You still look as good to me as the first time I saw you. *Better*, dammit. You're still the best thing that ever happened to me."

Minutes later I found myself sitting alone and staring unseeingly at the letter Matt had signed and left behind on the desk. After all these years, how strongly he still affected me. *Qué hombre.*

And yet, my being with him had brought no comfort; my body was cold and empty, there was a septic taste in my mouth, a residue of pain in my womb. We were no longer joined. We still lived and slept together, and he entered me almost nightly; but something was amiss. No matter how tightly he held me, I felt excluded from his life, his thoughts: he was sealed up inside himself. Che had put a malediction on him, a curse.

"Alicia, excuse me . . . "

It was Doreen. "Did he sign the letter? If you want it to go out in the evening plane I'll need to type the envelope."

When I handed it to her she took it but didn't go, stood scrutinizing me instead.

"You all right, hen?"

I nodded.

"You don't luke it."

Shakily I lit a cigarette. Blessed tobacco, it never let you down.

"The kettle's on the bile, how 'bout comin' and havin a wee fly cup with me," Doreen said, putting on the brogue to cheer me up.

Her good spirits were infectious. What in God's name was I moping about? Things were tough, but no cause for a permanent long face.

Resolution: starting tonight I will lighten up. I will put on a new face, a smile like Doreen's, go to the party with Matt and really shake my skirts. Forget pain, forget nightmares. Tonight I cut loose, I get drunk and laugh, dammit, *laugh.* And I make Matt laugh too, make him come out of himself, forget Che and the guerillas and all that.

Horn blasts again; the truck bearing the reunion boys was trundling past. The three of them—Frits and Billy Joe and YoYo—had left El Cortez two days ago, accompanied by four local fishermen and two hundred cans of beer. Now they were back and Matt had hopped up on the running board to greet them.

The beer must have gone down well: Billy Joe was wearing a huge sombrero; Frits was stripped down to his undershirt; YoYo was brandishing a beer can in each fist, and together they were belting out a raucous and bawdy ballad.

As the truck jolted to a halt someone shouted, "Hey, there's E.J.!"

"Eli, Eli!"

"C'mon, buddy, get your chops into some of this beer!"

The boys leaped over the side of the truck—Frits landing splat on his drunken face—and fell on the protesting Eli, whooping and pummeling. With people gathering on all sides, Billy Joe and YoYo staggered boozily around and began tugging at the truck's tailgate.

"Looka all fish we caught," YoYo shouted.

But they had trouble removing the bolts, so Eli and Matt went round to help; just then the tailgate came away and dumped a great clattering pile of empty beer cans down on them. They fell back shouting and protesting, like children under a waterfall. When the clatter ceased, Eli and Matt retaliated by climbing up into the truck, picking up a box of iced fish and dumping it out on the others.

That started it. A fish fight followed, with the four bibulous native fishermen joining in: it was wild, sophomoric, hilarious.

They flung whole baskets of fish at each other, hurled lobsters and crabs and octopuses at the onlookers, sent the shaved ice flying like confetti. The fish slithered all over the road: *pinto* and *cabrilla* and *roncador* and *mojarrón*: mullet and skipjack and snapper and bonito. What a bouillabaisse!

When they were done with the game the men went staggering off to a nearby cantina, arms linked, hollering and singing, caught up in an intense moment of camaraderie and love. The platoon was reunited and the whole office reverberated with their happiness and excitement.

As I stood watching the phone rang.

"This is LoCascio," said a voice at the other end, coming through scratchily. "Unidentified plane heading this way."

"You've challenged it?"

"Yes. No reply."

I put the phone down and looked at Doreen. "What's wrong?" she asked. When I told her she frowned and shook her head. "You'd better sound the alarm."

"It's so stupid. Air raid alarms in El Cortez."

"Orders are orders."

Resentfully, I went into Matt's office and poked the red button on his desk. Immediately a siren outside shrieked with such violence that several nearby children got the crying fits. Matt's palace guard came running from all sides, dispersing to various emergency stations; footsteps pounded across the roof to the gun emplacement up there.

The months of air raid drills which Matt had inflicted on the village brought results: mothers snatched up their children and ran for it; homeward-bound miners dived into doorways; the beggars and squatters flew everywhichway. Moments later the only ones left standing in the Camino Real were the reunion boys: caught unaware, they stood blinking and gaping until Matt bawled: "Take cover!"

They panicked like chickens, flying off wildly, bumping into each other, darting and squawking. Only Frits Hartogs held his ground; in his undershirt, befuddled face tilted up, he seemed suddenly pathetic with his tubby figure, his helpless vulnerability.

The plane came into sight. It descended rapidly and swept right over the village, a small twin-engine craft, and up on the roof somebody yelled in Spanish, "Get ready!"

The plane turned, climbed toward the sun, but came back, dropping quickly now. Frits hadn't moved. People were barking at him but he seemed unable or unwilling to respond, until Matt sprinted out into the road, grabbing him and towing him out of the way.

"Do you recognize the plane?" Doreen's voice was tight.

It was absurd, I didn't want to believe Che was capable of dropping a bomb on us, on me, but the thought, the fear, was there.

"Guid Lord, what's he trying to do?"

I heard Matt yell: "Hold your fire!"

It was obvious: the pilot meant to land on the Camino Real.

"He's daft," Doreen said. "Stark raving bonkers."

The pilot came in uncertainly, wobbling in his flight, and had to pull back and zoom up at the last minute, wheels just missing the belfry of the church. On his second try he seemed more sure of himself, came with nose down in a long glide, cutting his speed, holding the craft with more control. He hit straight down on the bumpy road, bounced hard, socked down again, wheels kicking up spurts of red dust. For a moment the plane swerved, went out of control, and I gasped; but then its brakes held and it came skidding toward us, wing flaps extended, and squealed to a stop about twenty yards away.

On both sides of the Camino Real men trained their guns. Matt appeared and walked slowly up the road, hand on his .45. He stopped and waited. A bird shrieked in the sky, startling everyone.

The door of the plane opened and the pilot jumped down, the biggest, mightiest, black man I had ever seen: a colossus carved out of anthracite.

He put his shoulders back against the plane and looked around. Presently he smiled lazily and said in a soft sly hip drawl, "Whut have we here? Some of that famous Latin American *hospitality* I've heard about?"

He turned to Matt.

"How come y'all look so surprised?" he asked. "Didn't I tell you I was gonna drop in on you? Well I did," he chuckled, "I dropped right in on your cotton-pickin' *haid*!"

Now, relishing his moment of triumph, his little coup, Claude Copeland put his head back and began to laugh, epic laughter that shook the walls and rattled the window-panes.

CHE'S DIARY

March 26

. . . Caraballo came from the capital with a communication from Pacho, repeating order cease guerrilla activities. The asshole! He and the rest of the old-line party functionaries have always opposed us. Now they are cutting us off from all arms and supplies, trying to starve us into submission. We are completely on our own.

*   *   *

Later

. . . discussed Fidel's words with the men. Today the party represents only one element of a much larger revolutionary movement. We are in the vanguard, they are in the rear. Today one must be a revolutionary before being an accomplished Marxist-Leninist. Through our actions and successes we must prove to them that we are historically correct.

But meanwhile we are starving and ill. Survival must come first. The next month will tell the story. Either we win or we become martyrs.

*   *   *

March 27

. . . What a hole we are living in. Dust, mosquitoes, endless scorpions. And so little food to be found in these dry, empty hills. Yesterday Pombo returned with a dead cat, which we tried to eat. A cat!

*   *   *

Later

. . . at 13 hours Pombo, Alejandro and Epifano returned with a car they had taken near Yanacuna from a stranger. U.S. passport identifies him as one Eli Jay Brickman. Driving with a girl, English passport, toward El Cortez. Probably a CIA agent or one of Mulligan's mercenaries with his kept woman. Carrying a large amount of cash, which Alejandro took, along with his car and belongings. Alejandro certain the gringo was an agent, felt they should have shot him on the spot. But consider the repercussions if he were a bona fide civilian. Much better that discipline was observed. We can't afford to have the army after us right now.

*   *   *

Turk

First dude I see when I come to town is big Claude Copeland, standing on the porch of the command post and towering over the Major.
Lord, is he big and black. "Hey, my man," he says, "you look ugly
and evil as ever."

I feel like growling at him, but the dog does it for me. Good old
dog, he always senses what's in my mind.

"In town you muzzle that hound," says the Major. I explain that
I forgot but Mulligan snaps out the order again. It means that with
all of them lookin on I got to try and make the dog obey. But the
dog hates the muzzle and starts backing away and showing his teeth.
This gives the boys the jollies and they start riding me, sayin things
like "Turk, not even your own dog likes you."

When I finally get him muzzled, Claude looks down and asks, "Has
that dog got a name?"

"Yeah, I call him dog."

Straightfaced, Claude says, "That's a boss name for a dog. Boss.
That's the pup you found in Nam, ain't it? You said you were gonna
bring him home and you did. I see you also brought home that
Chinese rifle you took off that dead chink. How are you, Turk? You
ain't got any better lookin."

"And you ain't got any whiter."

Lookin at him, I remember the first day Claude joined the company.
It was right after the manure hit the fan in Quang Ngai and the Cong
was ambushing us every other day and we were going right back at
Charlie and shooting the shit out of him, wiping out villages left
and right. Claude didn't have the revenge motive in him and he'd

25

get all shook every time we shot a dink or burned down a hootch, but he soon learned, he got it all together. The Major put him in my hands and told me to harden his ass up. For all his size and strength, Claude was still a boy when it came to war. I practically had to breathe fire but I finally made a man out of him. Claude learned to cut it, he became one of the best, a real hard charger, and there wasn't nothing I wouldn't trust him with, not even demolitions.

We had been buddies there, but we always liked to jive each other, so now, just to burn him a little, I says, "Been readin about you in the sports pages, Claude. Whatcha gonna do now that the Bears released you? You got yourself a job?"

Claude's mouth tightens, but just for a second. "Don't worry 'bout me, daddy. I've got a couple of years left."

"Anybody tried to sign you?"

"I've had some offers but I'm playing hard to get. You see, I don't really need the salary any more. I've got a piece of a magnesium mine in Calgary and a string of soul food restaurants in the USA. All I really dig now is the glory, the action itself."

It figured. After twelve years in pro ball he must of socked away a nice bundle. The big stars like him were supposed to be good for a hundred or two hundred grand a year, plus what they nicked doing hair grease ads on TV. Even the spades did commercials now. Claude had obviously got well over the years. Anybody that could afford to fly his own plane, even if it was only a Piper Cub, wasn't hurting for bread. Claude was a hotdog, all right. He was wearing a hand-tailored suit that must of run him a couple of hundred bills and his fingers were pimpish with jewelry. But the real tip-off was the look in his eyes, the look that says straight out without ever raisin its voice, "Fuck you, jack." There's no fakin that look. Either you got fuck-you money or you don't.

The black bastard, I envied him. But to keep from letting him know it, I stay on the attack: "What about your bum knee?"

"It was operated on two months ago. It feels good now, Turk, stronger and better than ever. That's why I came down here, to toughen it up running in these hills. Three hours a day should fix me up fine."

"Here's what I thought," says Mulligan. "Maybe he could work out with Fernando."

"Ever done any boxin, Claude?"

The Major answers for him, "He's ex-Golden Glove."

"I should warn you, this boy of mine is *good*. He's big and he can hit. He just turned pro six months ago and has already whipped every-body in the district."

"Shit, I don't care how good he is," Claude replies in that uppity hardnosed way of his, "he ain't gonna whup me. Nobody whups Claude Copeland."

"We'll see about that," I say. "Let's all meet at the gym later."

Then I turn and go inside with the Major to give my report. Not a trace of Eli's car did I find; it was probably on its way to some used-car lot in the capital by now. Then I tell Mulligan about Alfredo Aguilar: "You remember him? A young grunt, he's been working here about a year—in the ice plant, the infirmary, down in the mines."

"What about him?"

"Ain't sure. It's just a hunch. He came through my checkpoint today, right after you took off, hitchin a ride on the back of a beer truck. A week ago he came through Punta Prieta in a Land Rover with some government officials down from the capital."

"So?"

"So how come this young-un is ridin up and down the length of the province when he should be chopping copper and saving his pesos to get himself laid in Ranchita's on Saturday night?"

The Major pondered on it for a while. "That's the big question right now," he says. "To know who is with us and who the hell isn't."

"What's the mystery? Most of the people in this town are MNR sympathizers."

"You can't blame em. They see what's going on in this country and then they listen to Radio Havana, which says there's no unem-ployment in Cuba, no beggars, no whores, no shantytowns. I'd start thinking revolution too if I were them." Then Mulligan turns away and gets on the soundbox. He rings up each of the boys out on patrol and tells em to keep an eye out for Aguilar and to stay on his tail if they spot him.

"Anything else, Turk?"

"Nothing."

"Then at ease, sergeant. Light the smoking lamp."

Now comes the best part of the day. Now comes what makes soljerin for Mulligan really worth it. First I go to the bar and pour a White Horse for him, with water on the side. "There's champagne if you want it," says Mulligan. "Claude brought me a bottle."

"No thanks," I reply. "I can't drink that French piss."

Slowly now, I pour out a triple shot of Canadian Club and toss it down. The whiskey hits hard and lights the fire. As the flames shoot up I damp them down with a nice long swallow of cold beer. For two days out there on patrol I craved this doubleheader, dreamt about it.

I pour out another triple CC and take it and the beer back to my seat. This one I drink slow, not like my old man, who used to set up the shot glasses one after the other on the bar and toss them down bang bang bang like a crazy man. That was the way all the oldtimers in Sharon, Pa. used to drink. You'd see them belting down the double-headers in the Greek's saloon right after breakfast. That's why I never liked the mill; it gave a man a thirst he couldn't get rid of, no matter how hard he tried. And my old man sure tried hard. He just keeled over one day from the drink. Something in his gut had bust and he turned yellower and yellower in that hospital bed, with his bulging eyes turning yellow too, and right then and there I promised myself, "No mill for me, I'm not gonna have his kind of thirst. I'm not gonna die like that." A month later I upped and joined the army, at age 16. I got the hell away from Sharon and the mill and the deathly thirst it gave a man.

By now Mulligan has opened the Old Testament. "What's it going to be today, Turk? Proverbs or Ecclesiastes?"

"Proverbs, please."

Leaning back in the big leather chair I sip my brew as Mulligan starts reading, in his deep strong voice:

"My son, attend unto my wisdom and bow thine ear to my understanding . . .

I listen for a while and let my mind unreel.

"For the lips of a strange woman drop as a honeycomb, and her mouth is smoother than oil . . .

Thoughts of Betty came to the fore. She was probably sittin in the ward right now with her hair hangin down like weeds and her eyes all hollow and dark as caves. I felt sorry for her but then anger replaced the pity and, like always, began to turn me against her. The harlot, she brought it down on herself.

"But her end is bitter as wormwood, sharp as a two-edged sword.

"Her feet go down to death: her steps take hold on hell . . . "

The words were true, so true I couldn't stand thinking about them. I look round instead at the Major's booklined cubbyhole. Mulligan's read everything in sight—the histories, the biographies, even the novels. He's smart, the Major, and he knows as much about his trade as any Colonel or General. He should of been wearin all kinds of brass now, especially with his war record, only he was too much man for the chickenshit U.S. Army.

"Drink waters out of thine own cistern, and running waters out of thine own well.

"Let thy fountains be dispersed abroad, and rivers of waters run in the streets."

Mulligan's voice brings me back and I feel the hatred beginning to simmer down. I take a swallow of beer and tune into the sermon again.

The Major reads on, quietly and steadily. He didn't have to read to me, of course. He owed me no favors. Nor did the Bible mean that much to him; Mulligan was a lapsed Catholic. But he knew what that land mine had done to my eyes and he appreciated how I felt about the Good Book. He knew I'd read it all my life and had carried it in my hip pocket all through Nam, for luck and solace.

"For the ways of man are before the Lord, and he pondereth all his goings.

"His own iniquities shall take the wicked himself, and he shall be holden with the cords of his sins.

"He shall die without instruction: and in the greatness of his folly he shall go astray."

Finished now, Mulligan puts the Bible down and goes out to the main office and calls the reunion boys in. They gather near his desk and start examining the pictures and stuff on the walls. He's got some of his medals and decorations hanging there—the Silver Star he won in Korea, the Bronze Star with a V for Valor he copped in Viet Nam— but they take second place to the photograph of Ngo Chanh Kha.

"You remember him?" I ask Claude. Claude was there the day we found Ngo living in a village shanty with about twenty other kids. They were walkin around in rags and most of them had diarrhea and rickets. Mulligan called in the medic and ordered the rest of us to dig up supplies and cook food for them. Later we dressed the kids in GI gear. They were so thin and tiny it was like playin with dolls.

Ngo was far from the best-looking of the bunch but the Major felt the deepest for him. The boy-san was in bad shape: his parents had been blown to bits in a bombing raid. He was still suffering from the shock of it and couldn't speak word-one. Ngo understood Mulligan all right when he spoke in dink but he couldn't reply. All he could do was stare back with those broken eyes of his.

"Ain't that the kid that used to be our houseboy?"

"Right."

"Damn, how the time goes."

"Weren't you gonna adopt him and bring him back to the states?" asks YoYo, all the time spinning out his fool toy.

"The doctors advised me not to uproot him," Mulligan answers. "They thought at the time that the shock of a new country wouldn't do his trauma any good."

"Wonder what happened to him," I ask. "Wonder if he got out of Nam after the V.C. took over."

"I shouldn't have listened to the doctors," Mulligan says. "I should have taken him with me when I left. I hate to think of what Charlie might have done to him."

We all gaze again at Ngo Chanh Kha, who is small and slim and sensitive-lookin. There is a sliver of a smile on his face but his eyes still have a broken look about them.

"Just think of all the orphans we made in Viet Nam," Eli says. "It's enough to give anyone a trauma."

"We? How about the Cong? Takes two to make a war, you know," says Billy Joe.

"Yeah, two so-called civilizations ready to blow people to bits in the name of freedom and progress."

The words pap-papped out of him like firecrackers, drawing everybody's attention.

"You really feel that way?" asks Mulligan.

"Yeah, and so do you, even if you don't realize it," Eli says roughly. "That's why you adopted that boy—not out of love but out of guilt. We fought a stupid meaningless war over there and you know it. For all we know we might have murdered Ngo's parents at Chu Tau."

The impact of the words, Chu Tau, hits just like a goddamn mortar shell. There was a stunned silence and then, pow!, all hell broke loose. Feelings were real high, everyone turned on Eli for bringing Chu Tau up, a subject we had buried behind us in Viet Nam.

"Let's get this straight," the Major said. "What happened at Chu Tau had nothing to do with that kid. His parents were killed in an air raid—"

But the room is in an uproar, everyone is hollerin at Eli and he's hollerin back, going on about Viet Nam and how evil and wrong it was, with Chu Tau the symbol of it. The Major comes right back at him, demanding to know how it was possible to fight the Cong without getting our hands dirty. And so on. Man, what an uproar, what a scene! I found myself lookin over at Eli in perverse admiration, begrudgin him a ration of praise. Five minutes in town and he blows the place sky-high. You had to hand it to him, he had balls, he had a sack of nuts this big!

I was surprised to hear him hit the war so hard, because in Nam E. J. was more hard-assed than most of us, volunteering for those zippo squads that did most of the burning of villages and homes. He had a lot of enemy kills to his credit, and seemed proud of it. But now he was changed. Now he talked so hard and fast against America that I could hardly keep up with him. Here and there I got the gist of what he was sayin: the war was a complete mess, the people didn't know what they were dyin for and we didn't know why we were shootin them; it was a big blood-bath, a series of atrocities, and we were no better than a bunch of storm-troopers, and who the hell did America think it was, tryin to police the world. Eli even rang in the ancient Greeks to prove some theory or other about democracies not being able to survive if they go to war continually beyond their boundaries.

Mulligan leads the fight against him. Sure Viet Nam was dirty and brutal, he says, but it wasn't meaningless.

The meaning of Nam was that it happened.

What did we learn from it? Brickman asks.

Now it was Mulligan I had to try hard to keep up with. America learned plenty, he says. It learned that the post-war world wasn't the bowl of cherries it was supposed to be, that our nuclear bombs and threats weren't enough to contain the enemy. They wanted to compete with us but not on a grand scale, not in a holy war. They wanted to take us on in a small dirty war, down in the mud, in a fringe country. It wasn't a test or power but of wills: they wanted to see if we had the guts and hardness to fight this new kind of war, a war nobody could truly win, a war without exalted principles or motives.

Here the Major got pretty windy and highfalutin himself, pushing his own theory why democracies fall. He also rang in the ancient Greeks and said that without their tough spearmen, the Greeks wouldn't of given anything to the world because they wouldn't of lasted long enough. Look what happened when they became so sophisticated that their common soldiers would no longer fight to the death. They sat around tittering about art and the Acropolis while a bunch of roman farmboys overran them and beat the jism out of them.

I didn't really want to think about Nam again, nobody did, but what the hell, the words just rose up suddenly inside me and pushed their way out.

"Eli," I heard myself yellin, "everybody knows it was a bad war, but we didn't ask to be there. We was sent there and ordered to fight, and fight we did, durn it. Then they spat on us for it. We fought their war and died for them and they spat on us. That's what Nam was all about."

"Roger that!"

"Yeah, you tell em, Turk. We were at the end of the pipeline and no one gave dinkydoo about us. No one!"

"That's right, that's the way it was."

"They forgot us. They stuck us in that jungle and gave us a gun and then they forgot all about us."

"Right on, stud, right on!"

"We killed a whole lot of innocent women and children," Eli argues. "Don't you think that was wrong?"

"Sure it was wrong. But everything was wrong about that war. Tough for us, tough for the dinks."

"That's right, that's where it is."

"What we did was nuthin next to Charlie. Talk about storm-troopers. We were like boy scouts next to Charlie. Did you see what he did when he took over the country? Those guys are worse than Hitler ever dreamed."

"You know what our crime was? Allowin' ourselves to end up in combat. We were too dumb or crazy to play the game. Instead of working an angle and landing some safe rear-area assignment, we ended up in the swamps going after Charlie. That's what we should be ashamed of—of not dinky-dawing out, goddammit!"

"Yeah, that's right—we shoulda done what Frits did. He was the only smart one among us."

We all check Frits out, but he ain't lookin' any too happy. He's sittin' with his belly hangin' out, kinda fat and sad and depressed. His head's hangin' down and his eyes are fixed on the floor.

Frits had changed so much since the war that I hardly knew him. It wasn't just the fifty pounds he'd put on, it was the way he carried himself. He'd always been quiet and moody, but he could get his act together when he had to. It wasn't like him to be so spaced-out, hardly aware of what anyone was saying.

Maybe it was having been born again that was screwing him up. The guy had become some kind of Jesus Freak. He'd tried to interest me in his church, but I told him I had no use for any religion where the preachers took from the poor while riding around in Cadillacs and golf carts.

God's words were in the bible. All of religion was in the bible. Why go to a church for counsel when the Good Book offered it to you, day and night, without it costin' a nickel?

But Fritzie couldn't go it alone. He needed somethin' to lean on, an organization to prop him up. That wasn't for me. True Christianity was between man and God, not man and some institution. I tried to get him to see it my way, but he wouldn't listen. He just kept on tryin' to proseletyze me. He wanted us to pray together, even suggested that I help him bring some of the other guys into his church, the Pentecostal House of Something or Other. But I told him to forget it, that the only house these guys would ever join was one with a red light over the door.

Mulligan finally put an end to the argument. "Enough of this," he said. "We're here for a good time, not a political debate. Nam is over and done with. Let's try to forget it the way everyone else has. Let's go and have some fun instead. That's what I invited you down here for."

The Major shoos us out of there diplomatically. We head toward the gym in silence, but takin some of the anger and heat of the quarrel with us. Eli's face was still kinda clenched up and as for me, the skin on my face was still pricklin.

But I was madder at Mulligan than Eli. The Major hadn't given me the chance to truly speak my heart. Maybe I didn't know dick about politics or the ancient Greeks, but I knew a thing or two about livin with evil. And that's what the argument was all about.

Inevitably my mind went back again to the house in Texas and Collins' basement apartment. The man lived like a hog with empty beer bottles everywhere and cooking grease splattered all over the wall behind the stove. He had six or seven kids, all of them brats, and the tiniest ran around in rags with nuthin underneath, crapping and pissing all over the place. Collins and his wife didn't care. They were fat and rednecked and drunk all the day and night. Spoiled rotten civilians! But even when drunk Collins looked at Betty in that certain way. Yeah, I knew he was evil the minute I set eyes on him, but what could I do, the Viet Nam war was in full swing and Fort Hood was jammed with recruits, they came piling in every day on the Saigon Express, and there wasn't another room to be had in town for a married couple. If we quit the boarding house we'd end up sleeping on the street.

"You keep away from my wife," I told Collins. "If I catch you even lookin at her I'm gonna kick your head in."

Fat lotta good that did me: you can't reason with evil, you can't threaten it. All you can do is stomp it out.

Betty didn't help things, that's for damn sure. The bitch flirted like a harlot with him, pushin her chest out and wrigglin her can every time Collins passed by. She wasn't really out to entice him, just to aggravate me. That's how she got her jollies. In her own way, of course, she was as evil as Collins.

"You don't realize what you're doin," I told her. "You can't play around with a hog like that."

She just laughed coarsely and cruelly. "I'm just having some fun. God knows you don't show me any. You're more married to that damn bible than to me."

In the end it happened just the way I knew it would: Collins broke in on her one night and raped her in the john. Then, because he knew I would kill him if she told, he tried to slit her throat with a knife. Somebody heard her screaming and managed to break the door open before he could finish her off. The doctors saved her but she was just as good as dead after that. The state took her off and tried to fix her deranged mind with electric shock but all they did was frizzle what was left of the grey stuff. She was still sitting in the insane asylum down near Raleigh.

Now the bible words came back: *"Deliver me, O Lord, from the evil man: preserve me from the violent man: which imagine mischiefs in their hearts: continually are they gathered together for war."*

It wasn't until I reached the gym and spied Fernando that my temper started to cool. To hell with E.J. and the others. There was no delivering them from the evil man. That much I knew. Like Betty, they'd have to learn it the hard way. And learn they would. It was only a question of time.

But seeing Fernando really brought me around, cheered me up. Damn, but the boy looked good out there, skipping rope in the middle of the gym. The gym was nothing more than a woven palm hut and the floor was just swept hard-packed earth. It smelled of urine from the open latrine in back and the light was sullen, but Fernando gave the place class. As I watched him skip rope with that rippling grace of his, a tingle spread through my chest.

"Hey muchacho come on over and say hello," I called out. Fernando comes skipping over, so fast that the rope is a blur. He's big, over six-four, and his thick big-muscled chest and shoulders taper down to a narrow waist. His face is dark and unmarked and he's got the chopped-out profile and black glittering eyes of a hawk. All the boys say nice things about him.

Then I lead Claude into the tiny locker room in back, show him where to suit up. Undressed, that nigger is somethin to see: a man-mountain, a black Atlantis. He weighs a good two-fifty but none of it is fat and he has as much speed as power. I remember the last time I watched him play on TV, back in the states. On the first play of the game the quarterback faked a pitchout, half-spun and gave the handoff to Claude, who was waiting in his tracks. And then, zap! He took off up the middle, exploding so fast out of the line that everybody on the field was stunned. He shot through the Colts like an arrow through cheesecloth and was gone, long gone, before anyone could even holler.

Presently Claude began loosening up his bad knee, which has two big curved crimson scars on either side of the kneecap, stretching and flexing it in a slow methodical businesslike way.

"Got to be careful of those cruciate ligaments," he explains. Then, when it feels right, he binds the knee up carefully with an ace bandage and tapes it firm.

He's brought an old sweat-suit down with him a gray shapeless thing with *Edmonton Cubs* stenciled on front in washed-out letters.

"My lucky suit," he says.

Claude had played in the Canadian League when he got back from Nam. The American teams wouldn't even give him a tryout. They had never heard of him cauz all he'd ever played before the war was some high school ball.

"How much did they pay you up in Canada?" I asked him.

"Three hundred bucks a game, Turk, with a no-play, no-pay clause. But in the end I beat Mister Cholly at his own game."

"How so?"

"I took the team right into a tie for the championship. Then, three days before the big game, I walked into the front office and told Cholly I was quitting unless he laid a ten-thousand-dollar bonus on me. WHOOOOOEEEEee, you shoulda heard what The Man said. Curse? You ain't heard nuthin like it. Then he threatened to have me blackballed for life. 'You're outa luck, baby,' I told him, 'somebody already beat you to it!'"

Eyes glittering devilishly, Claude went on. "For the next three days they said, No, Never, a contract is a contract, where is your sense of honor? SHEEEeeiiitt, why is it that honky always talks honor when a black man mentions money? Why don't he just stick to the subject, which is *bread*, Jim, plain and simple *bread.* Anyway, I knew I had them. Cauz without me they couldn't win the championship. No championship, no money—no BREAD—for them. So in the end green talked loud to Mister Cholly and he listened to the call, just like he always does.''

"You sound like one of them black muslins, Claude. You hate all white men now?''

"No, I'm not a black musl*in*,'' he says with a sneer. "And I don't hate white men. I just hate white ideas, white *thinking,* you dig? You act like a man with me and we'll get along fine. You act like a White man, though, and you'll see some hate, Jim, you'll see it in your fucking dreams!''

"What kind of talk is this? We were buddies in Nam. There were never any black-white fights between us.''

"That's right, we were tight over there. But when I got home I found people wanted to treat me like just another nigger on the street again. They didn't give a damn where I had been or what I had done.''

"I got news for you. The same thing happened to all of us. We went home and the country turned its back on us. When you told someone you'd been in Viet Nam he looked at you like you had a social disease. That's why I cut out, Claude, and came down here.''

"Ain't you tired of soljerin', Turk?''

"You better believe it. But it's all I'm good at. And I just couldn't stick all those civilians back home.''

Claude nodded at that. "Right on. They hated us for what happened in Nam. We should have shot up half the country when we went back, we should've given *them* some shit instead of the other way around. But it's too late for that, Nam's just a bad dream, so let's forget it, let's see what that boy of yours has got. Let's see what the mother-fucker is puttin' down!''

When the fight commences Claude moves kind of slowly and stiffly, like he was unused to a boxer's motions. His shoulders are tight and his footwork lousy, but then, after Fernando pops him in the gut once or twice—he loosens up and starts getting the feel of the ring. Pretty soon both boys are moving and hitting well. I stay right with Fernando all the way, coaxing him along.

"Yeah, come on now, move . . . get under his jab . . . get to his stomach . . . come on, baby, timing . . . HIT . . . yeah, that's the way . . . fight . . . FIGHT . . . ''

It was one hell of a workout for Fernando, who needed practice against a big tough man like Claude, somebody who had the reach and weight on him.

"All right, all right now," I tell him, sometime in English, sometime in spic, "*otra vez,* baby . . . *eso* . . . come on, MOVE . . . hit . . . again . . . again . . . FIGHT."

The four rounds go pretty fast. Claude starts slowing down and getting winded after the third, but Fernando outboxes him from the start. The kid moves pretty good and hits Claude with a couple of right hands that would of hurt if they hadn't been using pillow gloves and headgear. Claude gets in several good chops too but the kid hangs tough and goes back for more. Everybody enjoys the workout and there is bo-coo applause when it ends.

Claude comes over and shakes Fernando's hand. There is a cut on the nigger's cheek but otherwise he's ok, tired and sweated, but grinning like a man who knows he's used his body well. He's a real jock and Fernando is eager to work out with him every day. So they fix it. Claude will get up at six and do roadwork with Fernando, then both boys'll come down here and put the gloves on.

Hot damn, for the next couple of weeks we're gonna have some *fun* around here!

Doreen

What a smashing party it was. Along about seven-thirty these scrumptuous cooking smells started drifting through the village; they put an ache in my tummy and spoiled me for work. Eli came at nine-thirty and I fled that office like a Glasga film audience fleeing God Save the Queen. The sight inside the rec hall was a'right: the food was heaped up everywhere, pots of soup, mounds of lobsters, platters of fish and steaming vegetables, dishes of turtle steak and *pez fuerte*. The big hall was crowded and smoky and dozens of waiters staggered around under trays of food and gallons of booze. At the head table sat the Major and his mates, under a banner reading:

198th Infantry Brigade
Third Battalion "Bravo Company"

The Major beckoned us to come sit beside him, and as we picked our way across the floor a mariachi band blared out a wild paso doble. By the time we reached the table a bowl of gazpacho soup and a clam cocktail and a glass of chilled white wine were waiting for us, and Eli shouted over the din, "McDonald's was never like this," and Alicia leaned over and placed a wine-wet kiss on my cheek. Then I was off and away, tucking into the food and grog, getting with it.

Scattered around the room were numerous tables at which sat the Major's soldiers and a slew of miners, engineers, surface men, and their wives. Free tables of food had been set up outside and the villagers and squatters milled around, shouting boisterously as they stuffed their gobs and peered in through the windows, bodies throwing off a terrible pong. Soon the sweat began dripping down my face and onto my clam cocktail.

Before long both Eli and I got right fu'. We chattered and boozed and laughed like a couple of nits and I found myself liking him even more now that he was beginning to relax. He was good fun when he got going and he did have these sexy brown eyes and roaming hands that kept pinching my hunkers under the table. I got even with him by tugging and tickling his cowboy moustache.

Over the coffee the Major got up and made a speech. First he formally welcomed the men and explained why he had invited them down: "Reunions of Viet Nam veterans are few and far between," he said. "The war was largely fought by strangers. The high casualty rate and rotation to the states brought this about. By the second year of the war we hardly knew the men fighting beside us. That's why I could come up with only fifty familiar names to invite down here; and of those fifty only five showed up. No doubt the turnout would have been much larger had the reunion been held in the states, but not by much, I think, because when you come down to it, Viet Nam is one war most Americans would rather forget. That also goes for the guys who fought it. We didn't come home conquering heroes. We were the first Americans to have lost a war and the country was vaguely ashamed of us, even as it was glad to be rid of the whole thing.

"Some of us—" and here he paused and briefly marked Eli, "—have been arguing the right or wrong of Nam, but I didn't really invite you down for that. I invited you down because I'm one guy who hasn't forgotten the war. I'm one guy who's not ashamed of you. I know what you endured—the wretchedness, the horror, the waste and loss. Better men than us fell and died there; let's not forget them. And let's not forget what we went through: fear and courage, weariness and relentless misery, wounds and death. You didn't make that war and you didn't like it, but you fought it, you cut the mustard. Not only that, you earned on the battlefield something no man can purchase, no matter how many credit cards he owns—the love and respect of his comrades. This is what binds us together, the noblest friendship of them all: a friendship forged under enemy fire. So I say to you, hold your heads up high, dammit: you went all the way through a miserable thankless war and came out the other side, with honor. You've got a lot to be proud of and I salute you. Three cheers for the Bravo Company! Hip hip—"

"HOORAY," the men boomed back at him.

Flushed and excited and a little drunk, Mulligan said, "And now let's celebrate, let's show them what kind of men we are!" He raised his glass triumphantly aloft and shouted, "I can outdrink, outdance and outfight any mother's son in the hall!" With that, he flung his head back and gave a wild ear-piercing *grito*. Next thing you know the mariachis had stuck up rousingly and Mulligan was out on the dance floor, whapping his hands and heels in a loud and ferocious fandango.

That was only the beginning: as the Major rollicked about out there, the waiters began pouring the stronger liquors—rum and tequila and mescal—and my head started swimming.

"Och, I'm getting right fu'," I told Eli.

"What?"

"Fu'. Full up. Pissed, old boy, *pissed*."

"That's better. Why didn't you say so?"

"Can I help it if you don't speak English?"

Next to take a bash at entertaining was Billy Joe Marshall, who came clumping out on the floor in his high curve-heeled riding boots, a guitar slung over his shoulder. Think of it: a real live long-haired cowboy! Far fooking out! He was tall and skinny with a long hard slant face and he wore tight Levis and a flaming orange shirt topped by a bolo tie, and when he opened his mouth out came this mushy incomprehensible drawl.

"What; What's he saying?"

Eli chuckled and paid me back in kind: "What's the matter, cain't you speak English?"

Billy Joe proved to be an awright singer: he ran down some old Jimmie Rodgers songs, then sang some ballads I had never heard before, not even in the cinema or on the wireless. "I learned this 'un out 'n Col'rada City 'n I wizza bronc rider," he'd say by way of introduction. Or: "This hea sayong is sunthin Casey Tibbs, greatest of alluh rodeo cowboys, made up one night n a bar n Durango while we wuz drinkin beer together." Twang twang twang.

Next the Captain introduced Billy Joe's mate, the one they called YoYo. If he had a surname, nobody used it. YoYo also wore pointy-toed cowboy boots and blue hard pants and a tight bright shirt, but there any resemblance to Billy Joe ended. Where the other was skinny enough to fall down the stank, YoYo was a pudgy wee bloke, baby-faced, bowlegged and potato-bellied. And that's not all: stitched in black on the back of his red satin shirt was this message: 1973 USA YOYO CHAMP.

He was still spot on as a yoyoist and gave a performance I didn't half enjoy. He must have had a yoyo secreted in every pocket—red, white and blue ones, a fluorescent kind, even a gold-plated one—and he produced them with the unperceived ease of a magician. Och, what he couldnae do with them. He made them dart and loop, describe fantastic arabesques in the air. One he spun out and went around the world with, another he manipulated and wove into a complicated cat's cradle. Leaping, swooping, humming—those yoyos flew around the hall like pigeons on the wing.

It was daft of course that a grown man should be this way about yoyos, but nobody dared laugh at him. YoYo was dead serious about his performance and gave it all the dedication of a concert pianist. The wee bowlegged runt lived and loved his yoyos the way a jazzman does his horn, an Irishman his words. As he whipped and whirled them about they sang the song of his soul.

When he was done everybody cheered him and he clumped off in triumph. Next the burly footballer Claude Copeland got up and stood conceited and gorgeous in a cream-colored two-button suit and ruffled lace shirt, singing in a deep melodious near-beautiful voice:

> *When I find myself in times of trouble*
> *Mother Mary comes to me*
> *Speaking words of wisdom*
> *Let it be, let it be . . .*

Next it was my turn. For just a tick I felt the fool, but then the big-hatted grinning musicians started blaring "A Hundred Pipers" and I told myself, Och, what the hey, anything for a giggle. So I went and sang some right sparky Scottish ballads like "The Day We Went to Rothesay" and "Mickey Tams" and I danced some, too. Och, aye!

This took the berries, dancing a Highland Fling ten thousand miles from home, for a bunch of narks who didn't know a fling from a haggis. It made me feel like a stage Scotchman, a proper Harry Lauder; but they cheered and demanded more, so I kept going on, around and around, having a wee carry-on.

The next thing you know, somebody was looping an arm through mine and jiggin me around. "Hope you don't mind," Eli puffed, "but the music got my Scottish blood up."

He was pissed too and began plunging and kicking about uninhibitedly. It was donkey's since I'd danced like this; it took me right back to girlhood days and all those hiking parties in the Cairngorms where we used to skylark all night, and I felt as light on my feet as when I was twelve. When it was over Eli picked me up like a bairn and whirled me around and then we went stumbling and gasping to our seats while everyone in the place smashed his bluidy palms red.

The party was still banging away at three in the morning, but I was ready for my kip.

Eli took my arm. "Do you want to go?"

I nodded.

Tito Cota, his back to us, was in the office next door, shouting into the telephone. His two bodyguards were with him. As we went past the commandant came to the doorway and shouted, *"Buenas noches!* I enjoyed your dancing very much tonight. And now you are together," he leered, rubbing his two forefingers together obscenely. He was drunk, swaying on his feet, fat and short and dairty, like a tequila keg on legs. "I have just been on the telephone to Lagunilla," he announced dramatically, as if making a speech, "and I have some good news to report." He paused for effect.

"Che is dead. The MNR is destroyed."

Eli stopped and copped a squint at him.

"Who said so?"

"General Pabellón himself. They caught the *cabrón* trying to rob a bank. He is no more, the army has taken care of him, shot him dead. The army has cleansed the country of communist filth: long live General Pabellón, long live the army!"

"You think that was the straight scoop about Che?" Eli asked as we walked outside.

"Och, don't ask me. I havenae figured out what's goin' on down here."

The night air, smelling of slag and smoke and showing a cloud of soot against the red-streaked sky, reminded me again of Glasga: that acrid grey smog that sifted into every corner of the city, working its way into your soul.

Eli came over. "You all right?"

"Super. You?"

He shrugged. "I think I'm drunk. Let's walk a little."

We went in silence down the Camino Real. What a pong the furnaces gave off; worse than Glasga, I thought. But then a breeze came up, carrying the smell of the sea, a whiff of something cold and clean and pure.

I tried to think of something to say, but Eli suddenly took the initiative. "You're running away from some dude, aren't you?"

"How'd you know?"

"Men run from life; women from men."

"He wasny just any old fella. We were supposed to be gettin married. My husband-to-be got killed the night before the wedding."

"Jesus. What happened? Car accident?"

"Nothin so innocent as that."

It was funny, I'd hardly told anybody about this, yet here I was, ready to blab my guts to Eli, a bloke I hardly knew.

"He sneaked off the night before our wedding to see an old girl friend, have a last tumble with her. Her husband was a seaman and he came home unexpectedly, catching them in the act. Hugh panicked and jumped out the window, forgetting it was three flights up. End of Hugh MacDonald. End of the story."

"Where was this?"

"London."

"What kind of guy was he?"

I'd known Hugh all my life. He was also from Glasgow and when he came down to London he stayed with me for a while. He was an engineer, something to do with aeronautics. He must have gone through a dozen birds when he suddenly asked me to marry him. I was only eighteen. We'd been friends, not lovers.

"But you said yes anyway."

"Och, I knew we weren't in love. But it didn't seem so important then. I was in a dighted state. The girl I was rooming with had just been shattered by a bad love affair. She tried to commit suicide in our flat one night. I found her in a sleeping-pill coma, had to rush her to the hospital myself. Later Roma became a Lesbian. Eventually I became involved with her crowd, lots of queers, night people, a very weird lot. I began to go to pieces myself, have stupid affairs. Then one night I drank myself unconscious. Couldn't remember a thing I said or did. That really scared me. It was like dying.

"So when Hugh MacDonald came around suddenly, saying let's have a bash at marriage, I said why not? What have I got to lose? What's so wrong about marrying for companionship and fun and security? They're just as good as true love, aren't they?"

Eli made what might have been an affirmative noise.

"Och, but all this hen talk must be boring you."

"Shut up. What happened when he got shot? How did you take it?"

I hadn't felt a thing at first. After everything with Roma, my feelings were pretty well protected. Or so I'd thought. Also, I'd always been self-reliant, having left home when I was fifteen, the first of my crowd to go down to London. Anyway, I found myself taking everything in stride. I buried Hugh, said goodby to Roma, and went on the road. That's where it hit me, months later, in Piraeus. I was walking around waiting for my boat, looking at the tug boats and listening to the gulls . . . and the next I was back in Glasgow. I was a little girl again, waiting on the banks of the Clyde for the steamer from Dublin to dock. My dad was on it, returning from his holiday, and he'd promised to bring me a present, a special surprise for wee Dollie, and I could hardly wait. The boat whistle hooted and the ferry came in and as he walked down the dock and crossed the quay, I ran to him, shouting daddy daddy. But he turned his back and started moving away, the package under his arm.

Hey, da'! I cried, and it was like a dream; I was chasing after my father, falling and clutching his legs and crying daddy you promised, but when I looked up I saw the face of a Greek cop and I realized I was down on my knees on a Piraeus sidewalk. A crowd had gathered round. I was weeping and sobbing.

"I spent a month in hospital and when I got out, I decided to move on rather than go home. I've been movin' ever since, here and there, hangin loose."

We went into the one cantina that was still open on the Camino Real. Eli ordered two *copitas* of tequila, but he didn't touch his drink when it came. He just sat there, looking at me.

"What are you thinking?" I asked him.

He just turned away at that and went to the far corner of the cantina with its raw-wood floor and walls and smell of *caña* in the air, and put some coins in the jukebox. When he returned to the table he sat fiddling with his tequila glass and listening to the cheap strident music. He tipped his chair back and, leaning against the wall, ran a hand roughly over his face.

"I feel drunk and hungover at the same time," he said. "Is that possible?" Then he raised his glass and said, "Here's to us."

The taste of the tequila made him choke; tears came to his eyes.

"Keerist," he growled, wiping his moustache, "you're right—that's the worst drink in the world. It tastes like ether."

But then he called the waiter over and ordered another.

"Where's your home, Eli?"

"Home? I lost my home when I sold my rig."

"Everybody comes from somewhere."

"I was born in Jersey City, but my parents died young. I spent seven years in an orphanage and was out workin' on the trucks when I was thirteen. So I know all about bein' on the road, baby. I discovered it long before you hippies did."

"I'm no hippie. I've worked all me bluidy life, same as you."

He looked over at me.

"Yeah, I guess you have. That's us, a couple of working stiffs. In my next life, though, I'm going to do it all differently. I'm going to ask for a credit rating on my parents. If they aren't Triple A, I'm not coming out of the womb."

I laughed and asked him about his parents, if he remembered them.

"Sure. Even though I was pretty small I remember my old man on Saturday nights. His one big pleasure in life was havin' himself shaved by a professional once a week. But y'know, if you went to him and asked him for movie money, he'd give you the dime he'd saved up for his shave. He'd do without to make you happy."

"How'd he die?"

"He worked himself to death."

Eli knocked back another shot of tequila, biting into a lime to cut the taste.

"Let's split," he said, turning and signalling for the bill.

We strolled through El Cortez, going down somnolent streets with sleeping beggars in doorways under ponchos and newspapers. From out of the darkness came a dog; he stood in the middle of the road, growling, eyes glinting menacingly. I grabbed Eli's arm. "Let's go back."

"That's Turk's mutt. He's got a muzzle on."

"I don't care," I said, my voice rising, "let's go."

As we hurried along Eli snorted with amusement and said, "I like that. For some reason it tickles me that you're afraid of dogs."

"Why?"

"I don't know. It's kind of old-fashioned and European."

"Och no," I said, "it's not good. Even wee puppies terrify me."

He smiled again and put an arm around me, hugging me close. I felt my juices rise, the muscles in my buttocks tighten. A daft snatch of childhood song popped into mind:

> *Hey Jock McCuddy*
> *Ma cuddy's o'er the dike*
> *An' if ye touch ma cuddy*
> *Ma cuddy'll gie ye a bite.*
> *Hoch!*

"You're too much, you little Scotcho," Eli said. And he kissed me on the mouth and made me tremble from the sweetness of it. I wanted him so much but was afraid. The fear hit me every time I was faced with an intimacy; there was an emptying in my loins, a dying.

I felt like running up the Camino Real to the furnace on the hill, but before I could move his arms went tighter around me, held me rooted, and I was pierced with desire again. But suppose I failed to please him? Suppose he lay in my arms as had Hugh MacDonald, thinking of some other bird as he moved against me, each thrust of his hips a stab of betrayal?

The ground was like foam under me. I sank, my courage gone. But Eli was there to buoy me up. He led me to the hacienda and through the damp sweet-smelling garden, where earlier today we had sat having tea. And here was Eli again, his hands and mouth, so good, passing on the gift of love, the warming strength that fills your loins and ribcage and throbs in your throat and mouth. Hunger for sex and food and love gripped me, cries came from my mouth, and soon I took Eli inside me, the heat spreading, my toes and fingers like hot coals, and we were wrapped and coiled, joined forever . . .

"Oh God I love it—"

"—um—

"—Fill me up—fill me—"

"—soon—"

He put his mouth on mine and it was incredibly delicious and it went on and on. Then, suddenly, as we reached our peak, he raised himself and with a great knifing lunge sliced me in two, stabbing again and again. The spasms of pleasure exploded in me and I thought, Yes, this is it, but he wasnae finished, he wanted something more. Desperately he went after it and I tried to give it to him, let him drive deep inside, but it wasn't enough, and finally I heard myself crying out,

"—enough—oh please enough enough—"

But, fingers digging like talons, he gave my body a wrench and piledrived me, making crazy inarticulate sounds, setting off a frenzy of orgasms, deep-shooting tremors that shook and wracked me . . .

. . . then it was the middle of the night, darkness all around and the alarm clock ticking and a rooster misrepresenting the dawn by a good two hours and Eli asleep beside me, the faint light from the garden sifting down and making visible the beads of sweat still clinging to the matted hairs on his thick hairy chest. His face was clenched

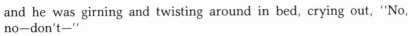

and he was girning and twisting around in bed, crying out, "No, no—don't—"

"Hey, what's the matter? It's me—Doreen."

He sat up blinking, grimacing. I went and soaked a towel, brought it to him. He wiped his face, then tossed the towel aside and got up. He went outside, into the garden, and didn't come back for the longest time. Feeling numb, disembodied, I made some tea and went back to bed and sat with my head all in a fankle.

Suddenly I remembered, with a dismal feeling: "Those bluidy bastard rebels, they stole me Maggie Bell tapes!"

"Whatever we're taking from you is for the revolution," Eli quoted.

"That was some bad trip you were just on. I do that to you?"

"It's got nothing to do with you," Eli said. "I really dig you. I'm lucky to have met you."

"What then?"

He just shrugged his shoulders.

I looked at him, knowing it was time to ask the question.

"Are you married, Eli?"

"I was, but it didn't last very long. When you're clocking two hundred thousand miles a year, it doesn't leave much time to be a husband." He smiled a little. "You're the first woman I've slept with in years that wasn't a groupie."

"Groupie?"

"That's what we call the chicks that hang around the water holes, the truck stops. They're hookers."

"It musta been a helluva life, drivin' a truck."

"Don't say that. Nothin' compares to bein' on your own, behind the wheel of your own rig, with a good paying load and your truck runnin' well. That feeling of freedom is the sweetest high in all the world."

"What will you do now that you've sold your rig?"

He stared across, eyes narrowing down to slits.

"That's a good question," he said finally. "That's a fucking good question."

There was nothing to do after that but take him in my arms and start loving him again.

Later, Eli just lay in bed, his arm around me, staring up at the ceiling, breathing quietly, thinking the night away.

Eli

The roosters woke me right after sunrise. Doreen was still deep in sleep, though, and didn't even stir when I creaked out of bed. She looked boss there, snoring away softly, smelling of woman, funkybutt sex. It was nice after all these years to have an all-night girl. The hookers never stayed; you just shot your wad and watched them leave. But now things had changed. Now I had me a girl that was here not for the bucks but because she wanted to be. It was a new feeling, a strange feeling—but a good one. I had regained my amateur status.

I went out, careful not to wake Doreen or the Señora next door. The morning was damp and smoggy and grey; I shivered, tasted acid on my tongue. My head was heavy and hurting behind the eyes. Too much tequila and boom-boom, not enough sleep. But that was the best way to stay young; it beat taking vitamins any day.

Somebody had been busy during the night; splashed in white paint across the face of the topmost mountain overlooking El Cortez were these words: ARRIBA MNR.

The *Rio Verde* cantina had just opened; inside it smelled of soap and water and of newly baked rolls. A cake of ice sat wrapped in burlap on the floor. I asked the bartender if he could recommend something for a hangover.

"Try a *cerveza*."

"For breakfast?"

"It's the only useful thing I've learned as a bartender: a dark beer definitely helps a hangover. But the beer must be dark, señor. *Oscuro*."

48

As the bartender poured the beer I asked him whether there was news of Che. Had he really been shot dead robbing a bank?

"His men tried to rob the bank, not Che himself. The three of them were shot down in the street outside."

"What's a guerrilla doing robbing banks?"

"Che needs much money. He pays his soldiers five dollars a day, compared with the regular army pay of five dollars a month. Is the beer helping your hangover?"

"A little. I think I'll try another."

"Bueno."

"How about joining me."

"With your permission. *Salud.*" He quaffed the dark beer, wiped his mouth, and said, "You dance well, señor. I saw you last night."

"Thanks. I was very drunk."

"Como no?"

As I sat drinking the Rio Verde began filling up with miners on their way to work, swarthy stumpy tough-looking Indians with wispy hair on chin and lip. I would have liked to talk with them but they spoke a dialect so crude and idiomatic that it made communication impossible. In a while I picked myself up and started walking through the village, watching the miners coming out of their whitewashed houses, the farmers clopping in on burros heaped with baskets of lettuce, onions, and lemons, the kids hollering their way to school. The acid taste in my mouth was from the pall of coppery smoke hanging over the village.

At the river as I stopped to light a cigar two soldiers came carrying a sopping-wet body up the bank to a waiting truck.

"Eli."

It was Alicia. She had pulled alongside in a jeep, Turk beside her in the front seat, armed with a carbine, literally riding shotgun. His cur sat in back amid a heap of things—jerrycans of gas and water, boxes of food—looking at me with those murderous green eyes.

"What happened to that man?"

"Ask Colonel Tito Cota."

"I don't understand."

"He gets a cut from every beggar in El Cortez. Anyone who doesn't kick in . . ." Alicia inclined her head toward the river.

"How can he get away with it?"

"This is a police state and he's the law around here. If you call him to account, he just shrugs his shoulders and says, 'Señora *Moolegan,*

I am only doing my bit to control my country's population explosion.'''

Alicia was on her way to La Laguna, the hacienda of her good friend Don Enrique Arguello, where a fiesta was to be held on Sunday. She invited me to come along.

As we headed up into the blood-red hills, we came across Claude and Fernando doing their morning stint of roadwork together. Clad in sweat-suits, they were staying abreast of each other as they jogged along to the tune of Stevie Wonder's latest hit.

The music was coming from a small casette in Claude's hand, a hard rock beat that really pushed the two athletes along. Fernando's stride was easy and loose, but Claude was dragging a bit, favoring his bad leg.

"Look at that boy of mine," Turk crowed as we pulled alongside them, "ain't he beautiful!"

A big grin cracking open his homely puss, Turk jumped down and hurried over to talk with the kid. I got out and said hello to Claude, who was sucking wind something fierce.

"How's the knee?"

"It's still there," he said, turning down Stevie Wonder.

"I'll bet you could go a nice cool brew right now."

Claude grinned and said, "How'd you guess?" Wiping the sweat from his eyes, he started doing kneebends. "How are you and Miss Scotland gettin along?"

"OK."

"You obviously like balling as much as ever."

"Don't you?"

"It gets better all the time, don't it?"

Up down, up down Claude worked.

"Remember that time we took ourselves off to Taiwan for a little Rest and Recuperation?"

"You mean Intercourse and Intoxication!"

I chuckled way deep down. "After eight months without a shower or a woman or a steak dinner, we really went ape didn't we? We must have hit every *museum* in town."

Claude laughed. "You went into one museum and didn't come out for twenty-four hours. You sure had yourself a time."

"What about that gal you were keeping in Tapei?"

"Them Tai women were *pretty* gals, weren't they? They weren't no size at all, none of em. Mine didn't weight more than ninety pounds soaking wet, but with her that was ninety pounds of sweet and juicy pom-pomming pussy. That bitch sure knew what the Good Lord put it there for."

Warm fraternal feelings were bubbling up. We used to chase up and down Tapei together in search of rock n roll, going from one record store to another, making the rounds of bars and dance halls that featured live music, hustling down narrow twisting weirdly-lit alleys crowded with people in Western and Oriental dress, drinking Jap scotch and smoking joints until the small hours of the morning.

Once in a while we'd find a group that could really get it on, like that night in the MAMA BLUES dance hall when the seven dwarfs came on stage. Not one of those teenagers was more than five feet tall and they looked comic up there, but when they started playing, man, they blew the smile right off your face. Those little Tai kids put down some sounds you couldn't believe, they were really into the music, playing a wild strange exhilirating set, a ricky-ticky, lie-tee-fie-ti, rock-around-the-clock cross between East and West, Rolling Stones and Ho Chi Minh, *sake* and Southern Comfort. They had a vocalist who sounded at times just like Mick Jagger, but when I tried to congratulate him on the fact he didn't understand a word I said. It turned out that none of the seven dwarfs spoke English; they were simply aping the lyrics phonetically, having memorized them off an LP.

Now when I reminded Claude of all that, he grinned and sighed and said, "That was a long time ago. Since then a lot of dust has hit the fan."

As he raised himself up to full height I saw how much older Claude seemed now, and changed. He'd been beat up on the ballfield: his nose was flat and he'd had some teeth walloped out: it gave him a tough mean look. But the big change was in his eyes: once upon a time they had glittered with hope and joy: now they were hard narrow slits showing the pent-up violence of a caged tiger.

"We got to have a talk one of these days, Claude."

"Um."

"I've often watched you play on TV. You made a lot of games for me."

"Pro football's ain't a game any more," he said. "It's a Roman Circus."

"Still, you've made out ok."

"Yeah, bread and circuses are big business these days. Last year I made more than the President of the United States did. That's got to be crazy, man."

I asked him about a gossip-column item which had said he was living with a famous jazz singer. "Yeah," Claude said. "I made it with her for a while. We even set up light housekeeping for a couple of years."

"What'd your wife think about that?"

"What wife? Didn't you know? When I got home from Nam there was a Dear John letter waiting for me."

As Claude squatted down and began stretching and testing his bad knee he said, "That bitch sure blew it, uuuhhhhHHHUUUUHHH! She gave me up for this numbers runner she met while I was off soljerin. That jody was good for maybe twenty, thirty grand a year and it must have looked pretty big to her. I was just seventeen when I got drafted and like everybody else she figured I'd never make it in the pros, having no college rep and all that, but did she ever figure wrong, ooowhhHHHEEE! It didn't cost me a cent to get rid of her. Anytime I get to feelin low, I just picture her in a two-room Lenox Avenue pad weepin over the million bucks that Dear John jive cost her."

"Has playing ball really made you that rich?"

"Yeah, and it's gonna make me even richer if these ligaments of mine hold up," Claude said, picking himself up off the ground. He dusted himself off, adding, "Got to stretch them some more, man." He chugged off, huge black fists thrust out before him like battering rams, blaring Stevie Wonder with every step.

Presently came a sweep of sandy waste: everything before the eye, desert and sky, was grey and toneless, except for some low spiny shrubs which put out whitish purple blossoms: improbable splashes of color in a dead landscape.

"How long before we reach the ranch?"

Alicia smiled. "We reached it a half hour ago: all this land belongs to the Don."

"Oh, far out. What does he do with all of it?"

"In the old days he had fifty thousand head of cattle, but then came the hard times and he lost almost everything. Now he lives on the edge, just as we do."

Up ahead were more trees like those I had seen yesterday: grey and bony things that resembled skeletons standing on stilt legs and clawing at the sky with their long, mad fingers.

"What kind of trees are they?"

"Boojum."

Alicia could not only identify all the flora and fauna growing along the road but could tell stories about their good and bad qualities: "You see that plant growing along the banks of the dry steam bed? *Hiedra maligna*, a kind of poison ivy. Right next to it is a jojoba bush whose berries have medicinal properties. In the old days they were used to cure certain diseases of the bladder. Children's scalps were rubbed with the berry in the belief that it would prevent baldness in later life."

"Stop the jeep," I yelled. "I want to score a bushelful."

Where the road began to climb stood another boojum tree with five rigidly upthrust branches silhouetted against the sky like a candelabra. A laborer sat under the tree, smoking a cigarette. His clothes were old but clean and well-patched. He and Alicia had a rapid and animated conversation in one of the local dialects; when it was concluded she gave him some food and cigarettes and a bar of *Palmolivo* soap. We drove on, only to come across another laborer on the down side of the hill.

"The men are volunteer road laborers," Alicia explained later. "They camp out here and work the road on their own. They survive on the food and pesos those who use the road can spare them."

"Are they MNR sympathizers?"

She shrugged her shoulders. "I don't know and I don't care."

A few minutes later Alicia stopped the jeep to talk with a *fayuquero*, one of the handful of truckdrivers who pushed and prayed their sclerotic vehicles over these roads. His name was Vicente Rodriquez and he was a fat salty old rogue who drove an old bugcatcher, a 1950 Mack truck piled high with all kinds of goods. Shirtless, red bandanna knotted round his forehead, he jumped down from his cab and boomed a greeting.

Rodriguez was not only a peddler on wheels but a combination of errand boy, mailman and courier. When Alicia told him that I drove a truck for a living too, he gave me a big *abrazo* and insisted I sample a mouthful of the *pulque* he was transporting to the north; it was milky, shitty-smelling stuff but one snort of it fired me up instantly.

"What kind of truck you driving?" he asked in Spanish.

"I lost my truck," I told him.

"A truckdriver without a truck is like a woman without breasts," he said.

"That's for sure. But in the states a trucker can't do what you're doing. They don't want you to be on your own. The government and the unions and the shippers gang up on you. You see that load you're carrying—the refrigerators, the cases of booze? An independent can't haul any of that back home. Only the big guys, the combines, are given the licenses for that kind of business."

"Can't you apply for a license?" he asked.

"You can apply.from now till doomsday and the goddamn Interstate Commerce Commission ain't gonna give you one. They don't want a freelancer to take on that work and neither do the Teamsters or the big companies. All they'll let you haul is produce—apples, oranges, peaches, that kind of stuff."

"And if you can't haul any produce?" Rodríguez asked.

"Then you haul air, you haul it from one end of the country to another."

"You can't live on air," Rodríguez said.

"You better believe it, hombre. That's why I don't have a rig any more, cauz you can't live on air, no matter how hard you try."

"Can't you work for the big guys?"

"Sure you can—if you agree to lease your tractor to them and let them cream 50% off the top."

"Fifty per cent! You gotta kick back fifty per cent to them? They're bandits," he cried angrily.

"Now you're getting the picture, amigo. Now you know why you're working and I'm a tourist."

"What happened to the USA?" he asked. "I thought it was a free country."

"Sure it's a free country," I said. "Free for the big boys to carve the pie up for themselves."

Alicia rejoined us, and immediately began pumping him for all kinds of information and gossip. Meanwhile, Turk fished a 12-gauge shotgun out of the back of the jeep.

"I reckon they're good for half an hour," he said laconically as he put on a pair of thick eyeglasses and set off up the hill, dog following.

Minutes later several shots were fired; the sound rolled overhead, hit the face of the hills opposite, and rebounded back with a sharp flat *smack* that flushed a covey of birds from a nearby thicket and sent them beating noisily north.

Turk fired another shot but Alicia and Rodríguez paid him no mind. The *fayuquero* had cracked open a case of round yellow cheese of which she eventually bought half a dozen wheels, in addition to a box of cane sugar and several kilos of fresh vegetables. They began bargaining furiously over the price, but once it was agreed upon he produced an immense gold-toothed grin and sang out, *"Muchas gracias, Señora Moolegan!"* Waving a big oil-stained paw at me, he drove off,

Cat diesel roaring and protesting like an elephant with a bullet in its hide.

The exchange with the *fayuquero* had put Alicia in such a good humor that when Turk returned with his catch—a brace of pheasants—she cried out, "Bravo, Turk!" and bussed him on the mouth. Turk's already parboiled face turned an even deeper red as he took his glasses off and swung himself into the jeep. Alicia sat beside me, proud and straight and beautiful, black hair rippling down her back and gleaming in the sunlight.

The sun had come out from behind its sheet of grey and we had picked up the sea route and were snapping along at thirty-five miles an hour, top speed for the province. But soon the surface of the salt flats turned soft and we had to back down again to prevent the brine from splashing up and fouling the ignition. It meant traversing long miles in either first or second gear. No matter: the sun felt good on our faces, we had time to talk.

Alicia told me about her father, Ed Hendricks, a Montana-born freewheeling, fun-loving old desert rat who had settled here right after the first world war. He had worked at engineering, prospecting and surveying when he wasn't out hunting pronghorn antelope and women, in that order of preference.

"Ed had so many mestizo wives scattered up and down the province that he swore he couldn't remember which one was my mother," Alicia recalled cheerfully. "All he knew was that he liked my looks as a baby and decided to take me home with him."

Raised not far from here by the Señora Blanca de la Mesa, Alicia had enjoyed a rare childhood. She'd spoken English and Spanish at home, ridden to school on her own pony, swum and fished in the Pacific, run free and happy as a hound over these hills. She had met Matt when he came down on a hunting trip right after Nam. One look and they were strong for each other. "We still are," she said, even though we fight like hell all the time now."

In a while the road began following along the crest of the high sand dunes lining the shore of a lagoon.

"Hey," Turk cried suddenly, "look!"

Not far from the shore, perhaps a quarter of a mile away, two whales surfaced in the vast lagoon and shot their jets of vapor skyward. They swam toward us, bumping and cuffing each other, rolling their immense bulk around, beating the sea into white curds. Next they dipped under the surface only to break water again, emerging in a mighty mass and crashing down with a great belly-whacking smack.

With wonder and awe I watched as the sea monsters sported around below, raising the waves on all sides.

Minutes later Alicia said excitedly, "The ballenas are making love!"

At first I wanted to scoff—whoever heard of whales making love?—but then as I peered more closely I saw she was right; they were engaged in prolonged loveplay. The female let big daddy know she was ready by bumping and rubbing up against him; he reacted by leaping higher and higher out of the water and thrashing his mighty tail around. Then, swimming at full speed, he cut across her path at an angle that was almost perpendicular and, lunging, thrust himself right into her. Mama Whale happily shook and shuddered all over as he rammed into her again and again.

The act of love took but seconds; then they were streaking off again, crossing the lagoon, the sunlight glistening on their dark wet backs as they celebrated the union with great lighthearted leaps and bounds. I felt like rushing into the water and swimming out to them. I wanted to touch them, join them, leap in the water and dive to the bottom, blowing bubbles all the way down . . .

All right. Talk about balling! Those goddamn whales were something, just by themselves they were worth the trip down. This country was too much. No wonder Alicia loved it down here, Matt too. And no wonder there were guerrillas in the hills. This turf was worth fighting over, yeah, maybe even dying for!

In a while we came upon Don Arguello's ranch, a group of dusty adobe and straw houses sitting high up in the hills surrounded by a palm grove and grazing fields. There was a corral and a miniature bull ring, very dilapidated. The Don was a stringy, elderly Spaniard dressed in faded corduroys and a patched workshirt, but courteous in the Old World way:

"My house is yours, señor. Be welcome. We are deeply honored having you for a guest. *Estoy a sus órdenes.*" His breath smelled of cheap brandy.

We were ushered into the ranch, a once-proud house embellished with handcarved balustrades and balconies. Now the wood was pitted and unpolished, the Indian rugs full of holes; but we were fed a savory luncheon of tortillas, frijoles, chicharrones and barbacoa cooked in a hole dug in the ground, the Indian way. Later, as we took our coffee out on the patio, a gang of cowboys came humping down out of the hills, whistling and shouting. They wore wide round felt hats and ankle-length boots and carried long ropes with leather balls on the ends.

As they tromped toward the bunkhouse, kicking up the dust, Turk said suddenly, "Hey, I know that dude."

He jumped up and called, *"Vaquero, como está?"*

It turned out that the cowboy worked on the side as a boxing referee; Turk collared him to pick his brains about the boy coming up from San Felipe next week to fight Fernando.

When Alicia and the Don also excused themselves and returned to discuss private matters, I got up and poured myself a *Crema de Menta*; it was supposed to be an aphrodisiac. Sure enough, I found myself thinking of Doreen, wanting her. Too bad she had to work today; she would have loved all this. She would have dug the ranch, that Don, all of it. That was Doreen, full of enthusiasm, open to everything. I'd never met another woman like her. They made 'em smarter and prettier, but not with that kind of spirit, such joy of life. And that Scottish burr of hers was like pepper on the tongue. I wished she were here now, talking Scottish, laughing that crazy big laugh of hers, embracing me the way she had last night, kissing me again and again . . .

I poured myself another *Crema de Menta*, but this time it made me sleepy instead of horny. I found a couch and had a nap, feeling rested when I woke. Alone, I began poking around the house and presently discovered a big musty room filled with treasured weapons of past days: muskets, flintlocks, muzzle-loaders. An entire wall was covered with ancient Spanish armor, positioned around a family coat of arms, whose faded motto read:

> *We are born to kill, not to die, and he who lives*
> *longest and takes most, is most man.*

When we left the ranch Alicia's mood was strained and subdued. She asked me to drive and sat wordlessly for close to an hour, chain-smoking.

"Anything wrong?"

After glancing back at Turk and making certain he was asleep, she said, "Don Arguello just told me Che has been offering five times above the going price for black market arms,"

"Why is he so desperate?"

"I don't know. Our previous information was that he was being supplied by the communist party. It must have been incorrect."

"Will he use the arms against you?"

"It's possible. He hates Matt's guts. Matt's never given him an inch and Che can't stand that: he wants to be Numero Uno around here."

She sucked hard on her cigarette and trapped the smoke deep in her lungs, as if to punish herself. "I shouldn't be telling you this," she said. "I don't want to spoil your stay here."

"You can't spoil it. What I saw today I'll remember for the rest of my life."

"You made a good friend in Rodríguez. He thought a lot of you."

"Same here. I wish I were in his shoes. I wouldn't mind making a living the way he does, carrying everything that people need, including the Six O' Clock News."

"I couldn't help hearing what you said about your problems. We're a lot alike, you know. As small, independent operators we're caught in the same squeeze between the power blocs, the government on one hand and the cartels on the other. If they're not trying to tax you out of existence, they're trying to take you over."

"But you seem to be doing fine," I said.

"We were, until the MNR started harassing us. The banks got scared and have made it tough for us to borrow money. Now that the price of copper has fallen we find ourselves running short of operating capital. We can't even afford new fittings on the main pumps."

"That's tough."

"If the price of copper goes up, we can make it. We've got a rich mine, Eli, one that hasn't realized a third of its potential. There are sizable and as yet untouched mineral deposits down there and if we can survive this bad spell and get the damn stuff out of the ground, we'll be all right. But sometimes I wonder whether the struggle is worth it. Maybe we'd be better off packing it in the way you did."

"I didn't want to pack it in, they forced me to," I said. "The biggies squeezed me until I cried Mama."

"I'm sorry. What will you do now?"

I shrugged. "I don't know. Do you people need a messenger boy?"

"Matt's already offered you a job. You could join our security guard."

"Thanks," I said. "But didn't anybody tell you—I'm a lover now, not a fighter."

It was the closest I'd ever seen her come to laughing. But then she turned her attention to the road.

We were crossing the salt flats again; she dug into her handbag and came up with a pair of sunglasses. "You must wear these," she said. "At this hour the *salitrales* reflect the strength of the sun almost as strongly as snow does."

We drove straight on until Alicia abruptly pointed right and said, "Take that turn." It was a hard climb up into the hills and the jeep's wheels spun in the dry sandy grooves of the road and we skidded from side to side. Having finally attained the coastal ridge, we headed north again and came finally to a small burial grounds overlooking the dunes and the in-rolling sea below.

Two graves of whitewashed stones stood atop this lonely site. Each grave had a low driftwood fence around it and showed a simple wooden weather-scarred cross. The plots were decorated with sea-shells and black-and-white pebbles and local flowers. Alicia went from one grave to the other, fixing a wooden slat here, weeding a flower patch there.

Later I found her, standing and looking down sombrely at one of the graves. Without being asked she said, "The marker is my father's. He asked to be buried near the sea."

"And the other?"

"That's where my infant son is buried."

. . .

"I'm sorry. I didn't even know you and Matt had had a child."

We stood quietly: I could hear the sea slapping against the shore and a nearby seagull sounding its strident cry. The salt pans, ridged here and there by dikes, sat broad and white in the sun, soaking up the sea's essence; and once again I took something of this strong, harsh land into my soul. I tasted brine on my lips and felt the lonely grandeur of the hills pass through me, leaving a perception of the life Alicia had lived here, the joy and love she had known, and the pain and loss too. I thought of her dead child and of the children I had murdered in Viet Nam and I trembled for the great wonder and cruelty of life.

Later, as we neared El Cortez, I asked, "How did the baby die?"

"The umbilical cord was wrapped around its neck."

"But any decent doctor knows what to do about that."

"We had the doctor but not the equipment. He couldn't operate on me."

"Why didn't you have the baby in the capital? Or in the states?"

When Alicia turned and regarded me, her dark eyes were moist and desolate. "That's exactly what Matt said."

Then we were home, descending the rust-colored hills around El Cortez and pausing briefly at the first checkpoint, which was manned by Charlie Corrigan, a short but powerfully built ex-platoon sergeant with a black patch concealing an eye shattered by German shrapnel at Port-en-Bessin on D-Day. We turned into the Camino Real and bumped along. My head ached and there was a crick in my neck.

It was still the siesta hour and El Cortez was silent and shut. But outside the main office a group of men were milling around. Mulligan was there and so was Colonel Tito Cota, whose *pistoleros* were dragging someone out of the back seat of a car.

"That's the kid, Aguilar," Turk cried. "They got him!"

"Who is he?" I asked.

"That's the one we suspect is working for the MNR."

I stopped the jeep and Turk jumped down. "Where'd you find him?" he yelled at Mulligan.

"LoCascio picked him up outside Mezquital."

A venomous look bloomed on Turk's face and he snarled at the young boy, "Where's Che, you son of a bitch? Where's his hideout, goddammit?"

Aguilar, small and thin with a shock of black hair falling over his pinched sallow face, began struggling with LoCascio. Suddenly he got free and bolted down the Camino Real.

"Shoot him," Tito Cota bellowed. "Kill that *culata!*" One of the colonel's bodyguards reached for his pistol but Mulligan was there to yell, "No, you bastard!" and to smack the gun out of his hand.

Turk meanwhile had knelt and yanked the muzzle off his dog. Alicia cried out, but by then the hound was racing after Aguilar, catching up with him seconds later and cornering him. Here the kid made another mistake and tried again in his panic to escape. The snarling dog began to savage him. My eyes went to Doreen's horrified face in the office window; I heard Tito Cota giggling idiotically.

By the time Turk managed to drag the dog off, Aguilar lay whimpering and bleeding in a pall of dust. Turk picked the boy up by his belt and carried him inside like a suitcase.

The rest of us stood staring down at the dog.

He sat on his haunches panting heavily, big pink tongue dripping saliva, his eyes shining with triumph.

CHE'S DIARY

Morning, March 27

The raid on Lagunilla a failure. Reason not yet clear. Either our luck was bad and troops accidentally came upon the scene, ambushing the men, or we have been compromised from within. Must root out this informer, if he exists. Meanwhile the men are totally demoralized. We must mobilize ourselves, take immediate action to restore prestige, fighting spirit. Finding arms still remains the problem.

Mao: "An armory should be established in each guerrilla district for the manufacture and repair of rifles and for the production of cartridges, hand grenades and bayonets. Guerrillas must not depend too much on an armory. *The enemy is the principal source of their supply.*"

*   *   *

Later, March 27

Alicia M. seen heading toward Don Enrique Arguello's hacienda. Spent several hours there, accompanied by two bodyguards. Must ascertain reason for this visit.

The report had a strange effect on me, awakened old feelings. Been months since I've thought of her, of being with a woman. Hunger, solitude more real. Instinct for survival more important. Until today. Damn her.

Doreen

Eli looked swacked when he came in. He didn't sit down, just stotted around angrily, teeth biting into an unlit cigar, face gone grey and hard as a whore's knickers. I couldnae give him any time; it was Friday and we were working like hammers to get the payroll done. Like everybody else in the village, the girls had been harrowed by the business with Aguilar; and knowing he was being interrogated right next door didn't exactly boost their spirits. Neither did the look on Eli's face: one squint and you knew somebody was still mistreating the boy.

"Come on, get with it, hen," I admonished myself. "You're supposed to be setting an example." So I punched away at the adding machine and when I looked up Eli was away. I got up and went to the electric fire and poured myself a cup of tea, my sixth of the afternoon. I was becoming a regular tea Jennie. That dog, I thought. That bluidy brute of a dog.

Eli wandered in again, eyes blazing with fury.

"Have a cup of char," I said. "It'll do you good."

"How much longer will you be?"

"A good few hours, I'm afraid. As you see, we're operating here on one piston."

"I'm going to split. I've had enough of this."

He said it loudly, drawing all eyes.

"Let's step outside," I suggested.

Soldiers were stationed in the street. Armed with carbines and machine-guns, they stood eying the mob of miners who had gathered opposite and were squatting on their hunkers, waiting and watching like so many crows on a fence.

We walked around the crowd and crossed the Camino Real to the cantina on the far corner. The wind, blowing from west to east, brought a pungent odor from the dressing-sheds on the hill, and Eli growled, "Keerist, what a stink."

"We call it *Parfum du Sud,*" I said drily. "Quite a pong ain't it?"

YoYo was the only customer in the cantina; sloshed, he sat hanging over a bottle of beer, wheeling out his yoyo monotonously, like a robot. He was in such a stupefied state that he didn't even recognize us.

Eli went to the jukebox and played a record.

"How bad is it in there?"

"Right now Tito Cota is manicuring the kid's fingers with a pair of pliers."

A queasy shudder ran through me. "Can't the Major do anything?"

"He tried, but the colonel threatened to have him arrested."

In the silence which followed the record, I heard the slow humming of the yoyo as it rode up and down. Eli turned his gaze to the band of miners across the street.

"They don't give a damn that Aguilar belongs to the MNR. All they see is one of theirs getting beat up by the army and the gringos." Eli gave a sarcastic snort. "And the Mulligans want me to go to work for them!"

"What doing?"

"Joining Turk and the others in guarding the place."

"You make it sound like a daft idea."

"It would be like setting up house on the rim of a live volcano."

"Och, stop blathering."

"Your problem is that you're too dumb to be scared. You think the world'll always look after you."

"I'm just not going to walk around scairt, that's all. Life's too short n sweet for that."

"What would you do if I left?" Eli asked. "Would you come with me?"

"I've got a contract, mate."

"Contracts are like pie-crusts—made to be broken."

"Not by this lassie. I don't operate that way. Besides, you don't really want me to take off with you."

"How do you know what's in my heart? You got X-rays for eyes?"

"It's as plain as the nose on your gob. You're beginning to turn chicken."

"Shove that," he said.

"That's what they're saying," I told him, "that you've got a yellow streak in you as big as the boulevard."

Eli jumped up, face gone all wild. "Who said that? Who the fuck said that about me?"

Just then YoYo came to life. Putting back his head he shouted at Eli, "Don't worry about it, sport. Fug em all, fug every single fuggen one of em!"

"Tequila!" Eli snarled at the waiter. *"Más tequila, por favor!"* Then, checking me, he asked tightly, "Did somebody really say that about me?"

"Forget it, Eli. I'm sorry I opened my big fat trap."

When the bottle came he poured the dram and drank fast. Then he pulled his arm back and smashed the glass against the far wall. He sat glowering at the waiter, daring him to protest. It was a nasty moment; fortunately the bloke held his temper."

"Nobody calls me chicken," Eli yelled. "Nobody!"

Then he threw some money on the table and stormed out.

I sat alone and still, my heart hammering away, sorry for having provoked him. The pressure was on Eli. Not only had all his luck turned bad, losing his rig and all, but his hatred of the war set the others against him. I'd been a mug to pass along what was only stupid gossip. I'd fooked everything up. Dear God, when would I ever learn to keep my clanger shut?

I couldnae move out of my seat. I just sat like a nit, tears in my eyes. It took the five o'clock bugle call to shake me up, get me started again. Thank God for the office, the unsorted payroll. I threw myself into work like a demon, rushing this way and that, scolding the other girls for the slightest mistake.

Later I looked up and discovered Frits Hartogs hanging over me. Two of his mates—Billy Joe and YoYo—had entered with him and were lolling about boozily in back, ogling the girls. I waited for Frits to say something. Poor man, he was all in a fankle and stood shifting from foot to foot, sweating heavily, tongue stabbing at his cracked, white-flecked lips. He was a regular roly-poly, round face and body, pudgy wee hands, but when you looked into his eyes you liked him. He had a sad, puppy-dog look that made you want to pet him, tickle his ears.

"Miss-ah-Cameron—" he began, mouth working loosely, "do you— ah—have a moment?"

"Yes, of course. What is it?"

"We were won-won—wondering—" He could hardly get the words out. Pausing, he picked up a sheet of yellow typing paper from my desk and blotted his shiny bald dome with it.

"Yes?"

"—about—ah—dinner tonight." Here again he lost his tongue, began flailing his arms, imploring me with those big, sad eyes.

"What about it?"

"Should we wait—ah—for the—ah—Major, or—" His mouth was so dry that his lips actually smacked. "or go out and—ah—ah ah—eat dinner by ourselves?"

"You're still the Major's guests," I said. "Dinner will be served as usual in the dining room at nine."

"Thank—thank—you," Frits stuttered. He made to leave but could-nae get his legs moving; it was as if they were encased in cememt. He stood with his eyes bulging and adam's apple moving, trying to get coordinated. I was conscious of every eye in the room on us. He was like a great big protoplasmic blob and I suddenly lost all patience and compassion for him. "Go away and chase yourself, you big bluidy cheuchter," I muttered under my breath. "Leave me alone."

But he wouldn't—couldn't—go.

Finally I forced myself to ask, "Mr Hartogs, just what is it that you want?"

"I—ah—was—just wondering, Miss Cameron—" His head was jerk-ing around and his voice was thick and hoarse.

I coughed loudly, hoping he'd do the same and clear his throat, but he only mopped his head again with the damp, crunched-up copy paper and stuttered, "—ah—I was just wondering whether—I—could —ah—ah—ah—ah."

At last the penny dropped. What was in his head had nothing to do with what was happening here. The bloke was all out of synchronization.

Taking a deep breath I said as gently as I could, "Thank you, Mr Hartogs, but as you see I'm behind with my work and simply could-nae make plans for dinner. But be a pet and ask me again, will ye?"

He nodded quickly, showing both hurt and relief, and backed away, the sweat coming off him like a blasted stream. Plook that he was, he bumped blindly into Carmen's desk and spilled a whole tray of change, only to crack heads with her as she bent down to retrieve the coins. She gave a whelp of pain and began bleeding from the nose.

Frits' face turned the color of the hills outside. Billy Joe snickered loudly and YoYo mumbled, "Way ta go, Frishie, way ta go," and whipped his candy-striped yoyo around in an eerily humming circle.

After Frits stumbled out, followed by his doped-up mates, I went and locked the door after them.

Not that I was afraid of them—just careful.

CHE'S DIARY

Sunday, March 30

We have only one duty and it is sacred—to fight against imperialism wherever we encounter it.

Today we are ready. For too long we have endured hunger and cold, the criticism of others. Today we fight, here in these hills. Today we show Mulligan what *real* men are like.

Frits

"Look, Frits, don't sing me no sad songs. Everybody's got problems. I got a boy who's a dope fiend, Harry Simpson's got a bedridden wife, I could go on and on, but what the hell would it mean? Whether we like it or not, we still gotta go out there and sell. Produce! Bring in the damn money! That's all the company cares about, that's all anybody cares about. So go out there, buddy, and push dog food. Because if you don't make your sales quota this month, I'm gonna fire you. I hate to say it but I got no choice. Because if I don't make my quota, they fire *me*. That's the way it is. So get out there, you fat fumbling Dutchman. Get out there and push Needlebee's Dog Food!"

That *schoft's* hard-mouthed voice was shrieking inside my head like a dentist's highspeed drill, but without my pills there would be no silencing it. I must have been crazy to leave them home, to think I could do without them. But the doctor had been so firm: "You can't keep taking amphetamines without risking irreversible damage—"

Meanwhile the fiesta that Mulligan had organized for us continued. There was a lot of yelling and jousting. The men circled each other on horseback, trying to unseat each other with rawhide lariats with leather-covered stones attached, a scream from the onlooking Indians shattering the air every time a rider hit the dust; how he didn't break his neck was a miracle.

A morning of it: the dust, the yelling, the buzzing of the bolos, the gypsy cowboys shouting obscenities while their women watched inscrutably, reposing on sheepskins, dark nut faces shielded behind black shawls. Meanwhile the stink of spitted pig drifted over everything: a greasy unclean smell that seeped into your soul the way exhaust fumes seep into a car. It made me gag, want to puke—

"—riding—?"

"What?"

"You gonna do any riding, Frits?"

I wanted to tell him that the horse and I were incompatible, but I couldn't get my tongue to shape the words. All I could do was make gagging sounds in my throat.

"Come on, man, even Eli is gonna try it," YoYo said.

It was true: there was Eli attempting to mount a horse. He was pissed, the cowboys had to help him up into the saddle, he grabbed the reins like a stagecoach driver. After four days of talk about Viet Nam and what great heroes we were, everybody had got around to feeling immortal. Even Eli, the fool, the damn fool.

Sick, I was going to be sick—

They were getting ready for the first heat. Six riders were up on their mounts, swilling a last mouthful of tequila, tightening blue and red scarves round the top of their broad flat hats, shouting boasts and insults over the yapping of the dogs and children.

The spectators were making just as much noise as the riders: they shouted and joked, made bets with each other on the outcome, village against village, us against them, nah nah nah, you guys are sissies, your mother's a *puta, chinga* this and *chinga* that, they flaunted their virility like adolescents.

Moments later they went off, all six riders coming together in a great tangled clawing mass—there was no such thing as a foul and two men were belted off their horses. Then they broke free and went pounding at full tilt across the corral, horse's eyes bulging insanely. The bumping and jolting was part of the horsemanship; Eli got socked by two riders at once and was nearly clobbered from his saddle; half off, clutching the beast's neck with one desperate arm, he wouldn't quit, hung on grittily, managed to finish the race dead last and earn a cheer for his dauntlessness.

Next it was YoYo's turn. He entered the next heat but never even survived the first collision, was dumped immediately on his back, letting out such a howl when he landed that everyone thought he was hurt, but it wasn't his back he had broken, just one of his yoyos. Pulling the shattered toy from his pocket, he held it up by the string for all to see. Silly tit, he was almost in tears.

Later his sidekick Billy Joe Marshall suffered an even worse humiliation. In Viet Nam he used to boast of his prowess as a bronc rider, how he had taken first money at the Rodeo de Santa Fe in the bareback go-round and how all the girls used to follow him around and beg him for a screw, blah blah blah, he went on endlessly about how great he was, and while none of us believed a tenth of it, we took it as gospel that he had competed for money as a bronc rider; after all, he had a card in the Rodeo Cowboys Association and he certainly looked the part, especially when he hunched that long lean flat-hipped body over a "gittar" and sang, "I'm goin where the water drinks like cherry wine, Lord Lord, I'm goin where the water drinks like cherry wine."

Only Claude Copeland refused to believe anything he said; he disliked the kid, insisted he was one-hundred-per-cent fake and fraud. "The punk's a pathological liar," Claude would say. "Even worse, he cheats at poker and when I catch him at it, I'm gonna waste him, Jim, I'm gonna stomp his ass from here to Hanoi!"

But Claude was almost as big a braggart as Billy Joe and nobody had much use for him either, except Eli. Of course, morale had gone down the pipe by then, the worst year of the ground war, the year in which we were obliged to go out on search-and-destroy missions designed to "sanitize" the province.

It went on for months, months of increasing violence and brutality, death, mosquitoes, dysentery, whores, killing, and suffering. There was nothing to fear in death, because we were already in hell itself. It didn't matter when you died, only how. The thing was not to be caught by Charlie, because if he took you prisoner he'd do what he did to Dave Lifschitz, an old boyhood friend of Eli's. He'd found Dave one day shot to death in a ditch with his hands tied with wire, maggots and flies crawling all over his black, stinking wounds. But that wasn't all. Some VC had sliced his prick off and stuffed it in his mouth. That's how Eli had found him, his old Jersey City buddy, staring up from a ditch with his eyes and ears full of dirt and his manhood hanging out of his mouth.

Turk: "Charlie'll do the same to you, if you get caught, if you don't kill the fucker before he kills you."

So we killed, with a vengeance, and Charlie killed back, we wasted everything in sight, soldiers, peasants, children, what did it matter, life was meaningless, life was shit, we were shit, the Vietnamese were shit. That was our discovery of the year, our big insight into the nature of things.

The more we killed, the more our government rewarded us. The bigger the body count, the oftener our commendations, the longer our leaves. That's what changed the war, turned it from a normal exercise in barbarism into a study in industrial slaughter: a technology obliterating an ideology. Those who killed well were rewarded with time off in Saigon, a chance to vacation with the bar girls, black-marketeers, pimps, cowboys, and street thieves. Rotation to the states came fastest to the mostest: those outfits that killed in job lots got shipped out of Nam first. We were obsessed with killing, seduced by it.

That day in Chu Tau when Eli Brickman discovered his mutilated buddy rotting in a ditch, we found it quite easy to obey his orders to waste the village. We knew he had shot his wad, but it didn't matter; in the Viet Nam context wasting that village was perfectly logical. Our government wanted the jungle sterilized; we sterilized it. Our commanders wanted bodies; we provided them. What difference if they be enemy or friend, soldier or civilian, man, woman, or child. Bodies were bodies.

So we went into Chu Tau, a village like all the others in Quang Ngai province, and this time instead of weeding the villagers out, shooting a few here, a few there, we shot them all. It was just a question of numbers. We did the job wholesale instead of retail.

It really wasn't very difficult: we simply herded them together in their burlap rags, pointed our sixteens at their brown, sun-shriveled oriental faces and squeezed the trigger. And as it went on, as the screaming bodies flew, toppling backwards, flopping into puddles of blood, and the smoke and heat of our weapons filled the air, my face began to pound, my body to swell. I became immunized against all feeling. I was zipped up tight, impervious, indestructible . . .

Looking up, I suddenly found myself back at the fiesta. It had come time for Billy Joe to ride.

Billy Joe.

Long after the killing at Chu Tau had finally purged everyone, Billy Joe was still going strong. He had flushed a woman out of a hovel, from under a pile of dead bodies, and had started beating her, smashing again and again with the butt of his rifle, while she just stood with numb staring eyes trying to understand what was happening to her. But how could she understand if Billy Joe himself couldn't? Later he swore that he didn't know what he was doing, that he thought he had been tripping out on acid.

"It was like a fantasy trip, a 3-D war movie, and I was so high it didn't seem real, none of it," he had said. "I didn't know I was killing anyone, I swear it."

He'd been totally blown out by the war. He had death on the brain, walked around in a helmet on which he'd painted BORN TO DIE.

The longer he stayed in Nam, the nuttier he grew. That crazy grunt lived to kill and killed to live. He loved the war, couldn't seem to get enough of it. None of us would go near him. He wore his hair down to his shoulders and carried a .45 and a knife and a look that said, "Fuck with me, man, and I'll skin you."

He'd been bad news in Nam, a man you feared as much as the dinks, but even with all that it gave me no pleasure now to witness his present humiliation. He sat up there on a horse with a chance to prove himself. But one look was all it took to know he'd never make it: he sat like a clay man, passive in the hands of the potter, and didn't even survive the start. One toss of the nag's head and he went flying, hit the ground with a thunk. He lay motionless for the longest time, then suddenly began grinding his face into the dirt, round and round like the bit of a drill, and everyone howled with laughter as he lacerated and abused himself like that, but I could only feel something like terror squeezing my bowels.

To make things worse for Billy Joe, Claude Copeland rode in the next heat and not only rode well but won it. He looked preposterous, his big thick legs curled like parenthesis around the sides of the small horse, but Claude knew how to handle the beast and proved an impregnable figure of strength. No one could dislodge him in a collision or stun him with an elbow. Eventually the *vaqueros* proved themselves faster, more skilful riders, but not before Claude collected two fat kitties and celebrated his triumph by standing in the middle of the corral, naked to the hips, colossal black torso shining with sweat, and tilting a bottle of beer back and letting the foam overflow his mouth and bubble down his face and chest and belly in rivulets of white. A pack of kids rushed out and surrounded him, shouting *"Viva El Negro!"* and swirling round him like the tides round the rock of Gibraltar.

It was here that I felt dizzy again, sick to my stomach. Must get away—fresh air—silence—

Push dog food, you fat fumbling Dutchman. Get out and sell Needlebee's Dog Food!

"Frits."

When I blinked the sales manager's face away Eli's replaced it.

"You all right, man?"

I had strayed far from the fiesta.

"—yeah, yeah—"

"You look wiped out. What's wrong?"

"Nuh-nuh-nothing—"

"Doreen said you needed help. What the hell's wrong, Frits?"

"Don't worry about me, I'll be all—all-all—right—"

"Bullshit."

Eli grabbed my arm and half-dragged me off with him. Through the crowd we went, brushing against the rough handmade woolen clothes of the peasants, passing a mother breastfeeding her baby with a tit as big as a balloon. There were shooting booths and a place where pigs were being cooked on the spit, fat sizzling and popping in the flames, flies buzzing everywhere.

My stomach was clenching and unclenching like a fist. "Wait—" I told Eli. I ran off behind a tree and was sick.

"The food get to you?"

"No. It's just that I'm—I'm trying to do without my pills."

"What pills?"

"Uppers."

"Jesus, man, no wonder you lost all your hair. No wonder you look a hundred and fifty years old. Didn't anybody ever tell you that speed kills?"

We had found our way to a quiet patch of earth, under some trees; at least here the air was clean, no stink of cooked meat, no flies.

I lay back on the grass, still trembling and twitching, stomach like water.

"What are you on now, Frits?"

"Nothing, I tell you. I'm trying to kick and that's the problem."

Eli said, "I hate to see you like this. Don't you have a doctor? Isn't anybody looking after you?"

"The doctors don't help, Eli. Only the blood of Jesus Christ can."

"You're really serious about that stuff, aren't you?"

"Don't talk about The Mission that way. They've been helping people a long time, Eli."

"I'm sure, but meanwhile you look awful, man. You ought check into a hospital for a while."

"No more hospitals. I had enough of them when they shipped me out of Nam. They put me in a psycho ward, Eli."

"It was bad, huh? But it would have been worse if they'd hit you with a court-martial for having bugged out of the war. At least you're not walking around with a dishonorable discharge."

"I wanted the DD badly, would have worn it like a Medal of Honor."

"The war's over now, Fritzie. People have forgotten how bad it was and they wouldn't respect you if they saw that DD on your record. Anyway, it's time you got Nam out of your system. You've got to bury all those memories and walk away from the grave, never to return again."

"The church teaches you that you can't ignore your sins. We've got to pay for them, for the blood we spilled in Viet Nam."

"The way I look at it, we already paid, in those godforsaken jungles. We suffered enough, Frits, why bring more down on yourself?"

"We have to go Christ's way—life for life, eye for eye, blemish for blemish—"

Eli was scowling and shaking his head. "They tried to drum that stuff into me when I was a kid, but I wasn't having it then and I'm not having it now, damn it. I'm not gonna live my life in perpetual guilt, not for anything I didn't do."

"And what about the things you did do—the people you killed at Chu Tau?"

"I suffered for that—I'm still suffering for it. Ain't that enough suffering for your fucking church?"

"Somebody has to die for us," I told him. "Somebody has to do what Christ did so that we can still call ourselves human."

"That's a tough outfit you belong to, Frits. It's not enough that we were all victims over there. Now they want us to become penitents to save our soul. Well, I say to hell with that. I'm not gonna become a martyr to satisfy the clerics. They want to die for pie in the sky, let 'em. But not me, kid."

My mouth had gone dry again and my body was beginning to shake. God, how I needed my pills, just a couple of tabs would do me fine. I'd been foolish to leave them home, to think that I could stay straight down here without any uppers at all. Maybe I could find some in El Cortez; surely one of the drug stores would be able to help out—

But I couldn't get up; my chest was still hurting, there was no strength in me.

"Eli—you wouldn't—wouldn't happen to be carrying, would you?"

"I've got some grass, Frits."

"Grass doesn't help. I—I need something stronger."

"I'll check some of the boys."

But Eli didn't move, just stood scowling at me unhappily.

"What a bummer to see you like this, Frits. Goddamn it, you deserve a lot better. Forget the pills, man. Forget Jesus. Get yourself some help. They've got these shrinks that work with Viet Nam vets, run these rap groups."

Fine advice. Can you imagine what would have happened had I followed it:

Mr Nelson, I'm sorry I failed to make my quota this month, but you see

*I can't work overtime now because I'm seeing a therapist three times a
week and—*

The look on his face, the scorn and contempt.

Nelson thought men who needed psychiatric help made rotten
salesmen. It was a sign of weakness, effeminacy. Only homosexuals
and bored housewives went to shrinks. Besides, there was no place
on your call sheet for couch time: the job demanded eight hours'
effort a day.

The job! I really wanted to tell Nelson to stuff it, but then what?
Selling dogfood was about all I could do. Even then it took chemical
sustenance to buoy me up. Talking to those hard-bitten supermarket
managers all day long put you in such a state that you felt like screaming. But it was always better after a couple of leapers. Those green-
hearted darlings made all the long drives possible; in winter through
the grey hard slanting Ozark rain, in summer through the Oklahoma
prairie heat, mirages shimmering wetly on the asphalt, FOOD TO
GO, $1 HOT DOGS, MALT SHAKES, AIN'T YOU HUNGRY YET,
IT'S FINGER LICKIN' GOOD, fighting the glare of the big diesel rigs
at night, trying to swallow greasy fried chicken in a Col. Sanders,
crawling into bed in a dark, dank boardinghouse room, knowing you
had to get up tomorrow and do this all over again, all for a lousy four
hundred and seventy-five bucks in take-home pay, plus one-half of
one per cent on everything over five thousand and the use of a white
company car with a big purple and pink dog on each door holding a
can of NEEDLEBEE'S DOG FOOD in his grinning mouth, but knowing at the same time you weren't fit for anything else. The big corpora-
tions didn't hire guys like me, they wanted Ivy League, mental health,
image, optimism, confidence; they wanted salesmen, not order-
takers; tomorrow, not yesterday—

"Oh, there you are. What's up lads?"

It was Doreen.

"The Major sent me for you. Everybody's waiting to go hunting.
Are you all right?"

I looked at her, wondering what she made of me, acting such a fool
yesterday, almost collapsing on her. I liked her so much, she was so
bright and alive, a joy to be around. That's what I had wanted to tell
her yesterday: how much I liked and admired her. But I had got the
shakes and had only disgusted her. I learned then what it must be
like to be a spastic; to live locked inside a bucking bronco of a body,
helpless to control it, brain exploding with rage and frustration.

Now I cursed this body of mine for having betrayed me. I cursed
life for the treason it was.

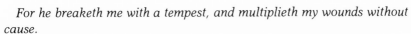

For he breaketh me with a tempest, and multiplieth my wounds without cause.

Eli was wrong. There had to be some righteousness in suffering.

Whom the Lord loveth he chasteneth.

But not even Turk who knew his bible, believed that. You couldn't call him religious, though. Reading the bible was one thing, living it another. Turk was like Eli: he couldn't accept that we had to face God's wrath before any of us who had been in Nam could be washed clean. Nobody could face up to that fact.

Turk and the others believed they could justify our having slaughtered the innocent. They simply dismissed it or excused it. But life didn't work out that way. Cruelty and indifference could not be annulled with more of the same. Accounts would have to be paid. We have to expunge the evil in us, burn it right out of our hearts and minds . . .

"Hey, Frits, watch it!"

I had wandered close to the edge of a ravine. Another step and I would have plunged a thousand feet into a black gorge. That shook me up, it really chilled me. Not the thought of death, just the realization how out of life I was. How could I reach the other men if I didn't pull myself together? To be a soldier of God took boldness, determination.

But then my head was pierced by a great pain, I heard Doreen asking what was wrong. I wanted to answer but couldn't, my head felt as if it had exploded, been blown to bits . . .

Eli

The morning after the fiesta we piled into a deuce and a half and took off for the mountains. Frits had thrown what seemed to be an epileptic fit; it was all we could do to hold him down, keep him from choking on his tongue.

That's what an amphetamine addiction did to you, speeded you up so fast that you needed tranquilizers to come down, feel normal. The tug of war between the two chemical substances screwed a man up something awful, made him worse than what he'd be on only one of the drugs. I'd seen it happen to a lot of truckers who ate pills to stay awake. In a couple of years they were like zombies, unfit to drive even golf carts.

"Maybe we should take him to a hospital," Claude said.

"Not down here," Mulligan replied. "They wouldn't know what to do with him."

"He's a lot better off with us," I agreed. "Maybe we can help the guy get over his screaming-meemies."

"How?"

"I don't know. We'll play it by ear, talk to him, stay with him."

"Maybe the fresh air in the mountains will help," Mulligan offered.

"Or baggin' a bighorn sheep," Billy Joe said.

"Are we really gonna find any bighorn sheep?" YoYo demanded of Mulligan. "Do they still run wild here or are you bullshitting us?"

"We've got 'em all right," Mulligan said firmly. He looked at us. "What say we all chip in and put together a big fat kitty for the first man that bags one of those beauties?"

"How much?"

"I don't know . . . twenty-five, fifty . . . "

"Make it fifty," Billy Joe insisted. "That bighorn's got my name on his forehead."

"That's what you think. He's all mine!" YoYo argued.

Voices rising, we all began yelling and jousting with each other, but goodnaturedly. This was how it had been in the war. We'd arrived a motley crew of strangers, but the bonds of war had joined us, turned us into kinfolk.

I'd missed that feeling, I realized. It was one thing to be on your own in the world, a free and independent spirit. That worked fine as long as things went well, but once the breaks started going against you, you needed family to back you up. Without kinfolk, your enemies would stomp you and kill you and eat your nuts for breakfast.

All right! Things were definitely picking up. You could just about see spirits beginning to soar as we headed higher and higher up into the mountains. Even Mulligan was wearing a big grin, clowning around. He'd been under heavy pressure yesterday. He'd wandered around alone at the fiesta, drinking hard, brooding, avoiding the festivities. The business with Aguilar was weighing on him. He couldn't avoid feeling responsible for the torture. It didn't matter that Tito Cota was doing the actual dirty work; it was being done on Mulligan's behalf, even if he hadn't asked for it. It was Mulligan who stood to gain the most from the boy's confession. That made him as guilty as Tito.

Matt was in a bind. He didn't want to condone torture but neither could he renounce Tito and quit his side. The class war had split El Cortez right down the middle, put him in with the likes of Tito. He didn't like the fat colonel but since he liked Che even less, he had to sit there and bite the bullet.

Matt accepted my offer of a cigarillo as we bumped along, climbing high. The sun began dropping out of sight, turning the hills around us dark and large.

"Enjoy the fights?" he asked, biting into the cigarrillo but not lighting it.

They were like nothing I had ever seen before: the horseman advancing slowly, carefully on the bull, moving his bolo over his head, keeping up a continual banter: "Hey, toro . . . you're a coward . . . a pig . . . a slut," and all the while waiting warily for the beast to charge. And when the charge came, deftly reining his horse out of the way and simultaneously whipping out his *cocobolo*, trying to wrap the lash around the bull's legs and bring him to the earth. Only once in five fights had a horse's flank been ripped open by the horns: a victory for the bull.

The most skilful of the *Rejoneadores* had in a fraction of that sidestepping moment performed the difficult feat of hooking the bull right off his feet, making him turn a somersault and land heavily on his back. The *rejoneador* had taken two turns around the ring for that, to great acclaim and accolades. Otherwise man and bull usually fought on to the point of exhaustion.

"Thanks for the fights, the fiesta. You must have worked like hell to put it together."

Mulligan shrugged and ran a hand over his clenched, craggy face. "That's all right, it was fun. The fiestas and the hunting are the best things about living down here."

"Listen Matt, maybe it's none of my business, but I have to say it. Why stay here? Why not clear out of El Cortez, leave this mess behind you? It's their fight, not yours."

Mulligan reached down beside him for a goatskin full of wine. "I've been considering it," he said. "But let's face it, every cent I have is sunk into El Cortez."

"It's only money. You'll make it back somehow."

"I'm going on sixty, Eli. At this age it's hard to start from scratch. On the other hand, I know I've been walking around these last months acting and feeling like the thousand-year-old-man."

"You could have a great life if it weren't for the political stuff," I told him. "This place is a paradise. Bighorn sheep in the hills, whales in the lagoons. If I were you, I'd sell the mine, find myself a shack on the seacoast and fish and hunt the days away."

Mulligan smiled. "I'm all for it, but I'm not alone. You don't know what Alicia's done down here. She took what was a ghost town and made it live. Nobody had ever run the mine at a profit before; El Cortez was famous for its failures. Even Anaconda Copper failed down here. Hell, so did the Jesuits before them. But Alicia had what nobody else had: a real love for this place and its people. El Cortez was just beginning to thrive when I met her. We've put everything into the mine—not just our money, but our lives. The earth contains not just copper but our seed, and I'm not about to give it up, not without a fight. Beside Alica was born here and wants to die here. If I walk out, I walk out on her."

Mulligan retrieved the wine skin and drank from it again.

"On top of that, I'd hate to let Che beat me. I refuse to believe the future belongs to terrorists like him."

"But the social order is rotten, it's got to erupt."

"So what? It erupted in Bolivia some years ago and look what happened: a radical regime took over and nationalized the tin mines and railways. Five years later the mines were almost bankrupt and the railways in ruins. Only assistance from Uncle Sam helped prevent a final collapse. And look at this country: for centuries the whites, a tiny percentage of the population, controlled the country and slaughtered the Indians left and right. A few years ago, a regime took over, with an Indian as president, a so-called progressive. And what did he do but prove himself the worst butcher of all. That's why the army stepped in. Hell, in the last ten years this country has had eight different presidents: six of them were assassinated, one was chased out of the country, and the other was strung by his neck from a lampost in the street.

"It sounds fine to talk about these problems in the abstract: social order, revolutionary seizure of power, land reform, the rest of it; but when it comes down to the particular, the words mean little in terms of solutions. Disorganization, corruption, violence, fraud are endemic in all the parties, left, right, or center. They're all a bunch of pistol-packing bastards and nothing will change until they change themselves. This country doesn't need Marxism to save it; it needs simple and basic human traits, like decency and kindness, charity and compassion, brotherly love."

"You preaching a Christian sermon, Matt?"

"Yeah, maybe that's what I am. Don't get me wrong, I'm a renegade Catholic, I don't believe in the idea of deity or of individual salvation in a spiritual eternity, but I do believe in Christianity as an ideology, a moral code. And that's what this country needs, not a political but a *moral* code."

"But the Church is strong down here, it's been preaching the Christian virtues for thousands of years."

"The Church, like everything else, is largely corrupt: the upper clergy are allied to the ruling class; the lower clergy are as poor and almost as ignorant as the peasants they preach to. Both levels of clergy have come to accept the outlook and values of the society in which they live. The great mass of people here ignore or reject the teachings of the church. The message of Christ, a positive message of action, goes unheard and unheeded."

"You ought to get together with Frits. He's more Christian than any padre I ever met in Viet Nam."

"I'm talking about Jesus, Eli—not Jesus Freaks."

We must have climbed a few thousand feet while talking, for now the night was cold and black. We were passing through a small mountain village standing on a plateau in a cleft of the hills. The village belonged in Africa, not the Americas: there was a tin-roofed verandaed *Presidencia* taking the place of the chief's hut, with thatched mud huts sprinkled round it, and a big bonfire flaring a sort of rough welcome. A tall gaunt man like a Moor stalked round the fire with a blanket over his head, and a woman knelt beside a pot making supper. Rows of eyes peered out of the dark huts like a cave of bats.

Our camp was ten minutes away, a small mud hut by the side of the road. Turk was there. He had a fire going inside and some fresh coffee on the boil. He'd just come down out of the mountains, having accompanied Tito Cota on a search party for Che. They hadn't found Che, just one of his bases. The information that had been squeezed out of Aguilar proved valid: guerrillas had been at the base maybe a day ago. It was a small one, Turk reported, with a crude bread oven, a tiny vegetable patch, and a butcher's block where some burros had been cut up with machetes. They had also found a couple of boxes of hand grenades.

Turk had brought along half a dozen of the grenades: home-made jobs fashioned out of empty fruit juice cans and lengths of gas pipe filled with sticks of dynamite and fired by detonators. The grenades were painted dark-green and looked lethal.

But it was time to eat and drink. Turk had prepared a tableful of game for us: roast quail and pheasant and hare. There was enough whiskey and tequila to float a truck. After dinner we cleaned and oiled the stack of 30-30 Winchesters Mulligan had brought along for tomorrow's hunt. Just before sacking out, each of us ante'd up for the kitty.

"If I win the prize, the next fiesta is on me," I announced.

"The bread's already spent," Claude said. "I've booked us all into Ranchita's this Friday night!"

"I wish I were there now," YoYo yelled. "I'd show those whores some things they've never seen before."

"You cain't teach an old whore new tricks," Billy Joe shot back.

"Maybe not, but I'd sure as hell like to try!"

The talk went from whores and sex to a discussion of the best brothels in southeast Asia. My thoughts went instead to Doreen. She'd been in good form today. In the midst of the fiesta she'd suddenly put her head back and shouted:

"CHLANNA NAN CON THIGIBH A SO'S GHEIBH SIBH FEOIL!"

The war cry of the clan Cameron.

SONS OF THE HOUNDS, COME HERE AND GET FLESH.

She was something, that lassie. I would have given anything to have her here now, tucked into my sleeping-bag with me, rubbing her goodies up against mine.

SONS OF THE HOUNDS, COME HERE AND GET FLESH.

I fell asleep, hearing the words echoing in my head. Next thing you know, I found myself being shaken awake by Turk, who was screaming, "C'mon, c'mon—grab a gun—move, damn you!"

Sitting up, I saw Mulligan outlined at the window, rifle in hand, ducking as a barrage of shots came from outside and socked into the walls, showering dirt all over us.

"What the hell is all this?"

It went on, the rifle fire, the shouts, the stumbling and thrashing around, the wild whinnying of a horse—

"Who's out there?"

In answer came the sound of a fire fight: rifles, carbines and machineguns, all aimed at us. I sat there stupidly, thinking, could this still be Nam? Was I back there? Had my whole life since then been only a dream?

But it couldn't possibly be. This wasn't Viet Nam, this was a hunting trip, a—

"Move! Git goin'!" It was Turk, snarling as he ran to a window and began firing his rifle. More machinegun bursts, short and hard. I threw myself down, tasted the dirt floor of the hut, digging my fingers into it. Real!

Someone threw himself down by my side.

"Here."

Mulligan pushed a rifle into my hands; it felt cold and heavy, laden with death. Instinct tussled with instinct. Finally I cast the rifle aside, seeing Mulligan see me do it.

"Turk, where are those grenades?" Mulligan asked.

From outside came more shots, whining, slamming into the walls of the hut.

His face lit eerily by the embers of the fire, Turk scuttled across the room, began fumbling around in his knapsack.

"Get down!"

"Christ!"

Mulligan and some of the others began returning fire; the room became industrial with the stink of cordite.

Chug-chug-chug-chug. I recognized the sound of an AK-47, the Russian-built automatic rifle favored by the Viet Cong, shooting off a full clip. Flat on his belly, Mulligan poked the rifle under the remains of the bullet-shattered front door and fired back into the night. Again a horse whinnied in terror.

"Sha, sha!"

"They're coming, they're coming!"

Running up, Turk whipped his arm around in windmill fashion, like a softball pitcher, and heaved one of the MNR's home-made grenades out the door.

"Give it to em."

"Fire, fire!"

The grenade detonated not far away, the tail end of the blast breaking glass somewhere in the hut. YoYo gave a battle-panicked scream—

"The truck—"

"There!"

"Hit them!"

Peeking out I could see the truck, figures running about in the darkness, muzzle blasts, sharp white spurts—

Came the starting roar of a motor; the truck began moving off, heading up into the hills, and soon there was only dust and darkness and overwhelming silence.

We stood in the vacuum gazing at each other: Claude was in his jockey shorts, YoYo was bare-assed naked, Frits was burrowed under a table, wearing the glassy thousand-yard stare of the shell-shocked. My face was garish with plaster-dust, like the Grand Panjandrum in a reverse minstrel show. We all looked at each other and sucked our breath in. Then we cracked, commenced snickering, giggling, laughing. It hit us all at once, the laughter did, but it wasn't good laughter, it was ugly awful laughter, a way of hacking out our shame and hysteria and fear. It left us with raw tight throats, eyes that were red and wet.

Mulligan sat watch that night. Highlighted by the flickering light of an oil lamp, his face looked skeletal, stood out like an emblem, a death's head.

Mulligan

We came off the mountain and hit it hard, keeping an eye out for the MNR. Turk, scouting up ahead, kept waving us on; we were alone in these endless hills.

Later the sun came out from behind the slate sky, just long enough to overheat everyone. I took it easy on the boys. They were in a foul mood, ashamed at the way they had disgraced themselves during last night's attack. For a bunch of ex-infantrymen they sure had folded fast. They were in lousy physical shape, too: Claude's knee had tightened up and Billy Joe was limping and moaning. The way they were humping it along it would take all of three days to reach El Cortez.

"C'mon, let's hit it," I yelled finally. "The way you're moving you'd think you were a bunch of old women."

"We're doing the best we can," Eli yelled back.

I was about to have it out with him, but thought the better of it. This wasn't the time for a fight. He wasn't the man I'd known in Viet Nam and I had to learn all over again how to handle him. What can you say anyway to a man that won't even stand up to save his own life?

I charged ahead, stepping up the pace, even though my own calves were aching and I was sweating like a racehorse. Che was counting on this, of course. Last night's attack was intended to break me down, but it had only done the opposite. I felt stronger now in my resolve to oppose him. His reliance on terror was a desperate act that proved he was incapable of achieving a mass uprising or of increasing his guerrilla band, training and supplying them. He had to limit himself to a small band of toughs taking refuge in tiny mountain hideouts.

These were his substitutes for the well-stocked bases a more substantial guerrilla force would have required.

One of these days we were going to meet *mano a mano* and when we did Che was going to learn a thing or two. He was going to learn what the soldier's trade was all about.

The guys collapsed by four-thirty and barely had enough energy to pitch camp. But we had put the mountain behind us, reached the edge of the desert; it would be a lot easier hiking tomorrow, flat dry land as opposed to steep rock-filled mountain trails that made you slip and slide and cut your hands. After a supper of tinned meat, soup and crackers, they crawled early into the sack. But they couldn't sleep. One's first night on the desert is unnerving; it's the immensity, the absolute silence—no crickets or frogs, just the flat earth and *you* and the vast sky overhead crowded with billions of stars. The weight of infinity, the silence, seems to crush down on you.

To cover their uneasiness and fear, the boys suddenly began talking loudly without pause, about baseball, yoyos, food, hunting, anything. They chattered like locusts, making no sense, just filling the void; and when sleep finally did come they lay muttering and tossing in their bags.

All except Eli, who lay staring at me, tightly. Finally he said, "Matt, let it be. Haven't you learned by now? You can't kill a revolution by killing revolutionaries."

"Che's no revolutionary. He's just a chicken-shit bandit."

"That's not the way the natives see it. To them he's a hero."

"He won't be a hero when I get through with him."

"I think you're wrong, man," Eli kept on. "If we learned anything in Viet Nam, it's that we can't win a guerrilla war."

"This isn't Nam," was my answer, "and Che isn't a guerrilla. He's a terrorist, a cheap-shot artist. There's only one way to stop him and that's to kill him."

"Haven't you had enough of killing? Aren't you sick to death of it?"

I shrugged my shoulders. "That's easy for you to say. You're not involved, you can get out. But for me it's the age-old story: kill or be killed."

*   *   *

As soon as dawn's first light showed I woke everyone up, forced them out of the sack. I didn't like the look of the sky, all dark and heavy. It was going to pour and we had to get moving and reach high ground fast.

"C'mon, pick em up and put em down!"

We made it just in time. It rained so hard that the water came pouring down in sheets from the slightest slopes. Turk and I screamed our lungs out to get them scrambling up the banks of the nearest gully. All the while the rainwater gathered in such force in the dry river beds that it came roaring down the canyon floor, a flash flood sweeping everything before it, bushes, trees, rocks, small game. It came with sudden overpowering ferocity, then was gone, leaving behind huge lumps of mud and clay.

"Lord, I've never seen anything like it," Claude said.

"It's a bitch, everything about this country's a bitch," Turk growled.

The weather toyed with us all day long, first giving us the back of its hand, unleashing one display of force after another, then caressing us gently, sprinkling a few raindrops here and there, bringing out swatches of bright red and purple anemones.

The flash floods came and went with startling power. Once we saw a huge boulder, easily half a ton, being swept along like a balloon. Meanwhile a north wind came up, cold and cruel, blowing right through us. Soggy-wet and shivering, we straggled along, Claude and Billy Joe far behind, Eli so mad at the world he couldn't speak. All in all, we were a pretty candy-assed bunch.

It got so bad that finally I couldn't take it. Gathering them together, I gave them a tongue-lashing, really got into them. It's time to stop dragging along, I said. Bravo Company used to be cold steel, but now look at you—yesterday's soup. What happened to your pride?

I ordered Turk to count cadence. They didn't like it, not one bit, but I didn't give a damn. They hadn't liked it in Viet Nam when I pushed them, but a soldier is only as good as his leader makes him, and I had made them good and they came to thank me for it, just as they would now.

So off we went with Turk Kohler bull-horning: "Hup hup hup!" Turk socked it to them the way he used to on the drill-field: "Come on, move it! You're suckin' wind like a buncha old women. You maggots, didja forget what it's like to be tough? You think life is all civilian good times? Well lemme tell ya, *this* is what it's all about— sufferin and hurtin, killin and dyin. Sure you wanna take it easy, sure you'd rather be watchin TV with a beer in your fist and your belly hangin out, but you can't right now, you gotta march or else you'll die out here. You call that marchin? Look at ya! If cunts were oranges you'd be a fucking Sunkist!"

Turk became a poet of profanity when he cut loose and I never failed to marvel at his performance. Such oath-making was a rare and
skilled art, worthy of critical appreciation, but the boys were having
none of it and recoiled into themselves, hunching their shoulders like
football players as Turk tonguelashed them across the desert floor.

Finally, maybe a half hour later, Eli broke.

"Enough," he yelled. "We're not in the army any more, can't you
get that through your skull? We're civilians and we don't have to take
orders from you or anybody else. So shut up and leave us alone!"

Continuing, he wheeled and let me have it, with both barrels, a
head-on blast. Eli was more than angry: his feelings of resentment,
outrage, and exhaustion were exploding like buckshot. I was the
villain in all this: a war-lover, a bully, a militarist. Faced by a time
of revolution, change, complexity, I could come up only with the old
obsolete answers: killing, war, strong-arm stuff.

When he broke off, ammunition spent, chest heaving, there was
a distraught look in Eli's eyes. He seemed unable to abide himself
for having lost control. But neither could he abide the rest of us.
Wheeling, he stomped off and charged on ahead, kicking furiously
at the earth.

My head hurt and I was woozy all over, as if I had just been
mugged. The poor bastard. Life had overwhelmed him; all he could
do was hit out. The irony was, I had precipitated all this by inviting
him down. It figured: nothing provokes like good intentions. Instead
of helping to renew our friendship, the reunion had endangered it.
What a mistake it had been to organize this party.

Alicia was right, the best thing was to pack them into a plane and
fly them home. Angrily, I cupped my hands and snarled, "Hup two
three four! March, dammit. Look like *men*, for Christ's sake! Try and
pretend you've got something hanging between those pantyhosed
legs of yours!"

*   *   *

CHE'S DIARY

Monday, March 31

Success. Mulligan's truck is ours.

For some of the men it was their first baptism of fire and they came through it well. They made Mulligan and his mercenaries look like *mulatos*. Be good to see the Great Captain's face today! How shrunken he must feel. He's learned who's master of these hills. Now the boot of history is on his neck. His last days are near!

Mulligan

We took a terrible beating. High winds and rain kept alternating all that next day, lacerating and punishing us. The boys were having a bad time of it: Claude's knee kept giving him trouble but he pushed on, face a slash of pain. Frits was in poor shape too, on the verge of another collapse, but he hung in, wouldn't quit. He had been like that in Viet Nam, I remembered. Whenever the going got tough and he seemed ready to disintegrate, Frits went deep inside himself, tapped a private reserve, came up with the strength and resolve to go on. The worse the going, the better he was. There was no explaining it; everything about the man was mystery, darkness, sorrow; yet you could always count on him to rise above himself, suffer his lot with an invincible heart.

Eli was the problem. Adversity wasn't toughening him. On the contrary, he had taken ill, turned feverish, yellow-eyed, diarrhetic. Not a word did he speak to me, but his hatred still communicated itself; it was as hot and palpable as lava.

At night the wind whipped across the desert and shook the stiff branches of the boojum trees, making them dance and moan: the effect in the moonlight was eerie. There were coyotes howling and the scolding of the cactus wrens was raucous and frenetic. Nobody slept much.

I lay awake listening to the sand slithering here and there over the desert floor, making whispering sounds.

The desert.

The boys thought of it as a place of emptiness and sterility, but they were wrong; it was seething with life.

Every piece of vegetation out there was fighting to store the water which had fallen; there might not be rain again for months, years. The trick was to protect that water from the other life encroaching upon it by growing a coat of natural creosin which sealed the moisture in and prevented it from evaporating in the heat. The coating also had a repulsive taste and was studded with thorns—protection against the ravenous thirst of stray animals and birds.

The desert taught a tough lesson, the blunt truth of nature: the law of life is also a law of death. Under extreme conditions every living thing is the enemy of all other living things: the fittest survive.

I could remember my first time here. It was summer, with the sun blowtorching the back of my neck. There were sharp-tipped burrs everywhere, endless reptiles and insects. Everyone thought I had gone off on a drunken binge somewhere. But it was the desert that had pulled me to it, with a force unlike any I had ever known.

I had wandered for three days across these sands, burning up, tongue thick and hot as slag, head swirling with insane murderous thoughts. I wanted to punish Alicia for having killed my son. She had killed Matt Jr. with her stubbornness, with her misplaced love for this contemptible country which built whore houses and jails instead of hospitals and schools. This country of bum politicians and cut-throat communists.

She had insisted that the child be born in El Cortez: "I'm not going to any cold impersonal military hospital in San Diego. Why should I turn myself over to a bunch of strangers when I can have my child at home, surrounded by people I know and love."

There it was. She wouldn't leave the place. Was *afraid* to leave it. When the odds went against us and we lost the child, I began to hate her. Never before had I hated like that, not even during the war. Then my fury had been directed against an abstract enemy, but here it was directed against a particular person, a single target.

It got worse as I slogged along. At San Pedro, a tiny village oasis where I had stopped to rest, I hit upon the perfect way to kill her. Poetic justice: I would somehow swipe an umbilical cord from a surgical wastebasket, wrap it around her neck, choke her with it, shouting, "See, this is how it felt, this is what you did to my son—!"

Madness.

I faced up to it, though. The desert does that to you. It won't let you hide from yourself; in the end you either shape up or fall apart.

Night after night I had lain huddled in my sleeping bag, listening to the wind, the sands. The desert speaks with a tongue of its own.

"Forgive, forgive," it kept saying.

But first I had to heal myself, become human again. The desert helped. It helped by reminding that only those who struggle survive.

I quit feeling sorry for myself and went back out there, into the heat, the wilderness, with just a pack on my back, a rifle by my side. I lived off the land, hunting badger and jack rabbit, experiencing the deep, profound satisfaction of eating what you kill. I discovered where the infrequent water holes were, which fruits of the cactus were edible. I burned every bit of fat off my body, came down lean and hard and alert.

The desert was a cruel bitch of a mistress, but I soon learned her moods and habits, conquered all fear of her. I even came to enjoy her silence and strangeness, her weird but prodigal beauty.

When I finally returned to El Cortez I was able to go to my wife and beg forgiveness of her.

I didn't like this country of hers, but neither did I hate it. It had taken a son from me, but what the hell, I still had another. Perhaps Ngo Chanh Kha wasn't my own flesh and blood, but I loved the kid and he loved me and called me father. That was enough. I'd probably never see him again, now that the VC had taken over all of Nam. He couldn't get out and I couldn't get in, but maybe one day all that would change. Anyway, he was alive because of me. He was my son and that was more than some men had and nobody could take it away from me.

Forgive, forgive.

It was uncanny how clearly the desert had spoken.

Now, once again, I found myself asking questions of it.

Am I doing the right thing?

Does what I believe make sense?

As I listened for a reply the wind blew hard and the fifty-foot boojum trees danced and clacked like wooden puppets, and the sands came swirling in too, humming and buzzing.

I caught my breath, straining to hear. But I couldn't make anything out, just sand talking to sand.

Doreen

Hell's teeth, but they were in a shocking state when they arrived, all grotty and red-eyed and exhausted. Most of them kipped out immediately. But not the Major. He just showered, ate, and flew right back out in his plane to reconnoitre the hills for a sign of Che. God knows what had happened out there; Eli couldnae or wouldnae say. For twenty-four hours he tossed and turned on the bed, sweating, shuddering, vomiting. Then he sank into a drugged sleep, skin a sickly mottled grey, lips the color of blotting paper. It was ghastly to see him like that, writhing around in pain. I stayed with him as often as I could, sponging him down, playing the helpmeet.

He made a long hard fight there in my room with the sunlight slitting through the drawn shades and the big Polish alarm clock ticking away on the night table, making strange calendar of our time together. My eyes drank him down as he tossed and groaned; into the depths of me he slid, deep down where the babies are made.

Alicia had loaned me a cassette player and some old tapes, and on one of them Buffy-Sainte Marie sang:

> *Don't ask why of me*
> *Don't ask how of me*
> *Don't ask forever*
> *Love me, love me, love me now . . .*

But when he was well enough to sit up he seemed to resent my ministrations. "Why don't you leave me alone?" he snapped during one siesta hour, face drained and sallow, eyes ablaze. Eli felt betrayed by his body; it made him dependent on me and he didnae like it; not

91

half. "Stop being so good to me," he ran on, "because when I get out of this bed I'm splitting, I'm getting the hell out of El Cortez."

Dinna fash yourself, I felt like telling him. Stop gettin' so excited.

"I don't need you. I don't need anybody."

"Rubbish. You're so tough, get up and empty that bleedin' bedpan by yourself."

He tried, stoving himself up on one elbow, gritting his teeth, giving it the old college try. But finally he fell back, completely knackered, groaning miserably. "Goddamn you. Stop doing for me, stop loving me so much."

"Och, lip up, you whelky snot," I shot back.

"Anybody who believes in love is a lunatic."

"Crikey, would ye listen to him? The cynic's message for the day. Because your head's all fooked up, you think everyone else's is too? You're a proper goosegog if you think that. The human race is as alive and well as ever and if you don't believe it, then *you're* the lunatic, mate!"

So said, I left him there and rushed out, blinking in the harsh light, hurrying through El Cortez, unreal place, men shouting and laughing, pong of chemicals, copper, children nattering away in Spanish. Then I found myself at the office, carbons to be filed, the girls popping their gum, feeling my love for him struggling like a crushed tree to raise itself and stand upright against the stream but knowing it was hopeless, the waters ran too swift and hard—

> *You're not a dream, you're not an angel*
> *You're a man*
> *I'm not a queen, I'm a woman*
> *Take my hand*
> *And though I'll never in my life see you again*
> *Here I'll stay until it's time for you to go*

But when Eli was finally well enough to get up he surprised me by making no attempt to leave. "I don't know what's the matter with me," he sighed. "I should clear out—we should *both* clear out—because we're sitting on a bomb and unless somebody defuses it fast, it's going to blow the roof off!"

"I'm no' leaving El Cortez," I informed him. "My Scottish upbringing wouldnae permit me to run from a fight."

"Your Scottish upbringing shortcircuited your brains. You're a trusting innocent mug and that's why men have always walked all over you. You're too good and too easy. I don't know why I have anything to do with you."

"I'll tell you why," I shot back hotly. "It's because you've got me to mop your brow and wipe your arse and cook meals and pull your peter and you *like* it, goddammit. You're not as hollow and dead as you like to think you are. You're still a man, E.J., you're still a member of the human race, and whether you like it or not, men need women. You need *me*. Maybe you'll never love me, but you'll always need me or somebody like me, because without a woman you're nothing but a primordial clod, a gargoyle, a clype, a biped! Now shut your mouf' before I give ye a knuckle sandwich!''

He grinned and made a pass which I managed to avoid—but not too emphatically. Next thing you know I was being dragged down on the bed and having me rump nipped. He began to manhandle me, gently, skilfully, and suddenly I heard him say, "I want you all the time, Miss Cameron. You're doing strange things to this hard heart of mine."

"D'ye mean it?"

"What can I say? Here's proof."

And he proved it, och aye.

Crikey, what a bother I was in over this one. I couldnae resist him, no matter what. I tried telling myself not to be such a proper mug, because no matter how much love I invested in him there wouldnae be an end-of-year dividend. Eli was going to leave; the tick of the clock was measuring our last hours together. If he was passionate and giving now, it was like a peace offering. Each caress was an apology for leavetaking, each kiss a way of saying farewell.

But so be it.

Nowhere in my birth certificate did it promise permanent happiness. I had him now, today, and that was better than nothing. He could stay until it was time for him to go.

So the inevitable was postponed, the condemned was temporarily reprieved. Life jogged on. Letters were typed, carbons were filed. Eli went and apologized to Mulligan; the old comrades made it up. Eli levelled with Matt, sounded his warning of doom, his intuition of an apocalyptic end. But his bodings went unheeded. As Eli put it later, "Fighters like Mulligan and Che can't be curbed. They cling to the old tribal psychology. They believe all the basic struggles of this life are irreconciliable and must be fought to the death."

"And you, what do you believe?"

Eli shrugged his shoulders. "It's not so original. It goes back to the prophets: wisdom is better than weapons."

But if we were sitting on a time-bomb nobody else seemed to notice it. Things went on as normal. A boxing match was announced for

Saturday night, Fernando Lopez vs. a lad from San Felipe. The furnaces on the hill cooked away. Patrols scoured the hills in daily search of Che. And every siesta and evening hour Eli and I went to bed and made love—desperate, tender, impassioned, end-of-world love.

Afterward he lay listening to Buffy-Sainte Marie, and I to the knockin' of the clock, the sound of time.

CHE'S DIARY

April 3

So Alicia wants to meet. After years of silence, she—

Who does she think she is, summoning me? She must believe she's the Empress of this province, the Queen Bee. What is she after, what kind of deal?

Mulligan

Turk was late. Having come off patrol half an hour ago he should have been here by now, reporting in, unwinding over a drink. It wasn't like him to hold me up. Restlessly, I went to the bar, poured a whiskey, flicked through the new Book of the Month Club selection that had arrived in the mail. *Come on, Turk, move your feet.* The next patrol was waiting to be briefed and sent out; there was a passel of work to be done, but as I got into it the church bell began tolling, slowly, dolefully.

I sent one of the girls out to find out which of the villagers had died.

The bell, it tolls for thee, friend Che. It sings the end of your days, my rebel chieftain, my plastic Robin Hood.

Right here, in the presence of my palace guard, my oldest and best army buddies, I had sworn revenge:

"That cuñado is going to get his. From now on we stop playing a defensive game and start hunting him, day and night. It means endless air and land patrols, road-checks, large-scale sweeps. It means sleeping out in the cold and rain, giving up workdays and weekends and holidays. But I'm going to find him and kill him. That much I promise you. I'm going to cut his head off and nail it up over the fireplace."

But swearing revenge was easy, achieving it something else. My hired hands were willing to fight; but willingness is no substitute for readiness. Basically they were a bunch of retreads and while I could squeeze a little more mileage out of them, they couldn't be pushed too far or too fast. We didn't really have the manpower to conduct endless large-scale sweeps and searches, not unless Col. Tito Cota helped us out. He had made a big show of committing himself

95

to the fight: "I'll go up into the mountains and stay up there until I stomp those *insurrectos* into the dust," Tito swore with characteristic bluster and braggadocio. But the next day the colonel opted out, claiming that he first had to approve the operation with his superiors. His will to fight was about as big as his brain.

So we were on our own, fifteen greybeards against the MNR. The odds were not what you would call tasty. We needed a break, a very big break, to beat Che. But he could be beaten; of that I was convinced. The papers in front of me told why.

Over the last month I had been accumulating an intelligence brief on Che. The information had been garnered from patrol reports, air recons, the testimony of informers, analyses by such shrewd professionals as Turk Kohler. What the brief did was break down the major elements a guerrilla like Che needed to survive.

Ideological motive. Strong. Give him that. It was easy to write him off as a scavenging bandit intent on loot and pillage, but all reports showed he was a much more complex figure than that. Evidently the leaders of the MNR, a bunch of chair-bound hacks operating out of the capital, wanted Che to quit his guerrilla activities and help turn the MNR into a political party. They had criticized him for his militaristic attitude, his "fetish of spontaneity," his "addiction to death and destruction." They believed bullets were no substitute for serious political work. But Che showed little grasp of, or interest in, serious political work. He was a man of violence and liked blood more than he liked red paint. He truly believed he could create a revolution with the help of a few dozen guerrillas and was willing to go it alone, without any party help. This had made them even more hostile. They began to vilify him, accuse him of things like "left-wing infantilism." But he had his own ideas about how to run a revolution, and the method of putting his ideas into practice interested him more than arguing with the guardians of Marxist orthodoxy. In short, he was a heretic, a tough obstinate fiercely dedicated revolutionist. If that didn't denote ideology, nothing did.

People. Questionable. No doubt many of the Indians around here sympathized with Che, but they weren't flocking to join his band. Neither were they chipping in with food and supplies; all reports showed that he had to pay hard cash for everything. Still, this might have been a tactical decision on his part, a way to win the hearts and minds of the population. What worked against him was that a lot of the miners knew him from the old days, remembered him as a pugnacious union deputy with a tendency to shout down, and eventually beat down, his opposition. Maybe they liked his cause, but they sure as hell didn't like *him*.

Space. Ideal. He had hundreds of miles of mountain and desert in which to hide. But the safer he was, the less contact he had with the people. What kind of revolution could he lead with no one to follow but a bunch of goats? Thus it didn't matter that the terrain favored him; sooner or later he had to come down out of the hills and show himself.

Bases. Clear-cut. He didn't have the manpower needed to maintain a variety of bases; neither did he have the resources to keep them stocked with food, arms and ammunition. He probably had one elaborate base somewhere stocked with every requirement for a long stay. Find that and we had him. But it called for the kind of manpower and energy which was impossible to muster around here.

Supplies. The key to it. With the party opposing him, Che had to go out and hustle for arms and ammo himself. This took time, money, organization. Now that he had stolen a truck from us he could move the stuff himself, but this also ate up energy and cash. By all reports he was paying big bucks for black-market arms. How could he do that and still pay his men? And he needed to pay them generously; the morale of guerrillas tended to deteriorate quickly. The men must live and work on reduced rations, under primitive conditions, with little sleep. Sooner or later this solitary, hunted life would break them down. Then too, they were Latins—they could hate that much, but not that long.

So. If Che couldn't buy the equipment, he had to swipe it. But how? Tito was keeping his troops close to home, where they couldn't be ambushed. It meant Che was compelled to strike at El Cortez, where the army kept a blockhouse stuffed with arms. I had a private cache of my own but nobody except Turk Kohler knew about it. The army blockhouse was the obvious target; must warn Tito to double his guard. It also occured to me that if we could find a way to sucker Che into attacking the blockhouse, we could entrap him and finish him off in a morning. But how to tempt him to attack? How to lure him down out of the hills?

Think, Great White Father.

A while later, remembering about Turk, I got up and walked to the window. And lo and behold, there he was, coming down the Camino Real, carrying something big and heavy in his arms.

As Turk came close, moving slowly and disjointedly, people rushed out of the cantinas and shops, only to pull up short, fall silent.

The deathknell sounded again, chilling me with an intimation of death.

I went outside. Turk came carrying his burden with the heavy ponderous gait of a deep-sea diver. His eyes were bereft and bewildered as he knelt down and deposited the dog on the ground.

The dog had died a painful convulsive death: his eyes were bulging out and his jaws were caked with scum and blood. Decomposition had set in; the smell was unmistakable.

"They poisoned him," Turk said hoarsely. "They poisoned him while I was out on patrol."

The bell tolled, just once, with an almost mocking sound, as the onlookers pressed close, whispering, "El perro, el perro—"

Turk rested on one knee beside the stinking corpse, eyes glazed, mouth hanging open, like a boxer taking the count.

"Pobrecito."

"Chingado."

Against the crowd's murmuring, jibing refrain, Turk looked round carefully, as if seeking out the culprit. His expression began to change as into his face came such a look of pure, animal rage that it made my scrotum tighten.

Then Turk stood up and went toward the crowd, mouth clenched, every scar and slash in his face leaping out with hideous clarity. The sight of him made them scatter everywhichway, like leaves before the wind.

Going to where his horse was tethered, Turk heaved himself up into the saddle, unslung his automatic rifle from its scabbard and cradled it in his arms.

Reining his horse down the Camino Real, he headed out of town, toward the blood-dark hills beyond.

Claude

RAP RAP RAP

It was more Turk's fight than Fernando's. He kept rapping and sounding the kid a good hour before the fight time, rubbing his neck and whisperin in his ear. He kept on signifyin, even when the kid went into the crapper:

"You're the best, the greatest, you're gonna beat the brains out of him, you're gonna do this and that and blah blah blah."

The old gunslinger wanted this fight real bad. He'd been walkin around for days with a demented look on him. To be still soldierin at his age, far far from home, was heavy dues for the man. He seemed lost down here, out of place. He'd always been a strange dude, of course. Even in Nam he'd gone his own way. The Lone Ranger, we used to call him.

I don't believe much in buddies, he used to say. It's better that way cauz it hurts too much when a friend gets iced. For all of that, though, I still liked the mother. He was a loser, the kind of dude that always pays big dues. But I had grown up with a thousand guys like that. Turk might just as well have been born black. His old lady had cut his balls off, some draftees had nearly blinded him by fragging his hootch, and now they'd killed his dog, the only thing he loved in this world. Yeah, he was a white nigger, all right. Turk was a member of the tribe.

"You're gonna waste him," he kept saying to Fernando. "You're the best, the greatest, and when you hit him he's gonna quit, he's gonna croak. You're the toughest, the strongest. You're the most man in this whole faggot country."

99

Fernando sat and said nothing. As Turk laced his gloves and snipped the plastic tips off with a pair of scissors, I studied the kid. He was scared. I could smell it. The fear-stink was something I knew about. I had sniffed it on a thousand athletes down through the years. I had sniffed it on myself, more times than I cared to remember.

Fear was a part of every athlete's makeup. It was neither a good thing nor a bad thing, just an emotion. The trick was to make something of it, convert it into a force, an energy. Goddamn if old Knobby Fitzgerald didn't come to mind. Old Knobby had been quarter-backing for twenty years but like as not he'd still puke his breakfast up before every game. He'd sit there in the locker room all white and sick and shivery. But then, when the game began, he'd go out there and whip that skinny old arm of his up and bullet the ball maybe sixty or seventy yards on the first play. Cookin old Knobby, he was *beeyooteefull*, he was in a different thing!

Fear could take away, it could turn your legs to lead and your head to mush, but it could also give, make you stronger, better. It was up to you to cook with it or not.

It was my hunch that Fernando would be ok by the time the fight started. The kid could use his hands pretty well—how well we'd find out tonight. Turk had taught him a lot and so had I. He'd come on strong over the last two weeks. His opponent, Perez, was a six-year pro with a lot more wins than losses, but the kid could take him—if he didn't choke up out there.

It was time now. Some dude stuck his head in the door and yelled somethin in Spanish. People had come from all over the province to see the fight. There was a mob outside—mostly Fernando's friends and family. They pressed round him, shouting encouragements and all. Fernando tried to smile; it came out a scowl. His face was tight and sour; I was hip to how he felt.

We elbowed the well-wishers aside and went through to the arena.

They had a kind of raggedy-ass setup for the fight. The ring was set outdoors, in the middle of a dusty schoolyard, under a necklace of bare electric bulbs. The air stank from cigarette smoke and DDT spray, which had been used to chase away the flies and moths. A nearby gasoline generator fed the lights, which dimmed every time the persnickety old motor coughed. The wooden stands were crowded with people. Others were either jammed into portable seats or hanging from the trees. There was a steady noise of talking, a scraping of chairs. In the 30—peso seats at ringside sat Mulligan and his wife, YoYo and Billy Joe, the whole gang. They had beer and cigars, looked happy and loose. Behind them sat the other big honchos of El Cortez, union leaders and engineers and the rest. There were lots of women too, some of them holding babies in their laps.

When the crowd spied Fernando they cut loose a roar. The dude could become a big local hero if he copped tonight. Next the referee came into the ring, wearing brand-new white sneakers, and the crowd began jiving him as he rubbed his baby shoes in the resin. Yeah yeah YEAH, there was a nice thing in the air, a feelin of something boss about to happen. Good to be alive, jim!

When I found my seat I stood tall and looked round, towering high above the natives, digging the scene. And letting them dig me, cauz they all knew me now, the biggest, toughest, baddest mothafuckah in the world! *Have no fear, Big Claude's here! Stick aroun and you'll see what Papa Bear's puttin down!*

I looked the señoritas over and locked eyes with one of them. Belita, the *madre superiora* of Ranchita's. I had visited her cat house pretty nearly every night; it was a dump but the girls weren't bad and the *madama* herself was a fine-looking bitch with a big ass and a shrewd head. When I kissed her hand, she laughed and said ironically, "Welcome to the *dulce vida*." She had heard about me, already had eyes for me. I looked the girls over and said I preferred her to them. She dug that. An hour later we were balling.

Afterwards, she dug her fingers into my arms, pleading: "Stay here. Share my life with me. Together we'll become rich."

She had plans to open a whore house in the capital, a *residencia de reunión* that would be like a palace, full of servants and paintings and fantastic bedrooms. "Such an establishment can never fail," she said. "Even if there is a revolution, nature will prevail. It doesn't matter if men are communists or capitalists, they will always want young girls."

She had the smarts and the contacts to build up such an establishment, make it go. All she lacked was the capital. I was tempted to accept her offer and give her the loot. Man, it might work out to be a good deal. I'd have income for life, Belita to do the dirty work, and all the chicks I wanted. That was part of the arrangement, Belita had said so herself. "You can make fuck with all the girls you want." GODDAMN, but she was tempting me! Something like that was perzactly what I needed right now. It could change my luck. Shoot, it could change my life!

Still, it was a gamble, it was a chance. I didn't know my way around down here, couldn't speak more'n twenty words of the language.

I'd have to marry Madama Belita, but even then the whole thing would be in her name. Law of the land, foreigners couldn't own property. On top of that, I didn't have eyes to end up as part-owner of a hookshop.

It wasn't that I had anything against whore-houses—hell, they were in the nature of being a public service—but there was Whitey to consider. If the word got out to mine enemy that big Claude Copeland, best running back in pro ball, idol of young America and all that bullshit, was whore-mongering down in South America, couldn't you just see the reaction? Couldn't you just picture the stories in Whitey's racist newspapers? Lotta people up north were just waiting for me to stumble, drop my guard. ooooOOOWWWWeeee would those blue-eyed mothafuckers jump all over me!

That was Whitey for you. Don' matter how hard you fight his battles, how many games you win for him. In the end he gonna end up fuckin over you.

But there was Miz Belita lookin at me, coming on like ninety, imploring me to come fly with her. *Fly!*

Goddamn, but I wanted her hard-rock ass! What to do, man, what to do?

Perez entered: a swarthy bull-necked thick-nosed club fighter. His face was badly scarred from all the hits he'd taken in his time. His supporters in the crowd sent up a big, raucous cheer, but he didn't even smile back: the dude was all business. He wore white trunks and high black sneakers with the letter "P" marked with gold studs.

As the referee called em together, I bought a brew and sat down beside Mulligan, who reported that the price on the fight was 7–5 Perez. I studied Perez for a while, then gave Fernando the once over. Turk was still hangin over him, givin him an earful, like a jockey to his mount.

I decided to bet a hundred bucks on Perez.

No special reason. I didn't know anythin about Perez. But I did know somethin about Turk. Once a loser, always a loser.

The fight was somethin else. Both boys went at it fast and hard from the start, throwing leather. Perez was fighting a defensive fight; cagy, cool, he kept stayin back, jabbin, tryin to open Fernando's guard. He seemed slow and had no left hand to speak of, but his right looked dangerous. Fernando stayed in close, hammerin away, workin on his body.

Yeah, all right, ALL RIGHT, we had ourselves a *fisticuff* fight here! Pretty soon I forgot all about it bein a tank-town match with a toot whistle instead of a warning bell. It didn't matter that the floorboards farted dust each time the fighters shuffled and stomped their feet. They were really doin their thing up there, ooooOOOOWWWWeeee! They were both good heavyweights and they really got into it, they gave it everything they had, and the crowd dug it and heated up and started shoutin things like, *"Otra vez! Abajo! Eso!"*

By the tenth round, with only two more to go, the feeling at ringside was that it would be called a draw. It was that close, but I figured Fernando would take it, as he was comin on stronger all the time, hittin sharper and harder. Perez looked worried. He knew he was in trouble. Between the tenth and eleventh, his manager talked long and hard to him, but it didn't seem to help: Fernando kept wadin in, choppin with both hands, workin on his body, pilin up the points.

Turk felt the win comin. He was standin up now, his big war-pocked face all swollen and bloody, hollerin, "GO ON IN ON HIM! HIT! HIT! IN THE GUT! ABAJO! ABAJO!"

He cut loose with a war-whoop as Fernando socked Perez in the gut and followed it with a right hand to the bridge of the nose.

When the toot sounded, I turned to Mulligan. "Looks like I can kiss my yard-note goodby. That's what I get for bettin against my own team."

The crowd gave an unexpected cry and Mulligan whonked an elbow into my ribs, "Hey hey, look at that!"

Perez had cut loose at Fernando after the whistle and was hittin him again, a hard right hook across the side of the head. As the ref rushed in and tried to separate them, Fernando stood blinkin dazedly, wonderin what to do.

That's when Turk blew his wad. "GET HIM, GET HIM," he started screamin at Fernando.

In that split second Fernando hesitated; instinct said it was wrong. But he was too much his master's puppet and could only do as bidden.

"KILL THE FUCKER! KILL HIM! KILL HIM!"

Obeyin now, Fernando bulled past the referee and threw a wild fist at Perez, who was ready for it. Duckin, he came up off the floor with his first left hand in five rounds. It caught Fernando under the jaw with a *chonk!* that knocked his mouthpiece out. The ref dived in again but by then the damage was done; Fernando was wobblin like a wino when he went back to his round.

Here, as the ref ordered the round taken away from Perez, Turk made another mistake. The stupid mothuh, instead of administerin to the kid and givin him a whiff of ammonia and orderin him to keep away from Perez, he blew his remainin cool. It was as if the roof of his skull had blown off and all his frustration and rage and resentment came out, steamin like smoke. He kept bad-mouthin Fernando, the words and curses and threats collidin and pilin up like derailed freight cars, becomin a shit-storm of shrieks and insults. Turk had gone dinky-dau.

It was too much for Fernando, who just didn't know what world he was in. He staggered out and tried to satisfy Turk, flailin his arms around like a busted windmill. Lord, what a mistake. Perez was waitin with a cold little sneer on his face. Seconds later he flicked his right out, clean and quick, like a snake's tongue, and hit Fernando once, twice, three times, the last an uppercut straight into the throat. As the kid went down pukin blood Turk leapt into the ring screamin GET UP, FIGHT, GET UP, FIGHT FIGHT FIGHT, and I shut my eyes, not wantin to see it, not wantin to be witness to the mortification of a man who had once been a mentor to me.

It was worse in the locker room. With the kid stretched out on the rubbin table and his mother weepin and wailin her beads, Turk would not quit. He kept rippin into Fernando, callin him every name his tongue could conceive. The dude was down and out but Turk was out of control. There was no mercy in his soul, only hatred and poison, and he kept spewin it out, splatterin it all over the fallen boxer.

Fernando lay there takin it, starin up at Turk through his bloody broken face, not saying word-one. But his eyes, Jim, they told everything. He had a look on him that was as mean and spiteful as a rattlesnake's.

Dolores

Eeho, did I ever draw a couple of gavacho bastards that Saturday night. It was my bad luck. I'd been wiggling my ass on the petate for three straight hours. Ranchita's was jammed full; every peon at the fight must have come by afterward, and they were all so drunk they started grabbing your cula the minute you came down the stairs. Three hours of that was long enough for any girl, so I headed for the kitchen where Ernesto the cook had promised me a big plate of *chilequiles*. I could just about sniff the crema de la leche and chile when these two gavacho bastards stopped me on the way out of the parlor. I recognized them as gringos from El Cortez. They had visited Ranchita's every single night and the word was they were bad news— mean when drunk, disposed to buy only one girl between them. I didn't dig that kind of freak stuff, so I tried to get away. But the one with the yo-yo grabbed me and said he was *muy caliente* for me!

I wanted no part of him or his cowboy pal. After having lived in El Paso's *chamizal*, I had no use for anybody who even *looked* Texan. So I didn't let on that I knew English. Instead I came on like a real dumb *puta* and started screeching away in Spanish, pushing my voice way up high, figuring it would scare them off. The other girls couldn't understand what was shaking. What a bunch of dumb bitches they were. *Mierda*, those greasers had no standards at all. Most of them didn't even know how to put makeup on and walk properly until I taught them. I didn't learn my stuff in no whorehouse either. I had good jobs in El Paso and L.A. I made long bread and went out with some sharp pochos. I'd still be up north if The Man hadn't picked me up for having no papers. The son of a bitch, whoever finked on

105

me should have his guts used for guitar strings. *Chinga tu madre,* you pocho pimp!

Anyway, I kept shrilling away like a *criada,* but it didn't work, they liked the shape of my titties too much. And me standing just five steps away from my plate of chilequiles! *Hijo,* let me tell you, I was mad, I had a bad ass, but what could I do? Madama Belita herself came over and laid the word on me. "You make those boys happy, Dolores. They got the pesos."

"Me *siento asolada,*" I growled. "I'm ravaged. And it's time for my supper."

"Eat tomorrow. Tonight get those dollars."

"Go to hell. I want to rest."

"Look," Belita said. "I'm going to hit them for fifty bucks. You can keep twenty."

"I don't want the twenty. I just want my chilequiles."

"You'll have your chilequiles and a dish of seviche too if you be a good girl."

I yelled that I didn't want to be a good girl and we started jawing away. In the end Madama Belita won, just like she always did, but not before I screwed another ten bucks out of her. I also made her promise to give me an hour off. Madama Belita was a lot easier to handle these days, now that she was getting it steady from El Negro. She sure dug that suede cat, and there were rumors that Claude was laying all kinds of bread on her. He wanted to go into business down here, though only God himself knew why. America was the place to invest money. Everybody was in business up there, they were all peddling something to each other. From coast to coast, the country was a great big *supermercado.*

When I went and sat with them, I was disgusted to learn that these turkeys drank coca-cola with their whiskey. *Jesucristo* what a couple of *culatas,* killing the taste of good scotch with that syrup. They tried to pour the same mixture down my throat but I spat it out and yelled that I wanted mine straight from the bottle, Johnny Walker, Red Label. Good old Señor Walker. Every time I tasted him on my tongue I thought of Pomona on Saturday night and me dressed tough, the toughest-looking *chicana* on the block, and getting into Luis' Camaro and finding that bottle on the white leatherette seat, seal unbroken.

Good old Luis.

Good old L.A.

This half-breed had herself one long bossa nova up there. Chinga the madre of the bastard pocho pimp who turned me in.

Señor Walker helped me relax a bit. I listened to the boys talking about the fight; they had dropped a bundle on Fernando and were mad as hell at someone called Turk for having loused up the fight. They kept bitching so long about the dude that it got to be a drag. I tuned them out and hummed along with the jukebox, *"Tu me acostumbraste,"* until the cowboy got up and played a lot of hillbilly stuff that spoiled my mood.

The cowboy, Billy Joe, reminded me of the blonde gringo son of a pocho bitch who got on the bus my first day in El Paso. He dropped his coins in the box, then turned and looked for a seat. All the seats were taken, however, except for a couple in the back, over the rear wheels. He came over to me, mouth curling up into a sneer. "Beaners ride the back of the bus when a white man needs a seat."

I shook my head, playing it as if I didn't comprendo but he started yelling and cursing, "Move over, chili-belly, git!" Then he grabbed me and I was going to kick his nuts until I remembered that I had crossed the river without papers and couldn't afford to get busted. So I crawled to the back of the bus, burning with shame and anger. Later I begged God to one day roast his skin in hell.

"Let's go, Dolores, let's make it now," YoYo said in Spanish.

Once upstairs the boys wanted the light out. The only glow in the room came from the *pitaya* candle lit under the Sacred Heart medal over the bed. They wanted me to make a show of undressing, but I wasn't about to perform and whipped my things right off. The little one just about flipped when I unhooked my bra and let it drop. His eyes jumped out and his mouth whacked open like a beer-top. I stepped close and gave him a good whiff. Next thing you know, he grabbed me and pulled me down on the bed, all the time kissing and tonguing my titties.

Billy Joe sat on the far side of the bed, just looking. He didn't even change his expression as YoYo climbed on top and started getting his nuts off. You'd think he was watching somebody in the dentist's chair. When YoYo got off he just unbuckled his belt, shoved his pants a few inches down, and took his turn.

Just a couple of jabs and Billy Joe started squirting. Seconds later he had his pants zipped up and was leaning back against the wall, smoking a joint. YoYo wanted to diddle around with me while they talked so I lay back and closed my eyes and tried thinking of something else, something nice, like my daughter Florencia, but as soon as it trickled into my head what these two gringos were talking about I perked up fast.

The *zopilotes*, they were planning to bust somebody's head in.

"Here's how we do it," said YoYo. "When Claude leaves for home we fly north with him and get him to land somewhere in the hills. We coldcock him up there and hitch a ride to the capital. By the time they find him, we'll have stashed the dust somewhere in the states."

"You sure got one fucked-up head on you," Billy Joe said. "How much do you reckon we can make on that nigger?"

"You see the way he dresses? You see the rings on his fingers?"

"Nothin, man."

"There's more. He wears a money-belt and it's stuffed with cash. I don't know how much is in there but it's a whole lot."

"If I know that flashy spade, it's probably all singles. Claude ain't worth messin with."

"OK, you tell me how we're gonna get rich down here."

Billy Joe replied, "We whipsaw the next payroll when it comes in. It must add up to something like fifty thousand big ones."

YoYo gave a low whistle. "Wow. How are we gonna do that? Mulligan's got armed guards all over the place."

"Most of them are busy right now hunting Che. Anyway, we got free run of El Cortez, don't we? Didn't we already walk into the payroll office just like that?"

"OK, it's easy to get in. How do we get out?"

"We have a jeep standing by," Billy Joe answered, "and we burn rubber out to the airstrip. We cop one of Mulligan's planes and fly to the capital and grab the daily Aeronaves flight to Mexico City. From there we can split to anywhere—Vegas, Rio, New York—"

"That's a great idea," YoYo said. "Except for one thing—we don't know how to fly."

"Who don't?"

"Aw, come on now, since when did you become a pilot?"

"In high school I was in the air cadets for a spell," the cowboy answered. "We practiced a lot on small planes."

"Are you bullshitting me again?" YoYo demanded. "Is this another lie of yours like the one about bein a bronc rider?"

"I ain't lying. I can fly one of those crates out of here."

YoYo made a face. "I don't know what to believe about you no more."

Billy Joe flared up, "I'll tell you what to believe—that you're nowhere and nuthin without me!"

They started badmouthing each other and it got pretty raw for a time, but soon it became clear that the little one, for all his noise, belonged to the bigger. YoYo was just that: a toy at the end of the cowboy's string. When he was finally told to shut up, YoYo obeyed but not before asking, "Why do you want to do Mulligan bad?"

"I don't, but we need loot, man."

"I don't like it. I got nothin against the Major."

"Neither do I. But what can we do, the well has run dry."

I was scared to look at Billy Joe and played it very dumb, careful not to hint that I knew even one word of English. When YoYo finally stopped pawing me he took out a packet of dope, sprinkled a little mound of powder on a newspaper, made a tight tube of a ten-dollar bill, and stuck one end up his nose. Next thing you know, SNIFFFFF, he was sucking the stuff up like a vacuum cleaner, breathing out and then SNIFFFFINNGGGG again. Eeeho, it really hurt to sit there and not be offered any.

Then it was Billy Joe's turn. The coke made him all flushed and excited, and he started reminiscing about some of the other jobs they'd pulled off. YoYo listened to him, nodding jerkily, giggling now and then, blinking and squirming around. *Hijo*, was he flying. "Yeah, yeah, we've done ok, we've really done ok," he kept saying over and over.

It was true. The two of them had done all right as a team since returning from Viet Nam. They'd ripped off a lot of supermarkets and banks without ever having been busted, not even once.

It took them a couple of more hits to get in the mood to ball again. Only now their freakiness came out. Billy Joe slid his hands under my butt and turned me sideways on the bed and put it to me hard. Meanwhile, Billy Joe greased me up from behind and wanted in. It was a drag, but I did it, I took them both. They were both real wild now, freaked-out. "Home run!" Billy Joe kept saying. "Four-bagger!"

When they finally finished and got dressed again, they picked up where they had left off. YoYo was still balking at the idea of the job. "It's too risky," he said. "There are too many guns around and it's too tough to escape. One little hitch—like the plane not starting— and we're lost."

"It'll start," Billy Joe said.

"Sure, you're gonna write out a written guarantee. You're gonna put a fail-safe clause in the contract."

"It's a lock-up," Billy Joe insisted.

"It's crazy," YoYo fired back.

"What do you know, grunt? If it wasn't for me, you'd be plowing fields for a living."

They were still barking at each other as they headed out the door of Ranchita's, without even so much as a goodby. Not that I gave a damn. To hell with them, the snowballs. And to hell with their big talk. They didn't have the *cojones* to pull off a fifty-thousand-dollar job.

I hurried to the kitchen and poked a fork into the chopped onions Ernesto had sprinkled all over my big steaming plate of *chilequiles*. I was hungry, this chiquita really had appetite. A couple of bites and I'd forgotten all about Billy Joe and YoYo, the *maricones*, the sons of goats.

Alicia

Let him be there. All the way down the coast I prayed hard and pushed the jeep recklessly. The road went through sand dunes that were soft and dank-smelling after the recent rains and my wheels spun in the stuff, rocking us from side to side. At Ricardo's Landing I headed inland to the main road and went south, passing El Marmolito and the onyx quarry. The quarry hadn't been worked in years and the slashed-open mountain gaped wide and deep, like a mass grave. Further along the road I passed the dessicated ruins of an old cattle ranch. What a land of the dead this was, marked with the tombstones of civilization.

A man jumped out on the road, waving a rifle and shouting, "Halt, halt!" I recognized him; the one with the patch over his eye, Charlie Corrigan. He looked like a pirate.

"What are you doing out here?"

"Fetching something for Matt," I lied.

"I'll go with you."

"No, I'm all right."

"But there's MNR in the hills."

"I've got this to get me out of trouble," I said, showing the .45 on the seat beside me. At the same time, I knew that if I should have to use it, all was lost.

At the junction of San Andres I turned right and picked up the coastal road again, passing the wildcat well my father had sold back in the 30's to an American oil company. They had pumped oil out for a year, only to have the well run dry on them, at two thousand feet.

111

A small boat came chugging across the lagoon: Raoul and his brother Carlos returning from Cedros Island with the booty from their fish traps. Raoul, wearing denims and a straw hat, lifted his one good hand from the outboard and waved. He had lost the other ten years ago while fishing with dynamite. According to Carlos, when Raoul saw his blown-off hand sinking to the bottom of the sea he had merely shaken his head and growled, "Dammit, it *would* have to be the one with my ring finger."

I could remember going out with them as a child and watching them fish for turtles, a tough business: the trick was to throw the harpoon in such a way as to pierce the outer bloodless edge of the shell without damaging the meat inside. The overhang was only about two inches wide, but damned if they didn't hit the bull's-eye nine times out of ten. *Qué hombres.*

Suddenly Bocca de Marron was only minutes away and my heart missed a painful beat. I stopped the jeep and shakily lit a cigarette, wondering for the hundredth time whether Che would be there: I wasn't even sure my message had reached him. It was all very dicey: Don Enrique had given the note and a thousand pesos to a man who knew a man who . . .

I found myself praying now. I prayed in Spanish and in English, asking God in both tongues to come through for me, to produce Che, make him listen to reason. Was God listening? They said He was munificent, but perhaps before He gave, a further sign of sincerity was required. I picked up the .45 from the seat and put the muzzle against my temple. "If this is the price I must pay, I'll pay it. If You'll save El Cortez, I'll pull the trigger."

Drops of rain began falling from the low black clouds which had drifted overhead. As the rain commenced to pelt down I drove on, working the wipers with the hand lever above the windshield.

I screamed when the rifle was fired and the bullet went whining overhead, but was relieved at the same time that Che had got my message. Two scruffy and heavily armed men came out on the road, eying me with suspicion and hostility. After searching the jeep they drove down the disused road leading to the fishing camp at Boca de Marron.

Just ten years ago the camp had been a beautiful sun-lit place, the shack covered with green vines and standing under the high fan palms fronting the beach where we used to skinnydip and eat fresh abalone and clams for lunch. Matt had just returned from Asia and the place had helped him to forget that hellish war and his bitter feelings toward the American government. We'd fallen in love, joined our lives here. The sun and the fishing had restored his spirits, given him a new purpose in life. He was done with the U.S. army, with generals who wanted him to fight but not to win, who wanted war but not victory. All he wanted was to forget Viet Nam and go fishing and hunting.

And make a baby or two.

Like most lifelong bachelors, he was crazy about kids, wanted them desperately; a son, anyway. After making love, he'd kiss my belly, whisper into it, "Go you little tadpoles, wriggle up there, find those eggs and hatch me a big fat baby boy with balls like a bull!"

But now, in the rain, the camp at Boca de Marron looked dismal and unromantic. The beach was littered with plastic bottles and dried kelp and lumps of tar. The windows of the shack were broken and stuffed with rags. Inside, the bed on which we'd made so much love was broken and rusty. The whole place smelled of damp and fungus.

Wearing jungle fatigues, Che sat behind a table, the white light of a pressure lantern bringing out the dark, deep lines in his face. He had lost perhaps ten pounds since our last meeting and had aged an equal number of years. He was unshaven and unkempt, with blood-shot eyes staring out of knife-holes in a bone face, but his presence was overwhelming, almost frightening.

"What do you want?"

"What, no greeting? Not even a *qué tal* for an old friend?"

"You're lucky I came. It could have been a trap."

Silence.

"Does your husband know you're here?"

"What do you think?"

He didn't say anything, just sat waiting with his hands spread flat on the table, the lantern hissing steadily. Three fingers on one hand were missing, I noticed. There were dirty seams where the stumps had been stitched.

He anticipated the question forming in my mind: "I had a little accident with a bomb," he said. His Spanish was barked out abrasively, as if the words were distasteful on his tongue.

"These days you seem to spend a lot of time with bombs."

He shrugged. "It's only by the exercise of violence that people can be made to understand us."

"Since when has any problem been solved by violence?"

"Tell that to the bastards who run the country."

This from someone who used to be a pimply, overweight butter-boy who followed me around El Cortez with a hand in his pocket, scratching his genitals. In those days he called himself *El Marlon*, after the movie actor, and the extent of his radicalism was to negotiate a pay raise for the miners by waving a stick of dynamite under your nose and threatening to set it off if his terms weren't met. One couldn't conceive of him becoming a guerrilla, inspiring and leading other men. But it had happened. Jesús Maria Salvatierra had gone away, trained in Cuba, fought in the revolutionary wars in Mozambique and Ethiopia. He had transformed himself, taken a new name, grown a new face. And what a face it was, with martyr written all over it.

"What are you looking at?"

"You. You're crucifying yourself."

"My life is nothing. My actions are nothing. I'm willing to die for our cause. Only the end counts—our ultimate victory."

"You're convinced you'll win?"

"We have the truth on our side. We're on the right side of history. The age of individualism is over."

"But you're alone, too. How many of you can there be—a dozen, two dozen?"

"You don't understand the historical situation. My task is to prove to the people, and to the Left, that their only hope of intervening effectively in the making of the nation's destiny is through revolutionary upheaval. Once they learn that the monopoly of the means of violence exercised by the oligarchy can be broken, there will be a tremendous unleashing of the explosive potentialities of the social order. Then my band will number in the millions."

"Mierda," I said. "People are sick to death of big talk, be it right or left. They want bread, not air."

"They're with me," he flared up. "You'll see."

"They're with you because you have machismo. They admire your courage and masculinity, not your Marxist slogans."

About to retort, he was seized by a fit of violent coughing which lasted a good two or three minutes, leaving him wheezing for breath.

"How long have you been coughing like that?"

He shrugged.

"You should do something about it."

"Don't worry about me. Only one thing can kill me: bullets."

I stepped to the shattered window and watched the rain drumming down on a wide arc of sea, transforming it into a luminescent sheet of silver.

When I turned back I said, "Jesus Maria, I haven't come to argue with you, only to tell you this: I fear for you, for all of us. You talk of victory; I see defeat. You talk of a new social order; I see only death. I've dreamt it. It will happen. My heart pains with the truth of it."

"So you've discovered your own mortality. Touching, very touching," Che said with a sniff of scorn. "Well, let me tell you something: I discovered that the day I was born. The milk I sucked from my mother's breast was the milk of death. Death is all we Indians have known. First it was the Catholic Death. Their soldiers lassoed us and dragged us off to work for the missions. They beat and whipped anyone who wouldn't accept God's word, then carried our bleeding bodies off to the church and baptized them. They preached the salvation of the soul, while ransacking the earth for silver and rubies.

"Next it was the Imperialist Death. French and English and American exploiters came here for the same reason—to get rich. They did it by shoving us down into the bowels of the earth for ten hours a day six days a week. Only now there was no talk of God and the soul. The cynicism and brutality came out into the open. They put one butcher after another into power. Do you know what one of them did to my father? He arrested him for trying to organize the mine workers and shoved a rubber hose down his throat and kept pumping water into him until he eventually swelled up and exploded like a balloon. I grew up on the story of his death the way other children grow up on fairy tales."

"I know all this," I said. "The country has been used by tyrants and their henchmen. But why punish us for that? We oppose them as much as you do."

"That's typical bourgeois liberal talk. Sure you oppose these bastards who have us by the throat. But all you do is stand by and make little clucking noises while we choke to death."

"Dammit, what would you have us do? Join you and become combatants?"

"We don't want you. All we want is your money."

"Matt says you'll only use it against us."

"Of course we will. Make no mistake about it: a revolution is underway and it can't be bought off. You'll get no promises for your dollars, only time. If the revolution succeeds, El Cortez will be ours; if it fails, you'll have won your gamble."

"Matt will never play that game."

"Then our meeting is over. Please leave."

I made no move, just stared across at him, recalling the hospital in which my father had died. In the ward next to him lay a man in the last stages of pulmonary tuberculosis, a skeleton with deep-socketed eyes; Che reminded me of him; he too was being burned down to the bone by the same deathly fire. Death was motivating his life, giving shape and urgency to it; he had too little time and so much to do.

But Che was also a man, a human being shouldering the burden of solitude and loneliness, the need to laugh and weep. And once upon a time he had wanted me, had hungered after me with desperate male desire. Nothing had come of it: he repelled me and no doubt he despised himself for having become enamoured of a bourgeois, a class enemy. But his desire kept showing through his attempts at concealment; that hand of his kept straying to his crotch. Pretending not to see it, I had avoided him and was easily able to abort the affair.

"Why do you keep looking at me?" he asked.

I couldn't find anything to say.

"Well, if you won't go, I will," he said rising.

"Wait."

Our eyes met; I made an effort to connect with him; my body trembled from the difficulty of it.

"What do you want, dammit?"

Panic flooded through me: I had a dream-like sensation of falling off a high building, turning head over heels in the darkness, a human pinwheel . . .

"I—I'm willing to go away with you," I heard myself saying. *Hijo,* the insanity of it. "Anywhere. You name it. As long as we leave this country."

He looked at me and as our eyes met something in his face moved. His eyebrows were flecked with tiny white flakes: the skin disease that every copper miner suffers. How like Matt he was: a true leader, all integrity and iron will and commitment. But above all, proud—and what proud man is not odious?

"Get out," Che told his bodyguard.

After the man left Che stood up.

"What makes you think I want you?"

The blood and hope were draining from my body. I felt like a skeleton that has been thrust out on stage and prodded into doing a grotesque dance.

Che fished a crushed-out cigarette butt from the ashtray, tossed it on the floor, and ground it under foot.

"You see that? That's what I feel for you," he said.

I stood there.

"Get out," he said tightly. *"Puta."*

I walked out and climbed in the jeep. It had stopped raining. As I drove off Che stood in the doorway of the shack, unmoving and inscrutable.

CHE'S DIARY

April 6

How she tempted me. Everything came back. The urge to run off with her—quit all this—have her every night in my bed—took hold of me. But I proved strong, stronger than ever before, proof that the revolutionary spirit burns as pure and hard as ever. Nothing and no one can stop me now. Crucial days are upon us and the time has come to live them. Nothing must deter us. We must live and fight magnificently—or die in the attempt.

Yoyo

From the way Billy Joe was hangin over Claude I could tell he'd never flown before. All that stuff about the Air Cadets was just so much doodly-squat. That was the thing that dragged me about Billy Joe, his runaway mouth. Otherwise we got along pretty good. He'd been callin the shots ever since Nam and we'd done ok, we'd teamed up and lived pretty high off the hog, except for a couple or three bad spots.

There were times when I felt it was a mistake not to have stayed on the farm after getting back from Nam. It would have been a lot safer—and smarter—than running with Billy Joe. But at the time I just couldn't see stayin home and workin my scrolls off for the rest of my life. After Nam, the farm seemed so durn boring, number fuckin ten. Besides, I didn't have eyes to marry a townie. Fuckin bitches, I'd never forget how they used to mouth off at me in high school:

"Say, Peewee, is it true your swinger is so small you use a peanut shell and a rubber band for a jock?"

Peewee this and Peewee that:

"You're too small to play basketball . . . you're too little to take me to the dance . . . get lost, shrimp."

That's when I started working out with the yoyo. I got so good at it that I won the state championship that year and the national the next. When I came back from L.A. with my trophy, I walked into Mazie's soda parlor and put it down on the counter along with the $325 AGVA check I'd got from Johnny Carson and the ivory-handled switchblade I'd ripped off from an Army-Navy on Hollywood Boulevard.

118

"From now on," I announced, "anybody what calls me Peewee is gonna get this dingus stuck in his hide."

They got the message all right and began crowdin round, wantin to know what it was like to go on tv and what kind of a guy Johnny was and all that. "He's real neat," I told 'em. "He said I was a credit to my home state."

I was pretty big around Mazie's for a long spell after that, but I wasn't unhappy when I got drafted and sent to Asia. There was a lot more happening in Nam then back home.

I could never understand why some of the guys complained about the war: sure it was rough and scary out there in the boonies, where Charlie was tryin hard to kill us, but for thrills and chills, Viet Nam couldn't be beat. We were lucky to be there, right in the middle of the toughest war our country had ever fought. It was a trip, a perpetual high.

Except for Chu Tau. That was the one shit thing that happened over there. It made me shrink to think of what we had done to them slopes. Killing soldiers was one thing, but destroying women and children was another. War wasn't supposed to be like that, a personal vendetta.

Billy Joe got mad when I refused to take part in any more round-ups. He himself usually had a Number One time clobbering those small, skinny, starving Vietnamese. "We really made the arms and legs fly!" he'd crow afterwards.

He sure loved a pile-on, did Billy Joe. Nam had given him a taste for blood. He just couldn't do without killing, was always wanting to waste some cop or pistol-whip a gas station attendant.

Scarin people outa their change was one thing, but cold-cocking them was another. Billy Joe didn't see it that way, though. He was a stone-cold killer and for months now I'd been growing more and more scared of him. His death habit freaked me out and made me real sorry I hadn't stayed home after the war, even if it was Dullsville, USA.

I had another chance now, though. The Major had offered me a job down here, workin for him. Maybe I should accept his offer. El Cortez wasn't much, but it did have a good whore house and lots of dope growing in the hills. Only bad thing was the war Mulligan had going against Che. I'd have to take part in some fire fights again, risk my neck as a mercenary. But at least that way I'd be on the side of the good guys again and wouldn't have to keep runnin with that crazy outlaw son of a bitch, Billy Joe.

Who needed the fucker, with his big talk of clothes and cars and breakin the bank at Vegas? He was gonna get me killed one day, and for what, some goddamned money!

Yeah, workin as a mercenary for Mulligan sounded good. He'd been the best damn officer in Nam. We all owed him a helluva lot. If not for him, we all woulda been snuffed out three minutes after seein our first action. Our platoon had walked into a Cong ambush and we froze under fire. Mulligan risked his life to work his way to us and bully us into action. We finally managed to shoot our way out of there, thanks to his bravery. What a soldier he was. He laid it on the line for Bravo Company, went the whole nine yards for us.

It was Mulligan who turned us into real pros, helped us get our shit together, whereas the rest of the units, they were full of hardcore chickenshit maggots that ran when they saw V.C., trippin over their dicks all the way. They pulled everybody down, the candy-assed sons of bitches, and if you tried to straighten them out, they'd do what they did to Turk, stick a frag under your hootch, put some TNT up your ass.

None of that happened in Mulligan's company. Nobody had it in for him, cauz he didn't bullshit you, expect you to risk your life for nuthin. He stuck up for you, even against the brass, and fought alongside you and gave you an honest answer no matter what. Mulligan was boss, he was a prince, and now that ratfuck cowboy Billy Joe wanted me to do him dirty.

She-it, what a life, what a bitching bind!

Suddenly Claude broke into my train of thought.

"Ain't that somebody down there?" he asked, bringing the plane around.

We looked hard but the dot on the desert turned out to be a wandering burro.

It was hopeless, searching for Mulligan's wife like this. Alicia had been missing for two days, but if the MNR had got her there wasn't nuthin we could do, and if they hadn't she'd get home all right. She knew the country and could take care of herself. Either way we were wastin our time up here.

Still, the mission was serving one good purpose. It was giving Billy Joe a chance to study Claude Copeland flying the small plane. Billy Joe was determined to go through with the job, no matter what. Just the thought of it made me squirm in my seat. It was too risky. Billy Joe believed we'd come out of it with enough bread to buy a ton of cocaine and become big-time dealers, but the odds said otherwise.

The odds said we'd likely get our behinds blown off by the Major and his palace guard.

I sneaked a glance at Billy Joe, who was hunched right over Claude, glomming his every move. The back of Billy Joe's neck was burned a farm-red; it reminded me of the coloration of my daddy's neck. I felt a chill spread from under my armpits, a death-chill. My old man could be in his grave right now and I wouldn't even know it.

Suddenly it hit me clear and hard: I flashed that the old man *was* gone. The farm had probably been sold off to some stranger, leaving me all alone in the world, and lost, just like that burro down there.

Then Billy Joe turns and gives me a sly little wink, as if to say, "I've got this flying thing pinned. There's nuthin to worry about."

Looking away, I sat biting my lip, feeling more shaky and scared than ever in my whole dumb-ass miserable life.

CHE'S DIARY

April 9, morning

Today we try our luck. The plan is set. Confirmation from within El Cortez came last night. At 6.30 I assembled all the fighters . . . reviewed the plan. Morale good. After today we'll have the firepower. Then we can concentrate on increasing our numbers, developing our army, working with the people. Our political influence on the peasants is still doubtful. We must be sure of their help—at least of their moral support. But first things first . . .

Alicia

From the road El Cortez was mysteriously silent. The checkpoint was unmanned and all work at the mine had ceased. *Jesuchristo.* Panic flooded through me as I gunned the jeep down the decline, ignoring the ruts and potholes.

They had gathered at the air strip, where Matt was shouting orders as I pulled up, a .45 strapped around his waist. His khaki shirt was shiny with sweat. "Take my plane up," he ordered one of his mercenaries, Charlie Corrigan. "Head inland, toward La Vuelta, then sweep north. Call in every fifteen minutes. Find that tank! Find it before Che can hide it!"

He came to me, face all twisted.

"Che attacked us this morning. We've got some dead and wounded, including Doreen."

"Doreen! How bad is she?"

"Bad enough."

"Oh, no—"

"And you went to him, didn't you?"

. . . .

"Answer me."

"Yes."

"Why?"

I shrugged.

"You're a fool," he said, struggling to contain his anger. "Don't you understand that men like Che have an absolute contempt for human life?"

He turned to the others. "I'll be at the first-aid shack. Call me fast if you hear anything."

As we raced down the Camino Real Matt described how Che had struck, using the truck he'd stolen from us last week. He had converted it into a crude tank by arming it with sheet metal and heavy weapons. He'd shot his way through the checkpoint with it, while his agents on the inside hit us from behind. Tito could have easily fought his way out, but he panicked and did nothing. All Matt and his men could do was ping away with pistols and rifles as the gun-boat sailed right through the village and up to the office and blew down a wall.

"Was anybody inside with Doreen?"

"Fortunately not. She'd come early to work."

"Matt, we're not going to lose her, are we?"

"I don't know."

I felt faint, had to put my head down between my legs to keep from passing out. Finally I sat up and shakily lit a cigarette.

"Why did Che attack the office? He must have known you weren't there."

"He wasn't after me, but our basement arsenal."

"What arsenal?"

"I've always kept its existence a secret. Only Turk knew about it. When the alarm sounded he followed orders, went right downstairs and locked himself in behind a steel door. Nobody could have taken him, not without a canon. The only trouble was, he wasn't alone. He had Fernando with him."

"The boxer?"

"Yeah, how about that? Turk turned out to be as naive and trusting as you."

"I don't understand."

"Ever since that fiasco of a fight, Fernando's been following Turk around, begging him, 'Let me prove myself to you, give me another chance, let me be your boy again.' Turk let himself be seduced. He even entrusted the kid with the secret of my basement arsenal."

"Which he passed right on to Che."

"Hey, maybe you're not so dumb, after all."

"But why did Fernando betray Turk?"

"Wish I knew. Probably he was a communist all along, an MNR sympathizer—"

"Poor Turk. He must feel like hell."

"Turk? He's past all feeling or caring."

"No—"

"Yes, dammit. He took the kid into the arsenal with him. They were going to make a big stand together, like real comrades." Matt broke off, a sour expression spread over his features. "Some comrade,'' he said sarcastically. "He shot Turk from behind, then threw open the arsenal door for Che to enter. Nice, huh? Real courage, eh? And these people would have us believe they are the hope of the future.''

El Cortez was empty and silent: not a sign of life on the streets, not even a chicken or a dog. Window shades had been pulled down, doors were shut, cantinas bolted.

We drew up at the first-aid shack. Vultures filled the sky overhead, their shadows flitting over us as we mounted the steps.

Turk's body lay on a stretcher set against the far wall. We stood over him. His open, unblinking eyes begged us to answer a simple question: *why?*

That was his fate, in death as well as life, to suffer without comprehension.

His body had already begun to corrupt itself; Matt covered it with a blanket.

Then he led me to Doreen's room. She lay in bed, tiny, white-faced, hurt. Rubber tubes were sticking out of her arms; her eyes were closed. A fly landed on her lips; Eli brushed it away. He sat beside the bed, holding her hand.

Unexpectedly, my insides yielded to pressure, began crumbling like the insides of a mine shaft in a cave-in. I found myself reaching out for Matt.

"Pull yourself together,'' he said. "I can't give you any time now. I've got to find that bastard Che. I've got to find and kill him before he holes up with those arms.''

Matt would not let me argue with him.

"I'm sorry,'' he said tersely. "That's the way it is. You tried your way, you tried to reason with him, and it got you nowhere.''

"But your way is worse, it's mad—''

"It's too late for talk,'' Matt said. "The only thing left is to fight.''

It was true: things had gone past all words. Blood had taken over. Matt was like a stranger; his face was unrecognizable, all hardness and darkness. Che had worn a similar look. The two of them were twin brothers now.

Mierda, what was with men, always worried about their pride and manhood and honor, always fighting and killing, hunting each other down—

But before I could say anything more, he was gone.

Eli

Stirring on the bed, Doreen opened her eyes and regarded me through a haze of pain.

"Don't happen to have a wee cuppa tea on you?" she asked, trying to smile.

"No, but I did bring you this." I showed her the blood-red Sacred Heart lithograph that Señora Blanca de Mesa had sent over. "She asked me to pin it over your bed and wants you to know she's praying for you in church right now."

"She's such a pet," Doreen sighed.

She closed her eyes again, wincing with pain, and I felt my throat tighten. She dozed off. Her pulse was weak but steady.

"I'll have my breakfast at work, mum," she mumbled deliriously. "Just let me sleep a wee bit longer."

I said nothing, sat holding her hand.

"I'll dry the dishes if you bring in the coal."

In a while her eyes jerked open.

"Eli," she said. "I'm so thirsty."

"I'll get the nurse—"

"No, don't go. I'm scairt, Eli. I'm scairt I'm going to die."

"You can't die—you've got a year and three months to go on your contract."

"Hah, that's right," she said, and looked at me. "I'm glad you're here. Your hands feel so good. They were the first things I liked about you. They're so strong and good. I love it when you squeeze my rump with them."

125

Outside a woman shrieked in Spanish, "My boy is dead, my precious child is dead!"

Immediately a great wailing went up.

"Who's that?" Doreen asked.

"Fernando's mother, I think."

"Fernando dead. Turk dead. How many more to go?"

Doreen was hit with pain and shuddered long and hard. I wiped the sweat from her upper lip.

"You'll stay here, won't you?" she asked. "You won't get killed chasing Che."

"I'll stay," I said. "It's not my fight."

Doreen cried out suddenly, fearfully, "Eli, will I be all right?"

I took her hand in mine; her fingers had turned cold and bluish.

"Listen to me blethering," she said. "I'm such a proper wee nyaff, tell me to shut up."

I didn't say anything.

"I'm such a bleedin' coward, Eli. I'm afraid to die."

"Don't talk like that."

"But that's how I feel, like I'm gonna die."

"That's the aftermath of being wounded: you feel sad and empty and morbid. It'll pass.

"I hope so. I don't want to die. I wanta eat fried bananas and listen to Buffy-Sainte Marie in bed with you again."

"That's quite a combination."

"Am I talking daft?"

She didn't wait for an answer.

"It's just that I keep thinking of all the things I love and wanta do again, like hiking in the Highlands or going to a Maggie Bell concert."

"Tell you what. The first thing I'm gonna do when we split from here is take you to a Maggie Bell concert."

"Wouldja? Wouldja really?"

"For sure."

"You think we'll still be together after all this?"

"I'd be willing to make book on it."

"You're not just sayin that, are ye? Do ye mean it or are ye just havin' me on?"

"I'm not havin' you on. I'm crazy about you, even if you can't speak English."

The pain hit Doreen again, refashioning the flesh on her face, tightening her cheeks, shrinking her mouth.

"Eli—"

"Hang in, girl."

Her shoulders sagged, her eyes were crushed and burning.

"Hold my hand."

"Here."

"I cannae feel ye."

"It's the drugs, don't worry about it."

She tossed and turned, sank into semi-consciousness, began talking wildly, "Wait for me—wait—the dog—the biting dog—help, Da'. The dog!" she shrieked.

"Doreen," I said.

"Who's that?" she asked. "Da'?"

"No, Eli."

"He's biting me," she shrieked again. "The bluidy hound is after me!"

She tried to rise up, twist away. She gave a scream, then fell back, another long shudder sweeping her body. She lay breathing harshly, fingers clenched on the sheet.

I bent close.

"Hey listen, I've got something to tell you. I love you, Doreen. I love you very much."

"You shouldny say it if you don't mean it."

"But I do mean it. I never thought it would happen to me, at this late stage, not after all the bullshit I've been through. But it's happened, all right. Don't ask me how or why, but there it is."

"Och," she said, "now I've got to get well. Imagine dyin' now, just when I've got a regular fella."

"You can't die," I said. "There's a whole pile of dirty laundry back at the house."

She smiled through the pain that was squeezing her face again.

"You bluidy male chauvinist pig, is that all your love amounts to—gettin' your knickers washed out?"

"Hey—it's *your* knickers I'm interested in."

"Would ye listen to him," she said in mock-anger, "the last of the red-hot lovers."

"Yeah, that's me, all right."

"Love 'em and leave 'em, you in your great big truck."

"That's right, except that I don't have a truck any more. I don't have anything, girl."

"Except me."

"Yeah . . . my wife to be."

"Wouldja? Wouldja really marry a nit like me?" she asked, tears forming slowly in her eyes.

"Why the hell not? Give me one good reason why I shouldn't."

"Here's one," she said. "If we got married, it would hafta be in Glasga. Me mum and dad are still there."

"In-laws. Cheerist, I forgot about all that."

"They're no so bad. But be warned. If it's in Glasga, you'll be called on to make a long speech at the wedding. It's an old Scottish custom."

"Really? What am I expected to say?"

"It's up to you."

"Can I talk about you?"

"If you want."

"Can I tell the truth?"

"Of course."

"That your butt is too big?"

"Och—"

"And your chin too small?"

"Eli, you're positively horrid!"

Suddenly her mouth popped open and she cried out. Then a short strangled rush of air burst from her body.

"Doctor!" I yelled. "Doctor!"

But her struggle was over. I sat for a long time.

In death the flesh of her face was relaxed; she regained her sweet, gentle smile.

Finally I rose and bent and kissed her mouth again.

I remember walking out of the room, but that's all. I don't know how much later it was, but I found myself standing in the middle of the Camino Real, unmoving, blinking in the white sunlight. I felt empty, shriveled.

I saw a jeep approaching. It was Mulligan, who got out of the vehicle, his face mutilated with grief, and said, "I'm sorry, Eli. I'd give my life to bring her back. She was one of the best and sweetest souls I've met in a long lifetime."

"Yes."

"There's so much I want to say. But the words feel lousy in my mouth. Do you know what I mean?"

I nodded.

"Let's talk later. I've got to go now. Corrigan just radioed from the air that he's spotted the truck. We know where Che's base is. I'm

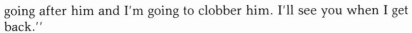

going after him and I'm going to clobber him. I'll see you when I get back."

Mulligan's jeep was heaped high with carbines and ammunition cases.

Something entered me from outside, as if from the depths of the earth, a force as old and harsh as life itself.

"Give me one of those guns," I heard myself saying, in a voice not my own. "I'm going with you."

Mulligan

"Matt, I beg you, don't go. Che's got what he wants from us. Leave him be, don't make things worse."

"That takes the prize. The man just massacred us and you sit there saying, Take it, like it."

"I'm not asking you to like it, just listen to sense. Che's ill, he's tubercular, he's on the way out. Why risk death to kill a dying man?"

"Che may be ill but he's not going to die. He's got the will to fight and that's all any man needs to stay alive. If I don't fight him now, then *I'm* the dead man, not him."

I turned away angrily from Alicia and finished suiting up. I had laid out all my old fighting gear—long johns, khakis, field jacket, the works.

"Look at you," said Alicia in dismay, "look at you getting ready to die with your boots on. *Jesuchristo,* I don't believe it, you're becoming a caricature of yourself."

I said nothing.

"For the first time in my life," she announced, "I hate what you are."

My resentment rose up swiftly. "Get the hell out! Go back to Che, do anything you want, but just leave me alone."

She started out but stopped, looking back in anguish. But then she made an effort to pull herself together. Fumbling around in her purse, she found a cigarette and with shaky hands finally got it lit, taking one deep drag after another, trying to calm down.

"I suppose you're right," she said finally, "there's nothing left now but to fight."

"That's the bottom line."

"It's not fair, dammit," she swore. "We haven't done anything to deserve this. We're not imperialists."

"In Che's eyes we are. This is exactly what happened in Viet Nam—we ended up on the wrong side."

"At this point, I don't care who's right or wrong. I just don't want you to go to war again."

"I've got to, Alicia."

"You said it yourself, Matt, when you came home from Asia: you used up all your luck over there. You were holding an empty hand."

"Don't tell Che that."

"Matt—"

She could hardly get the words out.

"I don't want to lose you. You're the most man I've ever met— please don't risk your life up there."

"I'm not going up there to die, Alicia. I'm going up there to *live*."

There were tears in her eyes again. "All right," she said after a time, "so be it. *Son las cosas de la vida.*"

Now I went to her, holding her close, looking at her.

"Do you really think I'm a caricature, a war-lover?"

She turned her eyes away.

"I've been in three wars and they were three too many," I told her. "There isn't a single good thing about war, but sometimes you just have to fight them. This is one of these times, Alicia."

"I know it. It's just that I don't want to lose you."

"And I don't want to lose you. Or our life here, what we have together. But that's exactly why I'm going up that mountain, *mi corazón*—to defend it."

Alicia nodded a little, then put her face up for a kiss. We clung to each other.

Then it was time to go, to get back into harness again.

While I dressed, my eyes went to the far wall, where some of my momentos were hanging: the medals and citations, the West Point credo carved in wood: "Duty, Honor, Country."

By themselves the words meant nothing, were hollow abstractions. But they took meaning from the actions of the men with whom I had lived and fought and suffered. They'd stood up for the words, paid with their lives to ennoble them. It wasn't necessary to believe in anything else except the men. To run from Che now was to spit on their graves, profane their memory, their sacrifice.

I said a silent prayer. I prayed for the strength to live and fight.

If I must check out of this world, let it be with courage and honor. I didn't want death but would accept it if it came. I'd had the simple pleasure of being there when the sun was shining and the rain was falling. I'd had the love of a woman like Alicia. That was a full enough cup for any man.

The whole gang had gathered outside: they were standing around uneasily, smoking, averting their eyes from Turk's body, a terrible reminder of the nullity and finality of death. I had ordered the body brought here because there was one last thing I had to do.

But first I had to talk to the men. "Let's get something straight," I told them. "The only ones here who are obliged to fight are those who work for me. The rest of you don't owe me a thing and if you want out, say so. I'll understand. It's going to be rough up there. Che is sitting on that mountaintop with a shit-load of weapons. We're going to have to blast him off and it won't be easy. People are going to kill and be killed. I invited you to this reunion to play, not die, and if you don't want to get involved say so now, before it's too late."

Glancing from face to face, I settled on Eli's.

"Come on, speak up. You've got every right to say no."

Eli's face remained all hard angles.

"All right, then. We're together again and you don't know how pleased I am. You've got my thanks, because now I know we're going to win up there."

I opened Turk's bible.

"Before we push off, there's one last thing to finish. Once a week I used to read to Turk from this bible. Today would have been his day and I figure the least I can do for him is to read the passage he liked best. It's got to be done now because I don't know whether I'll come down off that anthill alive. This may be my last chance to give an old comrade what's coming to him."

As they gathered round the stretcher, I reached down and pulled back the shroud.

"There he is," I said, "the remains of Ernest 'Turk' Kohler. He put his life on the line for a lot of people who hated what he stood for. He hated them back but still accepted the responsibility of caring for all the unwilling and untrained kids they dumped on us in Viet Nam. Everybody else had washed their hands of you—the Congress, the President, the people—but Turk gave you what he could. Somebody had to look after you. He was a son of a bitch in many ways, but he was no Pontius Pilate, standing by while his brothers got nailed to the cross.

"For that reason we owe him something, a measure of respect, maybe even love. Weep for him my friends, because he wept for us."

Cracking open the bible I began reading, feeling self-conscious at first, voice sounding false.

> *To everything there is a season, and a time to every*
> *purpose under the heavens:*
> *A time to be born, and a time to die: a time to plant and*
> *a time to pluck up that which is planted:*
> *A time to kill, and a time to heal: a time to break down,*
> *and a time to build up . . .*

As I intoned the words two black-shawled old women came by, took a look, crossed themselves nervously, and flew off in a clucking panic.

> *A time to get, and a time to lose; a time to keep and*
> *a time to cast away:*
> *A time to rend, a time to sow: a time to keep silence*
> *and a time to speak:*
> *A time to love, and a time to hate: a time of war, and*
> *a time of peace . . .*

Soon the truth and power and poetry of the ancient lament on the futility of man's strivings caught me up. I found myself moved by the words as never before.

> *. . . For that which befalleth the sons of men befalleth*
> *beasts:*
> *even one thing befalleth them: as the one dieth, so dieth*
> *the other: yea, they have all one breath: so that a man*
> *have no preeminence above a beast: for all is vanity . . .*

Upon closing the book I knelt again and placed it in Turk's hands. Then I got up and stood in the dusty, marooned street saying a silent and painful farewell. Finally I turned and said, "All right, let's saddle up and move out. We've got work to do."

"Hey, hold on a sec," Billy Joe said. He stooped down quickly and, before anyone could protest, gave a yank on the pouch hanging around Turk's neck.

Then Billy Joe straightened up. "Turk would of got a kick out of this too, Major," he smirked as he strung the pouch of VC gold fillings around his own neck.

CHE'S DIARY

April 9, afternoon

There are 27 of us, pinned down by gunfire from the air. We may have to fight it out up here. If so, some of us will die. But remember, a man who dies for freedom does not die.

Eli

My throat had tightened like a clamp, my eyeballs were threatening to bust right out of their sockets.

"You all right?"

It was Mulligan. His expression was calm, his voice low and controlled. He was a soldier again, a leader. You had to admire his professionalism. He'd been beat out at every stage of the war game by a raggedy-assed amateur, an irregular. A lesser man would have been all wild-eyed and rabid, hands trembling to unleash the hounds of war. But not Matthew J. Mulligan. He despised emotion in battle, believed that only fools fought with their hearts instead of their heads.

"You can still quit," he said. "You don't have to go up that mountain with us."

"Say that once more and I'm gonna have to kick your ass, mister."

He grinned and turned away, yelling into the radio set, "Keep on top of them, Corrigan! If anything moves, fire away. Keep them holed up till we get there. *Bravo Company is on the way!*"

The last words reverberated through the plane like a battle cry. Despite myself, I felt my body prickling all over. I was becoming a warrior again, a fighting man.

The others must have felt the same excitement and horror, because the air became charged, bodies were taut, eyes wide and white.

"We're united again," Mulligan said, "and does it ever feel good!"

He was right: we were suddenly linked, caught up in common cause. We breathed with one mouth, saw with a single eye. It was all for one and one for all. Mulligan was our leader and once again

135

we were invincible. We'd been through a hundred fire-fights together and survived every one of them, we were Major Matty's troopers and would rather fight than fuck. We were bullet-proof, we were super-men, we were the toughest, baddest asses in Uncle Sam's army—

"Hey," I thought suddenly, "this is ridiculous. It's insane."

I reached for a cigar, fumbling with the wrapper.

"Whatsa matter, E. J., got the shakes?" Billy Joe asked.

"What in hell d'ya want me to do, whistle dixie?"

Snickers followed this. But here, reminded of fear and death, the laughter stopped, faces went all hard. Slowly my eyes began to pick out details: YoYo biting his lips, Billy Joe scratching his crotch, Frits twitching away . . .

The small plane dipped. Looking out, I saw the whirling red-tipped propellors, the painted notice on the starboard engine:

USE ACEITE

ESSO

120

Mulligan made a sweeping turn over the sea before heading inland. Somewhere in that direction lay the San Pedro Martir mountains, where Che had been found.

It was a feminine kind of day: a gull was gamboling in the sky below, the edgy of the sea was dancing with froth, the sun was casting its tawny radiance over the salt flats.

"Hey look! Down there, in the lagoon!" It was Claude, shouting excitedly.

Three whales—two large, one small—were swimming along in the shallows. Unaccountably, they took off all at once and shot full speed ahead, toward the distant mouth of the vast lagoon.

He brought the plane right down over the shoals. A swarm of other shadows shapes were chasing after the whales.

"Killer whales!" Mulligan yelled.

They were like a submarine pack, swift and deadly. The grey whales tried to escape by darting behind some reefs, but the killers were easily able to cut them off. The grey whales panicked: the biggest reared skywards and fell back into the water with a splash, then took off and streaked toward the sea, leaving the other two behind.

"Go back and fight!" Mulligan howled. "Protect your own, you son of a bitch!"

The submarine pack wheeled in on their victims. The two dim bulks surfaced a few hundred yards away, roaring vapor through their nostrils as they blew hastily, desperately. Meanwhile, three of the killers, their high scalpel-like fins dissecting the skin of the sea, took off swiftly after the escaped bull whale; they were incredibly fast, like a pack of hounds pursuing a deer.

At this remove everything became slightly unreal: Mulligan was banking the plane, there was the noise of the engines, shouts of look at that, Christjesus oh man, until we came down over the shoals again, wheels almost nicking the surface. Mother and calf had become paralyzed with fear. Trapped, their backs to the rocks, they did nothing but roll over, show their bellies.

"No!" Mulligan howled as the killers attacked in full force, almost leaping out of the water in their eagerness to get at the whales. "Fight, fight!"

It was a combined effort: some of the killers seized hold of the baby whale's jaws and forced them apart for the others to tear out its tongue, others were slashing away at its belly, ripping open its flesh in a frenzy of rage and rapacity. Still others had turned on the mother, who was thrashing away with her flukes, churning up the sea into a storm of foam. Seizing a chunk of yellow blubber in his jaws, one killer stripped it the entire length of the whale's body.

In mid-lagoon another pack of killers had surrounded the bull whale. He broke surface in a mad swirl, blowing frantically, performed a kind of half-roll and then dived deep, his huge flukes churning up the sea into a green whirlpool.

Everywhere one looked the predators were attacking. Spreading swirls of blood stained the sea red as flesh and organs were ripped out, devoured. This place no longer had any connection with the rest of the world. The killers had forced their way into the baby's mouth and were pulling out great chunks of fat pink tongue; the calf rolled and twisted about in agony as they devoured her, gobbling down everything, blubber, entrails, blood, the works. Then the killer whales were wheeling in tandem, taking off, diving deep.

Suddenly all I could think of was Doreen, ripped open below the waist by bullets, everything all bleeding and torn. Nausea rose up and stung the back of my throat. I had to turn away.

But it was over. Just as quickly as they had come, the killers were gone, leaving behind the floating remains of the dead whales for the black-tipped seagulls to fight over.

Mulligan pulled hard on the stick and brought the plane up higher again and headed further inland. From here the lagoon looked peaceful and quiet; the sun glittered brightly; long rollers broke gently and whitely on the beach: nature at repose again. Up ahead was the peak of San Pedro Martir; we were rushing toward it at great speed.

My hand touched the cold metal of the carbine beside me.

To kill.

My God, I thought.

To kill.

I checked my cartridge belt, fumbled at one of the pockets where the clips were. My hands were like melted wax, no strength in them at all.

A trembling started in my shoulders and moved to my fingers. I squeezed the weapon with all my might, until my knuckles hurt.

Meanwhile, the plane rocketed toward the high brown snow-streaked mountain where Che and his men sat waiting for us.

Billy Joe

Corrigan was busy up there, buzzing round the mountain, diving and dumping shitstorms of machine-gun fire on the MNR. The puffs of smoke hung in the air like cotton candy, then drifted away.

Mulligan's voice sounded over the noise of the engines. "It's pucker-up time, boys. Keep your legs crossed."

He found a place to land just beside the mountain and we jumped out and moved fast. On the way up I did a little quick reckoning. Now was the time, now or never. With Turk dead, the Major would be needing a new boy. Why shouldn't it be me? I was tired of carrying YoYo through life; he had himself a big mouth and a tiny brain. I'd be a lot better off down here, working for the Major, keeping these spics in line. Once I got to be his sidekick I'd be able to work my way up, maybe earn a piece of the mine one day. That was looking ahead of course: annuities, old age. Not that I had anything to worry about. I'd be ok when I retired; I always had my music to fall back on.

It was hot as horse piss hiking along in sweaters and a field jacket, but the Major said it would be cold up on the hill. It was a long way up and I began to feel tired and achy. I lit up, taking a couple of quick hits of maryjane to put me in fighting shape. It helped, but not that much. Back in Nam, this was the time we used to drop some government-issue uppers. Yeah, Uncle Sam was always good for speed, ARVN for the grass and skag.

Wish I coulda had the dope concession in Viet Nam, instead of all them generals and politicians. I'd of been a millionaire today, struttin it all over the folks back home. Of course, they were such smalltown people that it didn't take much to impress them.

139

I fell to thinking of the stunt I pulled in high school, when I suddenly showed up one day in cowboy togs: twenty-five dollar stetson, hand-sewn Texas shirt, blue levis from Monkey Ward. I'd played hooky for two weeks, growing my sideburns, and when I made my surprise entrance, tall and slim, boots tip-tapping, a guitar slung on my back, you shoulda seen em sit up and howl. Even the cooks came out of the lunchroom kitchen.

Clint Eastwood!

Willie Nelson!

Sundance Kid!

Man, I sure knocked their eyes out. Watertown, N.Y. had never seen nuthin like it, nuthin! You shoulda seen how the chicks surrounded me, giggling and grabbing. But I cooled them by pushing right through to a corner and sitting by myself, real icy and hard. I could feel their eyes crawling all over me like red ants. And I could see how Lloyd Howard was looking at me, with different eyes now.

Just as I figured, Lloyd dug me like mad in that cowboy gear. He hadn't shown much interest before, but now he sure came around. I played hard to get, refusing his invitation of a ride home after school. He'd been giving the other guys five, ten bucks a throw, but I was shooting for higher stakes. Lloyd was gonna bankroll my way to become a bronc rider. All I had to do was play the game right.

Lloyd sure dug me in those tight cowboy britches and he kept coming on, day after day. Then, when his undies were practically on fire and he upped the ante to fifty bucks, I said ok. Twice a week, Monday and Thursday nights, I went to his room in the big house at Garden Estates. Seventy-five-thousand smackers that pad had cost his old man. Lloyd was only eighteen but he was already into two private incomes, one from his grannie, the other from his daddy. There he was, a high-school brat, pulling down twenty-seven-thousand bucks a year, tax free.

So twice a week we met in his room, where we did our homework.

It was easy to recall the room, with its bookcase stuffed with books and sex magazines, mostly them gay books showing young boys being sucked off. Lloyd liked to undress me, saying faggy things like my Big Tough Cowboy, but he himself never liked to remove anything except his shirt. He wore a big hand-tooled silver crucifix around his neck. I'd lay there looking at him and the crucifix as he copped my joint. Even now, I got a funny feeling every time I spied a crucifix, even in church. My stomach tingled and I thought of Lloyd, the look on his face as he moved up and down on me.

"Take five," the Major said. Everybody flopped down by the side of the trail. I rested a while, fighting the drug need, concentrating on the challenge at hand. Mulligan pulled a map out and started studying it.

I figured this was the time to make my move.

"Anything I can do, Major?"

"Just get yourself some rest. You're starting to limp."

"Don't fret over it. My leg might drag a little, but it's strong. And so am I."

Mulligan looked washed-out. He'd been carrying an M-16 and a grenade box and the strain had brought out the creases and wrinkles in his face.

"Why don't I carry that grenade box for you?"

"Thanks, you've got enough of a load."

"Turk would of carried it for you."

"You're not Turk."

"How do you know? Try me."

The Major squinted my way, studying me.

"Let me walk drag for you," I said.

"You don't know what you're saying. It's going to be tricky up there."

"Hell, it's a lock-up," I said.

"You're real cocky, aren't you?"

"There's nuthin to be afraid of. We'll take those spics with our left hand."

"The hell we will," the Major said. "They're more'n just spics. They're men, tough fighters. Anyway, what do you think we're doing up here—playing a game?"

"Sure," I answered. "The best damn game there is."

Mulligan let out an angry exasperated sigh.

"Get back down there," he ordered, mouth champing. "You're talking like a fool. And I can't use a fool for a drag man."

When I turned away my face was on fire.

"And another thing," the Major added, stopping me in my tracks. "If you think wearing Turk's pouch makes you his equal, you've got another guess coming. He didn't talk a good game, he *played* it. But he didn't like it, not for a single minute. He went to war not because he wanted to but because he *had* to."

You son of a bitch, I muttered as I walked back down the line, trying to keep from limping. Your fool mouth just cost you fifty thousand bucks.

Fifty thousand big fat hogs!

Frits

All hail war, the Universal Remedy, the Great Panacea. War is good to all, and its tender mercies are over everything. I am proud to stand here on this hilltop and urge all of you not to put your trust in Man, nor in the Prince of Peace, nor in the Messiah. Praise Ye instead the God of War, for His name alone is excellent, His glory is above the earth and heaven. Happy is that people whose God is war. My mouth shall speak the praise of war and let all flesh bless its holy name for ever and ever.

Amen and thank you, brethren. And remember this: Peace Sucks.

CHE'S DIARY

April 9, later

Patria o muerte.

Mulligan

It took everything we had to keep Che pinned down. Both planes alternated in the air all day long, one patrolling the mountaintop, the other returning to El Cortez to refuel and convey men and supplies. Meanwhile those of us on the ground hacked our way up and checkmated the escape routes. Next I took a recon patrol out for a quick look around. The mountain was covered with ponderosa pine forests through which a logging road had been cut. The road wound its way up to where the snow line commenced, about five hundred feet from which sat the ruins of an old Jesuit mission, now the MNR's hideaway. Che sat tough up there, deeply entrenched and in possession of a big arsenal of weapons and ammunition. We had our work cut out.

The book said we should hose them down good and hard even before attempting a strike. We should hit them with all kinds of heavy stuff: air fire, mortars, howitzers, recoilless rifles. We should go over the top of that hill like a vacuum cleaner, sucking it clean of life. But we didn't have the hardware. All we had were nineteen badly-armed senior citizens.

"Our only hope is to send a small assault party up the back side of the mountain," I said later at a briefing. "It's mostly rockshelf and we should have enough moonlight to be able to pick our way up. At 0200 a second party will fake an attack from the logging road and my assault party will storm the back wall with demolitions and try to blow Che out of his hole."

Here I realized how much I missed Turk; missed his nerve, his nose, his skills. Turk knew the secrets of gunpowder the way some Elizabethan scholars know the secrets of Shakespearean text.

"If we blow the place right, it should rout the MNR, send them screaming down the hill with their pants on fire. We'll have an ambush team set up on the logging road to pick them off."

Charlie Corrigan, eye-patch dislodged and showing the red leaky wound he had suffered in World War II, raised a hand and said, "And if you don't blow the place, Major?"

"Then the party's over," I said. "Pack your pajamas and go home to Mama. Got it?"

Not a word was said now.

I waited a bit before asking, "Any volunteers for the demo patrol?"

Again not a word.

I eyed the ring of men, trying to choose carefully. My gaze fell on Eli. It was time he was tested, made to decide once and for all which it was to be: the hoe or the dagger.

"Eli, I want you."

He looked at me, mouth tightening.

I waited, rooting for him.

Finally Eli made a noise in his throat which I took to mean assent.

Quickly now, I assigned two expert marksmen, LoCascio and Simpson, to the patrol, and fingered an additional twosome to act as a support team. "That about does it."

"Hold on," a voice said. It was Claude. He stepped forward, looking in his khaki woolens like a grandaddy moose. "I want in, too."

"I've got enough."

"Uh-uh. You need somebody to handle the explosives, man. I'm your boy. Remember, I learned the trade from Turk."

I remembered.

"You're sure?"

He nodded. "You know why."

I thought it over, then shrugged. "All right. Welcome to the club."

After that it was a cut-and-dried business of setting up fire teams and assigning them positions on the logging road. I deployed the teams in an inverted V formation, positioning the groups in depth with an all-around defense; since there was only one likely approach, each man would have a good view of the killing ground. Then I checked weapons. They should have been zeroed and tested, the ambush rehearsed; but there was no time for that, the whole ambush was a test of previous training and discipline. It remained to be seen whether these surplus soldiers could still fight.

The sun's shadows were lengthening across the mountain; in a few hours it would be cold and dark. I stared at the men and wondered about them.

"This is a one-shot operation," I said. "Either we finish the MNR off or we forget about it and pull out by dawn. If I don't make it down off that hill, then Eli Brickman is in charge. If he doesn't make it, the tin badge goes to Sgt Corrigan."

Turning to Charlie, I ensured that he understood all final orders: every fire team was to have at least one machine gun, with left and right limits of fire fixed to eliminate a danger to the ambush party. Every illume available was to be used—torches, flares, rifle grenades—but only when all possible guerrillas were in the killing ground. There must be no premature action: clear orders, explicit fire-control instructions, and clear assembly points and signals were essential.

Finally I handed the map over to Corrigan and said, "Enough talk. Let's go to work, girls."

We pushed off, traversing the shank of the mountain, boots crunching on the pine cones and needles underfoot. The dark sweet smell of the ponderosa trees permeated the forest. From the point position the noise we made seemed inordinately loud and I kept stopping to check but heard only the normal forest sounds. Soon I began to hurry the men along, wanting egress before the light, sifting down through the tops of the trees, disappeared altogether.

We tromped along, going from patch of light to patch of dark, like pieces on a chessboard.

Like most night patrols this one became a spooky business: a baby owl was ululating, an eerie cry that made your skin twitch, and the moon kept appearing and disappearing. Suddenly I lost sight of my checkpoints—two boulders on a nearby ridge. I stopped short, peering into the darkness ahead. The strain became unbearable, I was leading the patrol into enemy territory by radar. When the landscape became lit by moolight again I thought I saw a man's head pop up from behind one of the boulders. I hit the deck fast.

In a while I sat up shakily, knuckling the sweat from my eyes and thinking some survival thoughts. Turk Kohler should have been leading this patrol, not a clod like me. Turk had a true talent for the point: superb concentration, the stealth and grace of an Indian. It was a wondrous thing to watch him work, supporting himself on one foot while poking around tentatively with the other; only when he was certain the spot was free of twigs or leaves would he bring his other foot down. He could keep it up for hours, without ever losing rhythm or concentration.

Halfway up, while lying doggo again, I realized I had neglected an important detail: in this moonlight all faces and hands should have been blackened. *Ojalá!* I had no business making a mistake like that; it showed how rusty I had become.

If I couldn't rely on myself, how could I rely on the others? Who knew how they'd react in combat. They'd been hardened up in Viet Nam, but that was a long time ago.

I shot a look at Eli, sprawled out awkwardly, limbs all twisted. He seemed wrung-out, exhausted. Chances were he was still in shock over Doreen's death. Splendid! My second in command was a zombie—and I had picked him for the job.

But calm down, hombre, relax. Don't give up the fight before it begins; bury your fear before it becomes contagious. The MNR was in no great shape either. Most of those guerrillas were going to break down. It was a proven fact that seventy-five per cent of all new soldiers failed to fire their weapons in combat. They wouldn't shoot and they couldn't kill. Combat did that to a man. Any grunt who even pulled the trigger in action was practically a hero for doing just that.

Viet Nam gave us an edge over the MNR. Everyone in Bravo Company had learned how to subordinate his fear of death to the interest of the group. That's why we were going to be all right. Those guerrillas knew how to pull off a sneak attack but not how to stand up to hand-to-hand combat. We still had a few things going for us.

THOOOOWHEEEET! THOOOOOOWHEEEEET!

The cry of a baby owl, more mocking than menacing, shocked me out of my reverie. I looked around nervously. The moon had slipped out and was showing the ghostly silhouette of rocks and boulders. A few snow flakes fluttered down, chilling the back of my neck. Stars gleamed in the darkness.

El miedo tiene muchos ojos.

Fear has many eyes. Courage only one.

"Let's move out," I hissed.

We fall into single file. For many minutes I felt no sensation at all; my body had become numb. The men moved stooped over, hurting, mouths like slits.

We hauled ourselves up the mountain, slogging through drifts of snow that chilled and wet our feet. How many times before had I gone like this, hacking up some fool hill to kill a man for his political beliefs?

> *A time to weep and a time to laugh: a time to mourn and a*
> *time to dance.*

A time to love and a time to hate: a time of war and a time of peace.

At this remove it seemed as if my whole life had been spent at war.

Then came a great crashing sound. I threw myself to the earth, tiny charges exploding in my head. Footsteps pounded toward me. *This is it!* I thought. With cold shaking hand I pulled back the bolt on my M-16, rammed it home.

Then I saw it.

It was the biggest, proudest bighorn sheep I'd ever seen, a ram to end all rams. Bolting across the crest of the ridge, horns spiralling up into the moonlight, eyes shining madly, the animal was in panic as he flew. But even so, even in terror and flight, he was a noble sight as he accelerated toward the darkness beyond, head flung back, teeth bared, legs flexing and unflexing mightily as he leapt once, twice, three times and was swiftly, thuddingly gone.

Lying there, leaking sweat, finger jammed into the trigger of the sixteen, I took the beauty and power of the moment into my soul. It went deep, piercingly deep, and restored something in me.

El miedo tiene muchos ojos.

In a while I rose and gave a hand signal: the others resumed moving up at the usual intervals. Looking back, I could see their white clenched faces, hear them puffing and wheezing like marathon runners.

It was one hairy climb but at last we reached the lip of the final ridge. I peeked out over the top of the mountain: bare rockshelf marked here and there with boulders. It was cold, with a wind that kept whipping up flurries of snow. The moolight cast black fingers of shadows. Somewhere beyond the shadows lay the MNR. The rest of the men came up, faces working, breath steaming from their mouths. They tumbled down, weak with fatigue, and lay with their boots thrown apart, their eyes squeezed shut.

My watch showed we had made it in just a little under five hours. I unhooked my cartridge belt, eased off my field pack. "Keep an eye out, LoCascio," I ordered. "Wake me in twenty minutes."

I closed my eyes and slept. But did I? I felt the snow trickling down the back of my neck in long rivulets, heard the shrieking wind, and in my mind was a confusion of things.

"Hey, Major."

"Huh?"

"Come on."

It was LoCascio, shaking me awake.

I sat up, blinking, trying to clear my head. I felt wrung out, old.

The others were still sprawled out. I raised myself painfully, body cold and numb, and peered out over the ridge. All was dark but something was moving up there. Instinct said it was a man.

Finally the clouds streamed away and the rind of moon showed our objective: the ruins of the old mission settlement built two centuries ago by the Jesuits.

Between us and the MNR stood the remains of a stone wall which had once enclosed the mission. In its preserved place the wall was about eight or nine feet high, easy to scale, but there was a kind of rough tower at one end. In the dark I made out two faces up there. But one's eyes could be deceived in this kind of light.

Turning away, I looked down at my watch. I gave the men another five minutes, then woke them, signalling urgently that silence was absolutely essential. I assigned the support team, LoCascio and Simpson, to their position, then gestured for Claude and Eli to close ranks. They lay side by side, their breath steaming out and mixing into a silvery haze.

"How many do you see?"

"One."

"No, it's two," Eli insisted.

"I'd give my life for a mortar tube," I said. "We could waste the tower from here."

Countdown now: one minute to go.

My heart began to beat rapidly. The moon gleamed and for an instant framed one of the lookouts in its light. He wore a bandolier and carried a carbine—probably one stolen from my private cache. In the cold air his breath shone whitely. I wondered whether he had detected ours.

"Come on, Corrigan," I urged inwardly. "Come on, damn you—hit!"

It was time but there was no sound at all except for the sudden cry of an owl, a plaintive whimper like a child's crying. Then hit Charlie Corrigan did, with everything he had, raking the other side of the mission with machine-gun and rifle fire. The barrage sounded insanely loud in the stillness: tracers spewed wildly into the darkness, and a hundred—nay, a thousand—men seemed to be emptying their guns at the MNR.

There was a thrashing around on the hill, like that of a wild beast trying to escape a trap. More bullets and tracers went zinging into the stone flanks of the mission; flame spears leapt; there was the boom of grenades; vivid spurts of blue.

Men started screaming, like animals, birds, mythical creatures. Then came more volleys, whistles, shouted orders. The sky became lit with yellow and red as the MNR began to fight back. I had caught up with war again, had plugged into an old connection. The electricity coursed through me and made me shiver all over with excitement and anticipation.

Squinting across at the tower, I saw one of the guards rush out and take off for the interior of the mission.

I hissed at the others, *"Stand by,* you people!"

"AAAIIIII . . . "

A high fierce cry came from atop the mountain, an unbroken wail filled with primeval savagery. It rose and fell away, rose again to a pitch and held it.

Eli had his rifle in both hands and was shaking it as though to clear it of dust.

I grabbed him by the sleeve. "Eli—"

"Uh?"

I clutched him tightly, digging my nails into his flesh, and pointed to the lone guard in the tower.

"Take him," I ordered, handing over the bayonet. "I'll cover you."

Eli looked at me, grinding his teeth.

A huge black cloud came sweeping across the sky, heading slowly and imperiously toward the moon, like a queen in procession.

"Come on," I hissed as the darkness slid over and enfolded us. "Take him out. Kill that son of a bitch!"

Eli

"Go!" Mulligan said and I raised myself and started running, in a crouch, toward a boulder sitting some twenty yards away. I could hear my feet pounding and wondered why the lookout hadn't opened fire. It was the longest twenty yards in the world and my legs were thumping, lungs burning. But my mind was clear. It was ticking over nicely.

As Mulligan came up, footsteps hitting quickly, I peeked around the boulder and took a slap of snow across the face. My mouth tasted sour and black and dry, and the bayonet felt heavy in my hands. It really was me lying here, playing the avenger, with the snow pelting down and my bowels wanting to cut loose.

As soon as Mulligan made it, I took right off, plunging into the darkness without even looking back. I had to get away from him.

Presently the clouds dissolved and the disc of moon glittered and I became the biggest target on earth. I threw myself down waiting for a burst of machinegun fire.

Corrigan's fake attack sounded like the beginning of World War Three. The earth was shaking so violently that small boulders and rocks became disgorged and came sliding down the raked rockshelf.

The moon shone and the bayonet glittered. I looked down at the sleekly tapering steel, wondering whether I'd be able to use it.

I tried to conjure up some hatred. First I thought of Doreen, dead and gone from my life, her laughter stilled. But instead of hating the MNR all I felt was a deep pain. I couldn't even hate Consolidated Freightways or the I.C.C. now. They seemed so far away, so unimportant. I was past all hating, until all of a sudden the tipcart of my mind dumped a thought of Mulligan into my lap.

I scrambled up, ran forward.

As I pounded ahead, legs pumping, the high stone wall loomed up. Grabbing a handhold, I heaved myself up and over, coming down hard.

The wind was shrieking. I flattened myself against the stone wall, peering at the tower: it stood just a few feet away. I could hear the lookout hawking and spitting nervously.

Scrunching myself like a lizard, I started inching along the wall toward the tower. It was dark and then light as the clouds played games in the sky. The RAT TAT TAT continued, Corrigan was blasting away. I went with beating heart, watching the rainbow tracers light up the blackness. The earth quaked beneath me and the wind howled and brought a hot metalic smell. ZIIIINNGG POW POW POW, the bullets whipped here and there, the flurries blew pinwheels of white across the rockshelf, and I remembered my solemn promise never to kill again.

Slowly now, I inched my way around to the rear of the tower, boots crunching, bayonet extended. The tower was nothing but a crumbling ruin, gaping, exposed. The lookout was up there, draped across a heap of rubble. My temples pounded and sent little flashes of light across my vision. He was a small man with a squat body crisscrossed by ammunition belts. I crept forward, holding my breath, gripping the bayonet tightly.

All at once I was behind him. The moon appeared, showed him straightening up and shaking the snow off his shoulders. Again he cleared his throat and spat. My mind said Take him, but I couldn't move, my joints were either broken or petrified.

Then he sensed me and whirled around: I saw a wild tight face, frightened eyes, and then he came at me, lunging, grabbing for the bayonet, shouting something. I heard myself shout back, a hoarse cry. Suddenly his arm came up and grabbed my wrist.

I called on myself to fight, tried to find the strength. I no longer heard anything except the man screaming in my face. We both fought on, grappling with each other, strength against strength, predator against predator . . .

Billy Joe

First it went like the Major said it would and then it didn't. We brung some rain down on the MNR for a good ten, fifteen minutes, until the Major blew the lid off that dome. And how he blew it, the whole freakin night lit up like a disco and there was a bang that nearly split my skull in two. And then the spics came runnin, rats out of a burnin barn, and we just laid there and chopped them down, one after the other.

We must of offed a dozen enemy in thirty seconds. That part was easy, just a question of squeezin the trigger. But, then when we went up to finish the job, steppin over the twisted, blood-smeared bodies and headin up the logging road in the moonlight, we ran into a little surprise party.

We had just gone up over the saddle line. The moon had disappeared and it looked pretty weird up there, like them tv pictures of the moon—all rubble and pockmarks everywhere, the surface a cold grey crust. But then, zap! From the tumbled-down ruins of the church over yonder came a blast of fire that caught us lookin. Charlie Corrigan and one of his men were knocked dead and Frits, standin right beside me, went down hollerin, "I'm hit, I'm hit!"

Later on, down in a sheltering ditch, he discovered he'd only been nicked. But from the way he was carryin on, yellin and sobbin and whatnot, you'd reckon he was gonna die.

"Fritzie, Fritzie, take it easy," I urged him. "You're ok. Just think of the nice scar you'll have to show the bunnies back home."

But when Frits looked at me, his face all white, he just cursed me in Dutch and turned away and put his head down in his hands and began to sob and shake.

It was pretty hairy up there: the MNR had dug themselves a bunker and were firin everything from carbines to .30 caliber machine-guns. We'd lost four men all told and the only way we could take the MNR was by blastin them out. But how? Somebody tried heavin a grenade but it burst like a powder puff against the heaped-up boulders. Without artillery there wasn't a friggin thing we could do but sit tight and try to glom them to death.

We had no leader and everybody had a different idea what to do: "Let's heave every grenade we got and frag em to bits . . . Nah, let's set fire to the bunker . . . ''

Let's do this and let's do that, the shit really flew back and forth, and all the while the night grew icier and the wind cut like a whipsaw and I began to want out. It had been ok before, pickin them beaners off like rats, but now the fun was over. It was work and I discovered I didn't have much taste for it no more. It was too cold and I was too damn old.

Finally some of the guys crept off in search of Mulligan. The rest of us just lay shiverin in our rat-holes, occasionally peekin out and checkin the bunker. All was silent over there. The MNR couldn't go nowhere and neither could we. My teeth were chatterin like dice in a cup and I felt like pukin. Man, was I dragged. I needed a charge, a shot of skag explodin all through me, mellowin me out.

I smoked another joint, but it didn't help, my teeth kept chatterin and my hands shakin. All I could think was, I'm strung out, I'm strung out like a fuckin washline.

The guys came back maybe an hour later. No Major, only Eli.

He looked as if he'd been dragged along by a horse on the end of a rope. The skin on his face was all ripped and bloody and his clothes were in tatters.

He reported that both Mulligan and Claude had been hit. He didn't know how bad, only that they had definitely been wounded. They got it seconds after Claude finished placin the charges. He'd set the fuse and taken off fast with Eli and the Major coverin for him. He would of made it to the back wall if the MNR hadn't spotted him. They opened fire and Claude went down. Eli and the Major fired back, holdin them off. Finally Eli went to help Claude and get him down off the shelf. With Mulligan coverin him, he grabbed the big spade and started draggin him to safety.

Then it all happened—he hardly knew what. The charge blew, Claude and him went tumblin down the side of the shelf, the Major stopped a bullet. He was still layin there in the darkness, Mulligan was—somewhere near the back wall. Eli couldn't get to him because every time he showed his head, the MNR cut loose from the bunker. But he believed Mulligan was still alive. He had heard him groanin a little while ago, somewhere in the darkness.

"Let's go back and get him," Eli said.

"What about the MNR? Shouldn't we first take that bunker out?"

"How the fuck do you propose to do that?" Eli snapped. "You think you're Super Fly or Jack Gonads or something?"

Nobody said a word. We just sat watchin him, waitin for the word. Like it or not, he was in charge now.

Eli didn't dig the idea, though. You could see that as he sat there. He hated everythin and everyone. The wind came howlin down again, blowin sleet into our faces, whitenin them. Finally Eli turned and crept to the ridgeline and looked across at the bunker.

"Shit," he cursed. "Shit shit shit!"

The man was a stuck record.

I felt the cold rip through me.

Eli hunched himself up and cupped his hands and yelled across no-man's land as loud as he could: "Hey over there! Listen to me. We're willing to stop shooting. Do you hear? As far as we're concerned, this fight is over. You can leave your position. We promise not to shoot. We promise to let you free. I'll come over as a hostage. Do you hear? Let's stop this fighting!"

Next he yelled the same speech in Spanish and waited a bit, lettin the words sink in. Then he tied a white hankie to his rifle and stood up. "I'm coming over!" he called.

He started toward the bunker but didn't take no more'n five steps before RRRrrrriiiippppppp RRRrrrriiiipppppppp!

E.J. took a dive and practically landed in my lap as the slugs flew overhead.

As the MNR stepped up the volume of their firin, razzlin the air with the sound of weapon fire, E.J. started cursin again. He accused the whole damn human race of just about every folly and sin in the book.

Finally the MNR quit and all was silent and dark and bitchin cold again.

YoYo finally cried out, "How about it, Brickman, you're the big cheese—what the heck do we do now?"

Eli wheeled on him, eyes glarin. "Do? I'll tell you what I'm gonna do. I'm splitting, man. I'm walking down this mountain and going home. As far as I'm concerned, this war is over. You want to get your head blown off, go ahead—that's your business!"

He barked out the names of four guys and ordered them to accompany him around the mountain. "We'll try and retrieve Mulligan. If we can't get him off the shelf, it's his tough luck. He asked for this and now he's got it. Claude's in a protected spot, though. It won't be any problem finding and carrying him back to safety. Meanwhile the rest of you are on your own."

Eli didn't say another thing, just shoved the hell off and stomped off into the dark. I hunched myself up and, wipin the sleet from my eyes and mouth, tried to get warm. I looked up at the stars. They looked back at me.

A face appeared before me. It was Frits. He was breathin funny and his voice was comin from somewhere deep in his chest.

"Give me your grenades."

"Only got two. Why?"

"It's time to end this."

He looked at me and his eyes were like busted bits of glass.

"What in satan's name are you talkin about?"

He muttered somethin.

"What?"

He muttered it again: "All over now. Finished."

"Cool it, Frits. You're still shook up, man."

Abruptly Frits whipped his hand up and there was a .45 starin me in the face.

"The grenades."

As I slowly handed them over I could see more grenades strung round Frits' waist and bulgin outa his pockets. "Just what the fuck are you aimin to do, Fritzie?"

He didn't reply.

"Put that pistol down, man. You heard Eli. This party is over. All we gotta do is sit tight."

"What do you know," Frits jeered. "What do you know about anything?"

He turned and glanced across the ridge, face outlined in the moonlight. The .45 was still in his fist.

"Fritzie," I said again, feelin scared and helpless, "What's wrong with you?"

Frits paid me no mind, just crouched there waitin for the light to fade. As I looked at him a crazy thing happened. His head seemed to twist down into his shoulders, like a screw bitin into wood, leavin just a thing crouchin there, some kind of headless thing.

After mumblin something in Dutch he took off, zigzaggin toward the bunker. There he went, while the rest of us lay in the ditch gapin with disbelief. Finally someone yelled, "Jesus, give him some covering fire, let em have it, c'mon!" and we got with it, we cut loose with everythin we had.

RRRRIIIIIPPPPPPPP POWPOW POWPOW, the night exploded, we produced all the fire power we could muster and received even more in return. The night became alive with tracers, blue and white spurts. Somebody off to the right of me got hit and let out a scream. I hit the panic button and began firin an almost continuous barrage of slugs, emptyin the whole clip without even aimin. Now the maryjane hit me, my head was all light and tinglin, my body felt far away, and there was Frits ziggin across the open terrain, a headless animal. It was just like bein in Viet Nam, me shootin away, kick kick, the recoil joltin me, sockin my shoulder, feelin so high on dope that none of it seemed real.

But there was Frits bein hit by enemy bullets, Frits jerkin and twitchin like a marionette, arms and legs kickin out. He should of gone down because the MNR were murderin him. Suddenly I thought they can't kill him cauz he ain't go no head. I started laughin as Frits made it to the mouth of the bunker and drew his hand back and tossed a grenade in, followed by another, and then all at once holy shit that bunker blew and Frits blew and the whole mountain blew and lightning streamers swarmed before my eyes and a blast of heat hit me and knocked me bass over ackwards.

Raising myself to one knee, head spinnin dizzily, I peered into the smoke and whirlin dust. Frits was gone, the bunker was just a jumble of rubble, and there was no church either, just a kicked-over wall with a stone cross fixed on top, a cross that made me think of Lloyd Howard and how he used to go down on me wearing that big silver crucifix around his neck, and suddenly a sick pissy quivery feelin flooded down through me and I felt everythin between my legs go all warm and wet. Sufferin Mary, I was gigglin and shiverin and my dick was hard, it was spurtin off in my pants. Headless Frits had been blown to bits and I couldn't stop laughin.

Laughin!

Eli

We found Claude's body first; it lay in a painful sprawl behind a boulder just under the ridgeline. He was barely conscious; his right leg had been shattered by machine-gun bullets and the blood had soaked right through his heavy trousers and was all caked and filthy, but I didn't have any kind of medication to give him. All I could do was encase his leg in a crude splint fashioned out of some old slats of wood we had found.

I leaned over him.

"C'mon, Claude. You're moving out."

The morning sun was coming up, tinting the eastern sky with streaks of pink and red.

"Can you make it?"

Claude moved his shoulders.

There was an explosion on top of the mountain, followed by the rattle of fire. I listened intently, calculating its direction, and heard the thud of boots, more firing and shouting. Soon the firing and shouting stopped, a cloud of smoke came drifting down, bringing the stench of burning cordite.

Claude asked, "What's happenin' up there? Did you find the Major yet?"

"Not yet."

"What about the MNR? They gonna come after us?"

"I have no idea. All I mean to do is get you out of here, then look for Mulligan.

Claude lay back, closing his eyes in pain. He mumbled something I didn't catch, something about Madama Belita.

157

"You got a message for her, Claude?"

"It's the other way around. She had a message for me, but I didn't pay it no mind. She warned me against putting any money into Mulligan's mine."

"Money? You put money into the mine?"

"Yeah, fifty G's, man. Fifty of the big ones."

"You've been walking around with that much on you?"

Claude pulled the shirt out of his pants, revealing the money belt strapped round his waist. "There's five more thousand in there," he said. "You can have it if I check out."

"So that's why you came up this goddamn mountain—to protect your investment."

Claude didn't say anything.

"You're crazy, I said. "With all the loot you've got socked away, why risk your life for fifty grand?"

Claude looked at me, eyes dark and hollow. "That fifty grand was my last big chunk of capital," he said.

"But you told me you were a rich man."

"Not any more I'm not. I had some bad luck with my investments. Lost a quarter of a million bucks over the last five years."

"That's tough, Claude, that's a bitch, man. Mind you, I thought you were in some kind of trouble. But you're not flat broke, are you? You can always sell that plane of yours."

"It ain't mine. I rented it for this trip, just for a little image, if y'know what I mean."

The others who had been searching for Mulligan came up. I signalled to them. "All right, let's get Claude out of here. But be careful."

Claude quivered and groaned in pain as we lifted him, in a sitting position, his splinted leg sticking out like a baseball bat. It took all four of us to bear his great weight. Claude's agony stirred inside me and thoughts of him tumbled in and out of mind as we carried him downhill—how tight we had once been, chasing down rock and roll in Tapei, vop-vop-varooney, lady and gennulmen, THE SEVEN DWARFS! and talking about beating the bitch war goddess before she chewed us up with her steel teeth, but goddammit, the old hag had beat him after all, only this time Cluade couldn't blame it on her, just himself. He had been willing to kill or be killed, not to save his soul or his skin, but his bank book. His image.

Later I went back up the hill in search of Mulligan, wondering if he were alive or what. Traces of cordite still hung over the field of approach. The sky grew lighter. Minutes later I found LoCascio and

Simpson, who reported that all was quiet up top, that the fighting had ceased. They wanted to go and check out the mountaintop but I ordered them to accompany me. First we had to find Mulligan.

The next hour was a bad one. I thought I remembered where Mulligan had gone down but in the uncertain light every gully looked alike and we wandered around in circles, shivering and coughing in the icy air. We made a lot of noise but the fighting truly had ceased and nobody bothered us. We searched one crevice after another. Several times I thought I heard Mulligan moaning but I discovered after clambering across the rocks that it was only a trick of the wind; the same moan came from elsewhere. The wind was a lament and it sounded everywhere.

We came upon the back wall and the turret where I had killed the look-out. His body lay spreadeagled over the rocks leading up to the landing of the turret, smeared with blood. I must have fallen on him in a frenzy, chopping away with the bayonet. How easy in the end it had been to kill, to get back deeply into death.

The mountaintop was ripe with dead. Everything was all dead and dying, with a mingled stink of cordite and blood and dust hanging on the air, and vultures circling in the sky. Black broken legs, badly burned with flies clustered in the charred flesh, and trunks, face downward in the scorched earth, oozed bones and entrails like broken sacks of cement. And then came the dawn, the memorable dawn.

It was something, that dawn: it put on a show and we might have really enjoyed it had it not been for all the deathlings, annoying reminders of the night's debauch. They were everywhere and they were spoiling the morn, which came with a fat fireball sun rising up majestically and lighting up the sky with a blood-orange radiance. It would have been nice to sit and watch the sun unfurling itself, but the deathlings spoiled things, they made it impossible to concentrate on the performance. Inconsiderate dead men.

We found Mulligan a half hour later, lying on his side, arms outspread against the grey granite shelf. He was still alive. His face was ingrained with dirt and his eyes were like thumbprints of charcoal. His jacket was open, revealing a rip across the left thigh and belly. His intestines and bowels had been torn out and lay spilled on the ground, a bluish viscid heap.

"Help me out, Eli," he said thickly. "Do it fast."

I averted my eyes and contemplated the scene: Mulligan lying on the frozen turf, surrounded by an apron of granite and a shell-torn chapel thrusting its cross against the sky. And far across the mountaintops the redball sun turned fiery and lit the horizon from here to there.

"Do it, Eli," Mulligan urged. He seemed calm, ready to accept what must come.

I looked down, throat tightening.

"Quick," he said. "The pain began a little while ago."

"We can get you off this mountain."

"No," Mulligan said. "Too late."

"But—"

"Don't tell me you can't do it," he said, voice rising to a snarl.

I unsheathed my .45. The butt felt hot and grainy in my hand. Mulligan's face was dark and gaunt and stubbled, but composed. Tiny icicles clung to the hairs in his nostrils.

A shudder ran through me as the two sides of what I felt for him rushed toward each other and collided head on."

"Courage," Mulligan said.

The word meant nothing to me, absolutely nothing.

"Goodby, Eli," he said. "You did me proud last night. You did yourself proud."

A chill spread through my bones. I was turning to stone.

"You came through," Mulligan continued. "You fought the way you did in Nam . . . like a hero . . . "

That's when I shot him, right between the eyes, again and again, helpless to stop, squeezing the trigger until the entire clip was emptied and all that was left of Mulligan's head was some red and white pitted stuff like a smashed pomegranate.

We crossed the hilltop to the mission site. Everything was all blasted and ruined: hardly a single wall was left standing, except for the chapel front. Dead men were everywhere underfoot, an abundant crop. Most of them were MNR. It was hard to estimate how large their band had been because they had been blown to bits—an arm here, a leg there.

One guerrilla was still alive: he sat badly burned with huge red blisters on the flesh of his face, his dazed eyes staring out. Beside him lay the decapitated body of another guerrilla. His head lay a good fifteen feet away—the head of a young boy. Most of the MNR looked equally young.

We had waged war on a boy's club.

Among the deathlings we found Che's body. Those who knew him recognized him immediately, a carcass with one leg blown off all the way to the crotch. His face was crusted in blood. The eyes remained open. He had gone out like Mulligan: proud and unafraid and undismayed in the face of battle. He too had found in death a cause worthy of his life.

"Start gathering up the bodies," I ordered.

"The MNR too?"

"That's right."

"But—"

"Do what I tell you!"

Grumbling and bitching, the men went to work. It was a shitty task, scraping up the corpses, but it had to be done. We owed it to them, even to the MNR. We had lost six men, all mercenaries, except for Frits. These old men now shared something with the young men of the MNR. They shared a common brotherhood, the only true brotherhood of man: the brotherhood of the dead.

Soon I found the remains of Frits' body. There was very little left to him, just bones and blood and scarlet fragments of meat. Shadows flitted over us; the vultures were closing in.

Looking down at the remains of Frits Hartogs, I found myself talking to him, not knowing exactly what to say, but needing to say something.

Good Frits, poor Frits, crazy Frits. He had tried to make himself accountable for Viet Nam and Chu Tau, but the burden had been too much for him. He had collapsed under its weight.

For his sake, I prayed that there was such a thing as absolution, so that his soul would be received in heaven. If anyone deserved heaven, it was Frits. He had earned it last night by dying for us, for our crimes and sins. He had repented in dust and ashes for our having failed him and everything that makes men human.

If there was a God, I hoped that He would accept and embrace Frits, and not reject him as He continued to reject us.

Yoyo

The shit was really hitting the fan when we landed at El Cortez. The road leading out of town was jammed with people on the move. They were lugging nearly everything they owned, using either carts or burros or their own shoulders to carry the stuff. One man was piggybacking his crippled-up old mother, another was wobbling drunkenly under the weight of an old floor radio. What a sight they made, hundreds of em pushing and bumping along, hollering at their animals and kids, faces all scared and wild-eyed. There was nothin anybody could do to stop them, not even Alicia, who stood on the steps of the office watching them as they trooped by, the women shielding their faces behind shawls, the men flogging their burros, "Eeha, mula, eeha!" Even the beggars were clearing out, gimping along on crutches, wrapped in filthy sweaters and coats.

Tito Cota's troops were stationed on every corner, wearing white gloves and flashing submachine guns. But Tito himself was nowhere in sight. "He's hiding somewhere, too damn scared and ashamed to show his face," said Billy Joe. "Them boys of his ain't never gonna dirty their white gloves."

"Tito's had it, though," said LoCascio. "I hear the army is gonna court-martial him for what happened here. Some general is supposed to be flying down to take him into custody."

As he walked on ahead Billy Joe glanced my way and winked, "We got it made."

"Don't be so sure."

"Dig, we could walk off with the whole damn village right now."

He was right; in this confusion everything was up for grabs. Yet inside I felt all sick and miserable.

162

We walked into the office. E.J. had taken Alicia off to tell her the news about her husband; the place was empty. Cool-like, Billy Joe closed the door behind us and began casing the joint. The cabinet with the cash drawer was locked along the front by a big wooden bar held by an eyebolt and a combination lock. It wouldn't take much to bust it open.

"The dust is ours," Billy Joe crowed. "All those big fat hogs!"

The way he said it made my skin creep. "I still don't like it," I said. "I don't figger we can pull it off."

"You know whatsa matter with you," Billy Joe jeered, "you got a mouth disease—you can't keep it shut."

"Think what you want. But I still say it's too risky."

"We ain't gonna have no trouble."

"Says you."

"Yeah, says me—your meal ticket, your friggin master, and don't you forget it, you dumb hick."

My face was burning. I felt like spitting at Billy Joe, but what could I do, he had me backed up and pinned against the wall.

His plan had me copping a jeep and whatever tools we'd need to jimmy open the file cabinet, and him driving out to the airstrip and lining up the plane for the getaway. To hear him talk it all sounded as quick and easy as greasing a whore.

But my nerves grew real tight as the morning dragged on. It was no sweat finding us a jeep and enough tools for the job, but when Billy Joe drove off he took a long time in coming back. I killed an hour walking around El Cortez, watching the procession, half the town fleeing for its life. Then I stopped by the dispensary and watched the boys disposing of the dead bodies by stuffing them into these old barracks bags. There were no coffins to be had because the carpenter had left town too. After a while hanging around there got to be a drag, so I took off again and started poking around the back streets of the village.

It was spooky to see everything all dead and empty, backyards cleaned out even of their chickens. I passed one house whose front door was wide open, and decided to go in. It smelled of spic food inside—all them fried bananas and beans and crap. For a minute my guts churned over and I felt like puking, but I knew my nausea had nothing to do with the smell. It was something else that was making me sick.

I didn't want to rob the Major's wife. With the whole world tumbling down around her, robbing her would be like robbing the dead.

I looked round the house: it was pretty well cleaned out, except for a big wooden sofa, a wall mirror, some home-made chairs and a couple of oil lamps. They must of been poor folk, because the floors was made of dirt and the toilet was no better than a hole in the ground. Off the main room was a little dark curtained closet where they kept their religious images. Nothing was left now, except a small frame of a shrine. It had a color picture of Christ pasted on back. His face was real scary—all twisted and hideous with suffering. *Jesus died to save me and all of my sins. Well glory to God we're going to see Him again.*

That old hymn we used to sing in church popped into mind. I'm really going to sin today, I reckoned. I've sinned lots in the last ten years, but this is gonna make all them sins look like pablum. My guts squeezed together and the bile-taste rose up in my mouth. Robbing from a gas station or a supermarket was one thing, but robbing from the dead was another.

Jesus died to save me and all of my sins.

I was shivering and quaking now and feeling worse than I did up on that mountain last night. Up there I didn't feel I was doing any wrong. I was just fighting, that's all, and never in my life did I fret about that. There had always been wars and rumors of wars, the bible said it was so. Fighting was as old as life itself, and as necessary.

But this, this was something else. I felt right poorly now. I felt like I was gonna die, like the judgment time had come to pay for all my transgressions.

Dear dead Jesus, I prayed to the picture on the wall, can You forgive me just one more time? Will You let me live? If you do sweet Jesus, dead Jesus, I'll never burden You down again with the heavy discipline of my sins. I'll never make You suffer for me again dear Lord. Oh sweet Jesus please let me get through this day, dear God please let me live.

I'll quit these sinful ways of mine. That's a promise, dear Lord. Do You hear me? I'm telling you something heavy. I'm telling You that I'm tired of thieving and dealing and whoring. I'll change my life, sweet Jesus, if You'll only forgive me. Do you hear me O Righteous Judge? Spare me and I'll quit my sinning. I'll go home dear Jesus and live the upright way, the Christian Way.

I found myself down on my knees, praying for the first time in maybe twenty years. *That shows I mean it, don't it, Jesus?* Do You believe me now?

Then I picked myself up and went back into the big room. In the mirror my face was white and solemn; it was the face of a man who has made a vow. I felt better inside, a whole lot better. I had the joy of Jesus inside. So now I took out a yoyo; it was my favorite, a peppermint-striped job that I got when I was fourteen. I started it going. Oh yeah I made it *work* now. Goddamn, the juice ran right up through my body and out my arm. This was how I felt when I won the national championship, all hot and loosey-juicey.

Oh yeah! I gave that yoyo a real workout, make it do some *bodacious* tricks. Shubie-shubie-doo, I shot it over my head and under my arms and between my legs, I swung it like nobody had ever swung it before, cauz soon I was gonna be free. My sinning days was over!

I thought of the money that would be coming to me, my cut of today's haul. If I invested it, bought some trust deeds or bonds, got maybe fifteen per cent return, it would add up to around four thousand bucks a year, eighty a week. All I had to do was come up with another two hundred hogs a week and I'd be covered. Surely I could make that with the yoyo, playing juke-joints and American Legion halls and private parties. Hell, that was no nut at all. I'd be all right, I'd soon be stomping around like my old self, free and happy as a clam.

Somebody cried out. I wheeled around, scared as hell, yoyo cracking against the wall. But it was only an old woman. A witch, really— she must of stepped out of a book of fairy tales. She was all in black, with stick arms and legs, and had holes for a mouth and eyes.

She was dragging herself across the floor, jabbering something.

"Whadda ya want?" I yelled.

She kept jabbering and moaning, begging me for something.

"No hablo español," I yelled.

But she wouldn't shut up, just kept crawling toward me, all black and shriveled and smelly. Her face was covered with these awful sores, big purplish blotches.

"Get away!" I yelled. "Nobody here, vamoose!"

But she kept coming on, making these noises, these weird, desperate noises.

"Please," I said, backing off, "please leave me be, please!"

She stank. She stank of witch shit and graveyards. Then she put a hand out, a withered old claw, and screeched in my face. Falling back, shaking all over, I shoved a hand into my pocket, flung a fistful of money at her.

"There," I yelled, "it's everything I got. Now leave me alone—"

But she didn't even look at the money, just kept coming at me, reaching out with the black twisted claw, making the same horrible noises in her throat.

That's when I took off. As I bolted for the door, the claw came up, grabbed my sleeve, but then a second later I was breaking free, only to hear another scream break loose from her. AAAIIIIII, she cried as I pumped down the street with all my might. AAAIIIIIIIIII.

Billy Joe was there, standing across the street from the office as I ran up. "What's wrong?"

"Come on," I yelled. "Let's get going. Let's get this fucking this over with!"

"What hit you? You look hacked, man."

"Come on," I cried wildly. "Move!"

"Don't rush me," Billy Joe said. "I wanna know what's wrong. You ain't gonna crap out on me, are ya?"

"Quit bitching me," I warned. "Just quit it!"

Billy Joe studied me with screwed-tight eyes, then sniffed and said, "All right, let's go to work."

"What about the plane?"

"Don't worry, it's ready."

"Then let's do it. Let's score and get the fuck outa here."

We drove up to the office and left the jeep idling. Swarms of Indians were still heading up the Camino Real, going god knows where, wherever home was, a mountain village or some seaside shack. It was dusty and noisy, dogs were yapping, but nobody paid us no mind. I took the two tire irons and went inside the building with Billy Joe, whose face was grim and yellow. He was chomping gum a mile a minute.

The door to the main office had been locked, but no one was around and all it took to open it was one wrench on the tire iron. We went inside, where it was deathly quiet and empty. I headed right for the file cabinet and started clawing at the wooden bar, which soon ripped away with a loud splintering noise.

"Easy!" Billy Joe hissed, his back pressed up against the office door, a .45 pistol in his fist.

"Shut up," I shot back.

Two more heaves and I broke the bar off, flung the doors open.

And there it was, the green.

Holy Mary. There was a lot more than we thought.

My hands started shaking.

"Hurry," Billy Joe said. I started shoving the bills into an old suitcase. It seemed to take hours to clean out the cabinet; my shakes kept getting worse, I felt like I was gonna toss my cookies.

Finally it was done.

Billy Joe peeked out: nobody.

We walked outside, trying to saunter and look cool. But just as I slung the case into the back of the jeep, Eli came from around the corner.

"What're you guys doing with the jeep?" he yelled.

Billy Joe's hand went toward his .45, but I stepped forward and answered quickly, "Taking supplies to the doctor."

"All right, but bring those wheels back fast. We need 'em."

"Right, E.J.," I replied. Then I jammed the jeep into gear and we took off, motor roaring, horn honking, scattering Indians like tenpins.

Finally we hit some open road and I put my foot down and we hammered out to the air strip, bouncing all over the place, but *moving*. There was nobody on the strip except an old spic mechanic, who had his head stuck down in the armpit of an airplane and didn't even look up as we tearassed across to Mulligan's plane. Which looked old and beat-up and small.

Very small.

I studied Billy Joe. Now it was all up to him. He had turned the color of pus and stood staring at the flying machine, working on his gum.

He can't fly it, I thought. *He can't fly the fucker.*

We clambered in and I squeezed into a seat beside him up front. There were all these knobs and controls and things. Billy Joe's face looked sicker and more twisted by the second, as if someone had his balls in a vise.

"Can you really do it, man?"

His head jerked round. "Pop off at me once more and I'll carve you out a new asshole."

Slowly, fumblingly, he reached out, touched this, pulled that. Next thing you know the motors kicked over, coughed, got going. He started us rolling toward the end of the runway. He was still fumbling around but we were moving, bumping along. I smelled the leather and metal smell of the cockpit, the stink of high-octane gas.

A jeep came racing down the road from town: it was loaded with guys and even from here I could see they were armed.

Billy Joe saw them too. His mouth was clenched so tight you couldn't see his lips. He did something to get the motors revved up; their roar filled the cockpit and made it shake. I smelled gas again, a combustion smell. If ever this crate should crash and explode, it would be a hell in here, a hell of fire and brimstone and burning flesh.

We were turning now. Billy Joe seemed to know what he was doing, he had the twin motors blasting roughly but powerfully. We were beginning to take off—

Jesus died to save me and all of my sins.

Out on the airstrip the jeep was racing after us in a frantic attempt to head us off. The roar built up and reverberated through me and I recalled the old witch screaming AAAIIII as we shot down the runway bumping over the ruts and suddenly I realized the scream was coming out of me, but I didn't care and couldn't stop because we were lifting off the ground now and the plane was wobbling and straining and these big mountain peaks were rising up ahead, they were coming up so fast. They were blocking the way, we'd never clear them—

I screamed again as Billy Joe pulled back with all his might on the controls, his eyes bulging, and the plane nosed up and we made it, oh yes oh *yes* Jesus Sweet Jesus we cleared the peaks and were gone, *long* gone, streaking north with all those thousands of big fat beautiful hogs sittin between our legs!

Eli

We buried the dead on the hill overlooking the sea and the white salt flats. Some of the guys didn't like the idea of the MNR lying cheek-by-jowl with our boys, but Alicia silenced them by saying, "They're not enemies any longer, just dead men."

Since it was her family burial site, she was entitled to the last word. So our fallen and the MNR's fallen were united in death as they never could have been in life, under a long line of crude wooden crosses running down the length of the ridge. Each one of them got a military burial, Doreen included.

It fell to me to organize the graveside service. I looked up *Funerals* in Mulligan's big looseleaf book of U.S. Army Regulations and put together a plan that was little more than a parody of the original, but what the hell, that was where we were at. None of the required elements was at hand: neither military band nor colors nor pallbearers nor clergy. Not that it really mattered. Everyone was so shellshocked that for all we knew or cared the bodies could have been dumped in a ditch of swept away by a flashflood.

Billy Joe and YoYo had really zapped us. It wasn't just the suddenness of the robbery that shocked so, but the unfairness of it, the nastiness. It was like watching a boxer get knocked out, only to have some creep jump in the ring and start stomping on his body.

In the end we managed to get through it. First I sent a group up to the burial grounds to dig the graves. Afterwards I supervised the loading of the dead into the trucks and organized and outfitted a firing squad. Finally, a little after noon, we set off in a convoy, grinding through the heart of the abandoned town.

169

We should have buried the bodies right here, because El Cortez was more graveyard than village. Its jerry-built houses and huts stood side by side like tombstones. Windows were broken, doors banged in the wind, walls sagged.

The day was grey and damp. It had rained earlier and our tires whipped up gobs of mud and splattered the stuff all over the sidewalks and white-washed walls lining the Camino Real. How like Indo-China this street had been yesterday; Indo-China with its milling, struggling, pushing mobs of refugees, the yobos in their funny cone-shaped hats, the white-shawled women clutching their babies, the ox carts groaning under their loads. The grim, blasted, burned-out faces had flitted by yesterday like phantoms out of the past.

Now, as we chuffed up the hills ringing El Cortez, the mine across the valley stood out sharply. It too had been abandoned: railroad cars stood motionlessly on their tracks; the work sheds and shafts were empty. The fires in the great furnaces had gone out, smoke no longer billowed from the chimneys and layered out over the valley. The familiar stink of slag and smoke was gone. An awful pong, Doreen used to call it. But it was a living smell and I preferred it to this, the smell of the grave.

We climbed, passing the main sentry-box on the road; it had been chewed up by machine-gun bullets. Next came a long sandy waste and a stretch of road turned into a washboard by the recent rains. But the rain had also transformed the landscape: there were big bright fields of wild flowers everywhere, patches of scarlet, white and purple anemones sprouting with the joyous improvidence of a child's painting. It was spring, I realized, and the earth was renewing itself, seething and pulsing beneath the surface, erupting into life.

Further along we came upon a campfire and a solitary man sitting drinking coffee beside it: one of the road laborers Alicia knew. He flagged us down and Alicia, who had been sitting morosely, folded into herself like a bat, got out and talked with him.

"He's been waiting for us ever since word went out about the funeral," she reported.

By the time we reached the burial site we had taken on another two dozen riders—road laborers, farmers and villagers, some shepherds. The fat truck driver Vicente Rodríguez was also waiting for us up ahead, squatting beside his Mack truck with its exhaust pipe thrusting into the sky like a periscope. Most of these impoverished mountain folk had ridden their burros for hours to come and pay their last respects to Señor Mulligan.

Perhaps it was Che they wished to honor. But that didn't matter, as there was presently no difference between Mulligan and Che: in the grave they were as identical and equal as Siamese twins.

From the coastal ridge the sea looked as flat and grey as slate, with an odd whirlwind whipping the surface up into a waterspout. The road ran through a series of khaki-brown hills. Down on the right were the salt pans, gleaming dully with a sheen of sea water. The sky was grey but lightening; sunlight was poking out here and there, arousing in me a few crumpled emotions.

Gome, the gulls cried as they pumped overhead. *Gome.*

Here we were. The advance squad snapped to attention as the convoy pulled up. Alicia gave a little whimper as she spied the row of new crosses populating the ridge line, but she quickly stifled it, fought for control.

When she had fixed her face into an unflinching mask, I helped her down. A cold salty wind came in off the sea and smacked us hard.

Keer! the gulls screamed. *Koy-koy-koy.*

The bodies were placed beside the graves. The burial site seemed a squalid place now, everything all salt-stained and splattered with gull shit. The grey slats of driftwood had been nailed together carelessly and already the marker over Frits' grave was slanting in the wind.

"Parade REST," I yelled. The order was obeyed: people gathered round, heads were bowed.

The book called for Clergy, but there was no Clergy, just me reading the Twenty-third Psalm. Satan playing at priest. What a joke: Doreen would have split with laughter had she known.

"The Lord is my shepherd; I shall not want. He maketh me to lie down in green pastures: he leadeth me beside the still waters . . . "

The wind blew harder. Frits' rickety cross fell over, leaving him as solitary and forgotten in death as he had been in life.

"Yea, though I walk through the valley of the shadow of death, I will fear no evil; for thou *art* with me; thy rod and thy staff they comfort me . . . "

Frits' body was lowered into the grave. The wind moaned over this lonely banished place.

"Firing party, present, ARMS. Firing party, fire three VOLLEYS."

The four members of the firing party, all retired thirty-year army men, whipped up their rifles smartly.

"Ready, Aim, Squad, FIRE."

They fired the volleys over Frits' grave, the sound of the shots exploding in unison, again and again, and mingling with the panicked cries of the gulls as they flapped out to sea.

We marched down to Che's grave. His body lay at my feet. I felt nothing I was supposed to—no sense of revenge or triumph or vindication. All I felt was pity for this man who had to kill and die to learn the true meaning of love and justice.

"Ready, Aim, Squad, FIRE."

Next it was Mulligan's turn. My eyes went to Alicia; the wind had blown back the grey veil shielding her face, revealing a firm implacable expression as she regarded the sack of flesh that had once been her husband. She did not flinch. He was dead and gone but she would not allow herself to surrender to grief. She had wept all yesterday and last night, but that was in private; here she would be brave and strong and indomitable, even though inside there was chaos and agony.

Lifting my face I bawled at the firing squad: "Ready, Aim, Squad, FIRE."

The guns snarled, there was a thump as the two grizzled lifers flung the body of their former commanding officer into the grave and began dumping dirt, sea shells and pebbles on it. Alicia stood staring down into the abyss with dark moist unblinking eyes.

The rest of us went down the line, pausing finally at Doreen's grave. Staring down at her body, so small and shriveled, I wondered what would become of the life force it had once contained. Something I had read popped into mind, a story about a man watching television somewhere. Suddenly a strange program flashed onto the screen, a scene from an old comedy show of the 1950's. It played clearly for a few moments, only to disappear as quickly and mysteriously as it had come.

The explanation given was that the original transmission waves of the show had been floating around in the heavens all these years, alive and sharp as ever, preserved by flukey atmospheric conditions. It was comforting to think of Doreen like that, to envision that sublime life force of hers hovering free above the earth, ready to plunk down and invigorate somebody's life again, if only for a few transient moments.

Abruptly a pain shot up my spine; it was as if someone were stripping the skin off my back. The firing squad was waiting for my command but I could only stand there, unable to speak, filled with a despicable raw pain and with a need to crawl into the grave with her.

I felt a presence beside me: it was Alicia, who took my hand in a gesture of loving. We stood together for a moment, bodies touching lightly, joined together for an instant of time. Then I looked up and gave the command:

"Firing party, present, ARMS.

"Firing party, fire three VOLLEYS.

"Ready, Aim, Squad, FIRE."

The detonations died away and the opening notes of Taps sounded from a nearby portable record player. The bugle solo sounded cracked and tinny on the machine but then, as it kept building in intensity, swelling out, I realized that the bugler was trying to say something and wanted us to go with him, up and up as he reached for the heights, and for a moment this grey and sea-stained hillside wasn't so squalid any more, it was as fine and proud as the song of farewell being played over it. That bugler knew damn well whose epitaph he was sounding, men like Mulligan and Che's, poor bastards who had gone down in war for reasons you could only hope were worthy of them.

SONS OF THE HOUNDS, COME HERE AND GET FLESH.

Then it was done. The last notes of God is nigh drifted slowly and quiveringly out to sea and we stood all choked up with loneliness and sorrow.

Nobody spoke as we turned and filed back to the trucks, carefully averting our eyes. The hillside was returned to silence again, to the indifferent rocks and wind, the nesting dead.

On the return trip Alicia sat upright and staunch, still fiercely controlling her emotions. But upon reaching the outskirts of El Cortez she asked that the truck be stopped. She crossed to the lip of the hill and stood gazing down at the village. The houses and shops were unlit and desolate—dark empty shapes in the twilight. Everything was silent.

She took all this in for several long moments, then turned away and walked down the road, where she stood with her head down, weeping.

But by the time I reached her the tears had subsided and she had straightened up. The color of her face was patchy, her eyes were red, but she managed to find her voice.

"I'm sorry, Eli."

She tried to light a cigarette but her hand was too unsteady. I lit it for her as we walked down the road together.

"It was the sight of El Cortez that did it," she said, looking down at the village. "That's exactly how it looked when I first took it over.

I can remember standing here and gazing down at all that desolation and thinking, How will I do it, how will I ever raise that colossal wreck to the surface?

"And now here I am," she continued, "standing in the same place thinking the very same thing. What an eerie feeling. Only now I know there's no hope. That I'll never do it again."

"Maybe there's a way out," I said. "Maybe the banks will step in. You owe them a lot of money, it could be to their advantage to keep the mine operating rather than let it slide into bankruptcy."

"I doubt it," she said. "The banks'll step in all right, but probably only to repossess our machinery and equipment. They'll pick El Cortez bare and leave behind nothing but bones."

She bit down hard and struggled to contain her emotions. "Oh, *mierda*," she said finally in a choked-up little-girl's voice, "it hurts."

We walked on.

"I had always thought that if we failed down here, if the mine ever went broke, someone else would pick up the reins—a private owner, a copper syndicate, maybe even the state. I really thought El Cortez would stay alive no matter what, that it would still be here and thriving long after Matt and I were gone."

This was a mother's dream of immortality for her offspring: El Cortez had become her child, a substitute for the flesh and blood creature that had dropped from her womb with a noose around its neck. But that was only part of the story: Alicia wasn't just a woman with a misplaced maternal drive; she was one of the good ones. I knew it now as I had never known it before. This was a stand-up lady who had gone out and tried to remake the world, add to it. Most people talked about it, but few of us ever did anything about it. Somewhere along the line we chickened out and quit the struggle, settled for the easy way.

Not Alicia, though. She had got down in the mud with a bunch of roughneck miners and peons to scratch for copper and dig foundations and raise El Cortez from the deep. She hadn't made it of course. In the end the world had beat her, but then she had probably always known it would. The good ones always seemed to know it. They seemed to understand that the odds were against them, that eventually they must pay a price for their courage and humanity. It gave them a kind of grace: the grace of bravery under pressure.

"Let's go," Alicia said.

We started back to the truck.

"What will you do now?"

She shrugged.

"Why don't you come up to the capital with me, give yourself a chance to recover?"

"Thanks," she said, "but I'll stay here."

"I wish there was something I could do," I said.

"You've done enough already," she replied, then gave a big sigh. "Dammit, why does it have to be like this? Why can't people just live and work and have fun and be decent to each other? It sounds so little to ask."

She looked at me, tears welling up in her dark lioness's eyes. "What is it about us that makes go to war? Why in God's name can't we rise above ourselves and find the imagination to solve our problems and differences? Why do we go on hurting and killing each other?"

It was a question that I couldn't answer.

Alicia was the last person I saw the next morning as we took off from El Cortez in Claude Copeland's plane. Claude sat in the rear, his leg swathed in plaster and propped up on an orange crate, clutching a half-empty bottle of tequila in his hand. As we climbed and circled over El Cortez, searching for a tailwind, I peered down and spotted Alicia, a solitary female figure in a rust-colored serape crossing the Camino Real.

She stopped and looked up, waving a hand in farewell. She kept waving as we caught the wind and leveled off. The big plum-red hills around El Cortez came into view. I could see the topmost peak with its white-painted words: ARRIBA MNR.

An additional slogan had been spelt out with large white rocks during the night: EL CHE VIVE.

I noticed a man on horseback coming down the mountain trail, heading toward El Cortez. It could only be Don Enrique Arguello. No doubt he had ridden in like this fifteen years ago to help Alicia make a beginning. Now he came again, this time to make an ending.

The town began to shrink and the figure that was Alicia Hendricks Mulligan turned into a blur on the landscape, then a grain. And then she was gone, swallowed up by the earth's hungry, blood-stained mouth.

In a while I went back and joined Claude Copeland, taking a long hard drink from his bottle.

"How's the leg?"

Claude scowled. Tilting the bottle back he drank and roughed his mouth with the back of his hand. His face was loose and hollow-cheeked. He seemed smaller, shrunken, like a deflated balloon.

"I'm all right," he said. "Don't worry 'bout me, I'm gonna be all right." But his voice lacked conviction. His bravado was gone and he looked like an old man, a homunculus, who had crawled inside someone else's young body. His jowls were sagging and his face was stained with defiance, "I'm glad it happened this way. I'm glad I got my goddamned leg shot up."

"Why?"

"Cauz now some club owner will be denied the pleasure of announcing to the world that the smartass uppity nigger fullback Claude Copeland is all washed up. I'm gonna call a press conference when I get back and announce my retirement from the game because of 'war wounds' or something like that. That way Mister Cholly won't be able to cut me from his team and gloat it up in public."

"Do they hate you that much, Claude?"

"Mister Cholly has always hated any nigger that stands up and talks back to him."

"But he's paid you big money to play ball for him."

"Only because I made him even bigger bread in return. It's all money, Jim. It's the only thing that holds that bullshit racist society together."

I turned away and looked out of the plane's window.

All around us was blue sky and hard bright sunshine. The sea was as soft and green as a putting turf, and the waves were rolling in and licking the shore lazily, like a big old pussycat. The hills and valleys were covered everywhere with wild flowers. Mother Nature was doing a number down there, she was strutting her stuff all over the place.

Then the plane passed over the mountain where we had fought Che and his men. I could make out the ruins of the shelf where I had found Mulligan. All quiet on the mountaintop now. Not a predator in sight.

Motors loud and rough, we flew toward the capital.

"Listen," Claude cut in, "what I told you the other day in battle was for your ears only. Once I'm home I ain't gonna let anybody know I'm broke. I'm gonna put on the same show I always have."

"I hear you, Claude."

Suddenly the pilot shouted and pointed down at something. In the hills below was an air strip. At the far end of the strip light smoke was billowing from the wreckage of a plane.

Quickly, we landed on the bumpy strip and taxied toward the wreckage. Billy Joe and YoYo's bodies lay near it. Billy Joe's eyes had been ripped out by vultures, leaving two ugly, bloody holes. YoYo's head had been snapped at the neck and it dangled loosely, as if on a string.

"They must have landed here to refuel," the pilot said. "*Muy estúpido*, this strip hasn't been used in years."

They'd been stupid, all right. There was only one obstruction on the entire plateau: a boojum tree, a lone twisted black shape standing out like a skeleton against the sky. The air strip was plenty long and wide, an easy place to take off from, but the boys hadn't made it. They had been pulled irresistibly to that solitary tree, as if on destiny's leash.

I poked around in the wreckage, looking to see what I could find.

And there it was.

Claude's eyes widened when I opened the leather suitcase and uncovered all that money.

"Those two motherfuckers stole themselves a small fortune."

"Wonder where all the US dollars came from," I said as I riffled through the stacks of cash.

"That's the fifty thousand I gave Mulligan for my share in the mine."

"Well, you lucked out, Claude. Here's your investment back, every single penny."

Claude just stared down at the money. "How about that," he said finally. "Never thought I'd see it again."

I left him sitting over the suitcase and went back to the plane for a shovel.

"What are you doin'?" Claude yelled down the line as I went to work.

"Just what it looks like."

Claude's voice sounded angry.

"Leave 'em," he said. "Leave 'em the way they are. Let the buzzards claim their own."

I shook my head. "They're members of the club now. They're entitled to the same treatment as the rest."

It took me over an hour to dig the two shallow graves. As I worked I tried hard not to think of what Billy Joe and YoYo had done down here. I tried to remember them when first we met in Viet Nam. They had always been a little strange, kind of flaky. But not corrupt, not criminals. The war had done that to them, it had turned them inside out. They'd become sadistic in Nam, always on the hunt for victims, simply because they were such victims themselves. The only way you can stop feeling like a victim is to make someone else into one.

Well, it was finally over for them, the need to hurt others. They'd finally found some peace from their tormented lives. It no longer mattered what they'd done or thought. We'd gone past the point where those things meant a damn. Billy Joe and YoYo couldn't hear me now. Dead men have no ears.

But as I hacked away at the earth, I learned that the dead do have a voice. I could hear it now, crying out from beneath the ground, crying out in sorrow and anguish and shame at what had happened to them, begging us to never let it happen again, to put an end to war once and for all.

But enough of that. Enough of the dead and the dying, all this harking back. It was time to let these two and Mulligan and Doreen and Che and all the others go the way of the earth. The dead had been buried, now it was time to look after the living.

"Let's move on out of here."

Once we were airborne I ordered the pilot to turn the plane around, head back to El Cortez.

"Why go back?" Claude argued. "We can send Alicia her share of the money once we reach the capital."

"I know that," I said.

"Then why are we going?"

"Because I have to," I told him.

*   *   *

A couple of hours later I was sitting in Ranchita's over beers with Alicia and Don Enrique Arguello.

"You're sure?" she asked for the tenth time.

"I'm sure."

"But suppose we can't get the mine going again?"

"Worst comes to worst, I'll buy me an old Mac truck and make like Rodríguez. I'll push that bucket of bolts up and down these hills for a living."

"You would, too," Alicia said, expression softening, managing a smile. "You'd love it, too, wouldn't you?"

"It's a good life," the Don said. "You live poor but you are free."

"Let's drink to it," I said, raising my glass. "Let's drink to living poor but free."

We touched glasses all around and then Alicia excused herself.

"There's so much to do," she explained. "I must call the bank and discuss everything with them. Maybe they'll be merciful if they know you're going to help me with the mine."

"I'll go with you," the Don said, rising.

I told her I would stop by once I dropped Claude at the airfield.

"You've done enough today," Alicia said, taking my hand in hers and squeezing it gratefully, intimately. "Thanks, Eli," she whispered, brushing my cheek with her lips. "Thanks for being here . . . for everything."

The warmth of her farewell lingered on my skin long after she had left the room.

"You will be with her now?"

It was Dolores, one of Madama Belita's girls, one of the few who had stayed behind; the one who had spent time in the USA. She was young and pretty in a hard-boiled way.

"We're just friends, Dolores."

"Friends!" she scoffed. "I saw the way you looked at each other."

"How was that?"

"Like you meant business."

I had to laugh at that. "You've got business on the brain, Dolores."

"True enough," she said. "That's why I'm here. I'm going to take over one of the abandoned grocery stores and fix it up."

"Finished with 'the life' are you?"

"Forever."

"But what will you do for customers with your grocery store? This place is like a ghost town."

"They'll be back, wait and see. El Cortez will always have some life to it. People need a place to meet and buy and sell their goods."

"Well, I wish you luck," I said.

"Thanks," she said. "Meanwhile, would you like to go upstairs with me?"

She was flashing me a professionally seductive look.

"Hey, I thought you were retired."

"Not till I open my shop."

"Sorry, girl, I'm waiting for Claude."

"Where is he?"

"Upstairs with Madama Belita."

"Hah," she sniffed, "when those two go at it, the clock has no hands. You could be here till morning."

But she was wrong. As if on cue, Claude came down the stairs, using one crutch and the bannister to manuever his broken leg. It was hard work, though he looked anything but unhappy when he hopped his way to the table. He had a pleased smile reaching from one end of his face to the other.

"Looks like you had a good time, buddy."

"You might say I did," Claude replied, easing himself into a chair. "You might say we *both* did."

"Don't get too comfortable. If we don't get to the airfield soon, it'll start turning dark."

"Forget the airfield," he said. "I'm not leaving, Eli. At least not for the USA."

"I don't understand."

He and Madama Belita had been having a little talk. He had decided to go to the capital with her, where, with his money and her expertise, they would open a *residencia de reunión*.

It can't fail, Claude insisted. There hasn't been a whore-house in the history of mankind that didn't make money. It was still the best business in the world, except maybe for religion.

"What do you think?" he asked. "Am I talking crazy, man?"

He didn't wait for me to form a reply.

"With Madama Belita running the show, I don't think I can go wrong," he continued. "Anyway, what would be the point of going back to the USA? There's nothing happening there for me, nothing at all now."

Only problem was, he'd have to marry Madama Belita. That was the only way he could stay in the country and keep her happy. No marriage, no deal, were her last words to him.

"It means locking myself into the situation, locking myself up for good," Claude said.

"Well, what can I say? Maybe that's the key to married bliss— marry a madam. Think of all the fringe benefits."

"This is no time to joke. I'm putting my last bucks into this thing."

"I appreciate that. But I can't see how you can go bust. Madama Belita is more businessman than all of us put together. Just let her run the show, man."

"Run *me*, you mean."

"Maybe that's not such a bad idea. You could use the services of a personal manager."

Claude sat back and thought it over.

"I wish I had me a crystal ball," he said. "I wish I could look into the future and see everything to come."

"When you get hold of one, let me know. I'd like to borrow it for half an hour."

Claude looked across at me, hard. "You can't be too sure of yourself, either. Are you really ready to give up everything back home?"

"I feel the way you do, Claude. There's nothing happening for me back there."

"That's right," he said. "What the hell would I do if I went back? My fifty grand wouldn't get me very far in business. It wouldn't even buy me a house."

"It'll buy you one down here, though," I laughed. "A cat house."

"With me the Number One Tom," Claude mused. The idea of it made him brighten up again. "Why not?" he suddenly yelled. "Why the hell not?"

"You tell 'em, Claude. Do it, daddy! Fuck 'em all, is how I feel about it. Fuck the I.C.C. and Consolidated Freightways and Uncle Sam himself. Fuck that old greybeard and everything he stands for today. He had his chance at running our lives. We gave him our innocence in Viet Nam, man, and you know what he did with it. He exploited it for his own purposes, turned us into misfits, criminals and drug pushers. Who needs him, Claude, is what I say. Who needs the evil, dishonest, cynical son of a bitch?"

Claude said nothing, just sat thinking it over some more, brooding.

I left him then and headed out the front door, with Dolores following me, yelling, "Where you going? Stay a while!"

"Sorry, Dolores."

"Come upstairs and let me show you a good time."

When I shook my head, she ran and caught up with me, grabbing my sleeve.

"Whatsa matter, don't you like my chi-chis? You too tired to ball?"

"Another time, huh."

"You know what you need," she shrieked after me, "some Spanish fly!"

That made me laugh as I walked down the Camino Real to Alicia's office. That made me put my face back and laugh my head off.

—The End—